COLOR
OF
THE PRISM

THOMAS J. NICHOLS

Color of the Prism

Copyright © 2012 by Thomas J. Nichols

Second Edition: 2019

10 9 8 7 6 5 4 3 2 1

All rights reserved. No part of this book may be reproduced or transmitted in any form or by any means, including information storage and retrieval systems, without written permission from the author and publisher. The only exception is by a reviewer, who may quote short excerpts in a review. The author and publisher retain the sole rights to all trademarks and copyrights. Copyright infringements will be prosecuted to the fullest extent of the law.

This book is a work of fiction. Names, characters, places and incidents are either products of the author's imagination or are used fictitiously. Any resemblance to actual persons, living or dead, or locales is entirely coincidental.

ISBN-13: 978-1-7340054-0-0 (Paperback)
ISBN-13: 978-1-7340054-1-7 (eBook)

Published by Nicholson Books

Editing by Janet Musick
Cover designed by Spomenka Bojanic
Interior designed by Deborah Stocco

Publicity Contact: 281-602-3135

Printed in the United States of America

CHAPTER 1

The blazing desert sun threw its last glimmer of light over the mountaintops. The canyons below became hushed. Birds settled into their nests and darkness draped its mantle over the valley. The whitewashed walls of the elegant ranch house were dappled by the last luminous rays of light that shimmered through the eucalyptus trees. The dwelling was dark except for a single light that shone through the library window. The place was empty except for Reynaldo Guzman and Julian Espino Gatica, but even so, the two men spoke in hushed tones. Conversations such as this were not easy, even with one's most trusted associates. The fate of Arturo Aguilar was being decided.

Guzman sat in the high-back leather chair behind his oversized mahogany desk, sucking deeply from a Cuban cigar. Dark blotches of perspiration stained his starched white western shirt at the neck and plastered it to his chest. Death is not discussed easily, and the death of a lifetime friend is even more exhausting.

Through a cloud of smoke, Guzman gazed at Gatica, a tall, gaunt, heartless killer. He was a stoic, ruthless professional who could — and frequently was called upon to perform without concern for scruples, God, or country. Simply put, he was a man who would kill his mother for the right price. Gatica never knew his mother, a fact that might account for his cold, vicious nature.

Guzman stubbed out the remnants of his cigar and leaned back in his chair. He pulled out the bottom desk drawer and produced two glasses and a bottle of Maker's Mark. He tipped the bottle and poured them each three fingers of whiskey.

"*Salud*," he said as they clinked their glasses. "And may the dirty son-of-a-bitch burn in hell."

"*Salud*, don Guzman," responded Gatica. "He will do that, I assure you."

Guzman leaned forward, rested his arms on the edge of the desk, and studied his manicured fingernails. Lifting his eyes, he looked contemptuously at Gatica's dirty, bony fingers wrapped around the glass of whisky. Guzman's hands were always clean, but Gatica's were invariably caked with grime and filth. They finished their drinks, each deep in his own thoughts. The minutes ticked slowly by. In another room a grandfather clock chimed nine times. It was as if the timekeeper sounded the bell for the start of the next round. Guzman lifted the bottle and poured each of them another drink.

Gatica got up from his chair, taking the glass and gulping the stout whiskey. He leaned across the desk and poured himself yet another drink, turning the glass slowly, watching the whiskey swirl around inside the glass. Like the whiskey, his mind was spinning, trying to find the right words. Finally, he spoke. "I ask your permission to speak, don Guzman, on a most difficult topic, if you will permit."

"Say what you will. This is a very hard night for me. Ask what you will. You know this isn't normal for me to let someone question my actions, but I understand. This is different for us both."

"don Guzman, I have known you for many years, and from time to time, I did work for you without a word. You always paid me well, never tried to cheat me. I could see, always, why you were doing something, even if it wasn't my business. But this," he paused and let out a deep breath, "this is different. Hell, Aguilar is different. He has been like a brother to you. He is well-connected. His death will cause many problems. It'll be big news everywhere, not just around here — everywhere." He gazed vacantly around the room. Finally, his gaze rested on Guzman and their eyes met. "It'll be in the news like that big football guy, Simpson, who got accused of those murders, or like that guy they said blew up the Olympics. Aguilar is very big and he is friends with every politico, every big name in every cartel. They know him in Columbia, in New York, in Mexico. Shit, they know him everywhere. I tell you, my friend, he is big. Maybe too big for you to do this."

Gatica sipped his drink and sat down on the straight-back chair across from Guzman. "When he dies, there will be pressure on the police and they'll twist everybody. The newspapers will scream. *Senor*, I tell you, somebody, somewhere will talk. Somebody will point to you. They may not touch you for this thing, but if they think you have your hand in it, they will screw you forever. I don't know what this man did to you, but are you ready to pay this price?"

He guzzled the remainder of his whiskey and waited for a response. When none was forthcoming, he spoke carefully chosen words in a steady voice.

"We have worked together and have done a few things, but never anything like this to such a big man in America. I have great respect for you. You are a man with honor, but will it be worth the price to you?" Gatica asked.

Guzman leaned across the desk with his hands folded tightly. He looked to be in deep thought as he spoke, but his rage at Arturo Aguilar was evident in his voice and in his posture.

"You are right, of course. You have no right to question me, but this one time I will permit it." He stabbed his finger at Gatica's face. "There will be much trouble over this, but when someone violates his word, when someone violates your honor, then you must speak. Arturo and I have been like brothers, as you said. But you *pobrecitos*, all of you. You and Arturo were born in the shit of the hillsides or in the stinking barrios. You lived in the shacks. He was no different than any of you. But when he was little, their kerosene stove blew up. His whole family died in that miserable fire, but he got out without a scratch. The bastard! He should have died then."

Guzman got up from his chair and walked to the window. He stared into the darkness for a few moments, then returned to his chair. He lit another cigar and watched the smoke float gracefully toward the ceiling.

"Some nuns took care of him, then my uncle on this side of the border took pity on the nun's sob story and adopted that miserable bastard. To make a long story short, we grew up almost like brothers. We screwed the same girls. We fought the *pachucos* together. We ate the same food. We even did our first deal together. We got some dumb lily white dude from Indiana to think we had a load of marijuana, and we ripped him for about a thousand dollars."

Guzman laughed and poured himself another drink. "We thought we were the richest people in the world. A thousand bucks. We got drunker than skunks and got us some girls until it was gone. We were like brothers. They were good days. We grew. We trusted each other. Everything we did, we split. Man, we weren't stupid. We were smart. We went to college. We got to be real good. We could move weed, heroin, and cocaine. We could buy and sell anything. We even got to where we would move a load of dope one way and go back with a load of Levis or guns or computers. Everything paid. And you know something else?"

Guzman stared into the other man's eyes. "You know what? We trusted one another. There were five or six of us who got big, but we respected each other. We never ripped off each other's stuff or money. You have to have trust or you have nothing. But now, there is no trust. I am a rich man, Julian." He gestured around the library with its shelves full of the world's finest works of literature. An original Remington graced the wall over the fireplace. A pair of antique pistols that were carried by Pancho Villa was hung behind glass on the wall.

"Now I find my partner has cheated me. He tried to open up new markets. They didn't work out, so we lost money. One or two maybe did okay, but not much and that bastard kept quiet about all of this. There is no trust. He cannot continue to exist. It is that simple."

"don Guzman, I only question. Are you certain about this? Are you sure? You must be positive before you take such a big step." Gatica heard himself almost pleading.

"As I told you, I am a rich man. I know everything," Guzman said as he leaned back in his chair. Once again he watched as the smoke from his cigar climbed the soft currents of air up toward the ceiling.

"I know everything," he repeated. "I know what hand he uses to scratch his butt. I know what finger he uses to play with his wife, and I know how many times a day he farts." Guzman looked across the desk at Gatica and smiled. "A rich man can buy anything."

"It's very sad," Guzman said as he looked down. "Very sad. He got too white, too big in real estate, too many boards of directors, too greedy, and yes, too untrustworthy. He forgot his bond."

Guzman got up from his chair, walked to an antique oak chest, and pulled open a drawer. From its depth, he brought a tired, battered old shopping bag and returned to the desk. He tossed the bag on the desk, spilling its contents out onto the rich mahogany top. Some of the money fell onto the floor, some was spread across the desk, but most of it remained in the sack. Gatica scooped up the money and put it back in the bag.

"Count it if you wish. Forty thousand dollars now. The same when it is done."

"The amount is accurate, I know," Gatica replied.

"Take it and go," Guzman said softly. His voice sounded as if he were exhausted, if not physically, at least emotionally. "I will be fishing at Puerto Penasco in three days. I have a boat there, the El Mar. Find me and we'll talk again about some things. We need to finalize some plans."

Guzman looked at Gatica and smiled, shaking his head back and forth as if he couldn't believe it himself. "It has come to this. I never thought this could happen, but it did. Julian, when you see me next, be ready to tell me how you will do this. We'll go over things. I'll have some ideas of other things that I might have to do or people I might have to see."

Guzman walked to the library door and led the assassin through the house and out the rear patio door. Gatica slithered off the patio like a coyote slinking into the desert away from a hunter. "Better watch that old sack," he joked as Gatica slipped quickly into the darkness and started walking down the hillside toward the dry river bed a half mile away.

Gatica carefully picked his way around the scrubby bushes and prickly pear cactus as he made his way to the Santa Cruz River. He always was a cautious person, and knowing he would see Guzman meant that he would probably end up with a load of cash. What with robberies of illegal aliens and just the normal shootings and murders, he would be ahead of the game if a couple of willing shooters were with him. Gatica's business did not allow for slip-ups, and in this instance, he guessed correctly. In a way he was ahead of the game. He previously used Lupe Contreras and Sixto Bustamonte on small-time jobs. They proved to be both reliable and deadly, essential requirements in this line of work.

As he approached the riverbank he stopped and gave two short whistles. To his right, a soft whistle echoed his own. His people were waiting for him.

"Lupe, Sixto," he whispered. "C'mon, I got it."

Gatica's friends quickly made their way to him through the darkness, peered into the sack, and saw the money.

"Are we in business?" asked Contreras.

"*Seguro que si, amigo*," responded Gatica. "You bet your ass we are. From here on, no screwing around until we're done. We have work to do and we gotta be three careful *hombres*."

Gatica sat down and dropped his legs over the bank of the dry river. "Gotta be careful. No unnecessary risks." He looked up at Bustamonte. "You take the lead. Stay about twenty meters ahead of us and don't let anybody get close to us. No wetbacks, no *migra*, no nothing."

Gatica reached up, grabbed Contreras by the belt, and pulled him down to a sitting position. "*Compadre*, you stay twenty meters behind me. No closer; no farther. We all need to have eyeball contact with each other. No slip-ups."

Gatica twisted around so the dim light of the stars allowed him to see the face of his watch. "Ninety minutes, that's what it should take us to get back to the fence and across the border. We stay in the middle of the riverbed so nobody can jump us. We walk fast and get the hell out of here."

"Got my gun?" He held out his hand to Lupe, palm up.

Lupe handed him the tiny .22 pistol and smirked. "Goddamn man, why don't you get a real gun? Look at my .40 caliber. Look at Sixto's gun. Son-of-a-bitch, if we ever get in a real gun fight, you're dead meat."

"To hell with you," Gatica said as he playfully threw Lupe into the riverbed. "Just you cover our asses."

The hike in the soft sand of the dry river was grueling. They followed it south toward Nogales, carefully scanning the banks for anyone who might be a danger to them. They followed the river through the outskirts of town and approached the border. When they were less than a mile from the international fence, they climbed out of the river and headed southwest toward the slit in the fence which they normally used. They were less than one hundred meters from the fence when, from a rise off to the right, a spotlight suddenly swept over them.

"What're you doing?" a voice bellowed. "You Mexicans. What are you doing?"

From the authoritative tones, Gatica knew it was the Border Patrol, *la migra*.

"Just heading home, sir," he said meekly. "We've been working all week in the fields and are just going to our families."

"Friggin' wetbacks, get back on your own side of the border," the angry voice shouted.

The three Mexicans jogged toward the fence. "Yes sir, we're going," hollered Lupe to the Border Patrolman. "We're going." Gatica heard a pop and the shrill of a bullet speeding over his head.

"Shit head," Sixto yelled as they darted through the fence.

"Cheap-ass pricks," growled Gatica after they were safely on the Sonora side of the border. "Even pricks have to have some fun, but some day I'm going to take his toy and shove it up his ass."

Looking like ordinary workers on their way home, the three men walked hurriedly but cautiously for several blocks through the fringes of the tourist area until they came to Julian's pickup truck. He slid behind the wheel as Lupe got in the other side. "Get in back," Julian snapped to Sixto, "and keep your eyes open."

Moments later, the old truck headed south toward the outskirts of the city. He stopped at the Mexican version of a Super K-Mart and gave Lupe and Sixto money to go in and buy enough supplies for five days. "Get some ice chests, a few beers, and enough food to hold you over."

He sat in the truck with the money Guzman gave him, keeping a sharp watch, but saw nothing of concern. The men returned carrying what looked like enough food and drink to last them for a month. They dumped the goods in the bed of the truck and got in. Julian drove south, out of town. In less than an hour they left the highway and eased the truck up an old deserted road to an abandoned mine and the remains of several decaying adobe buildings.

"This is home until the job is ready," Julian said without a trace of emotion. "No screwing around. From here on, its business, and nothing else."

He showed them into the best of the old buildings and introduced them to their quarters: a couple of cots and a broken down table with an old kerosene lantern.

"I'll be back in a couple of days," he said. "Stay here. If anybody comes around, do what you have to do."

Julian walked to the truck and drove back down the rough road to the highway. By dawn, he expected to be in *Puerto Penasco* where he could get a room and sleep for a while. Now was the time to plan. Reynaldo Guzman, if nothing else, was consistent. Whenever he sent for Julian, it could only mean someone was to die. He always paid cash, small denominations of well-worn bills, always half up front, half upon completion of the work. Lupe and Sixto were good trusted helpers, but this was too big. They could access explosives and guns, but even the most trusted friend can surrender to greed. Aguilar was a good example. He was too greedy and betrayed his best friend.

This was not only a difficult night for Reynaldo, but also for Julian. What about his friends? Would they, too, have to die? This was a hard choice to make, but friendship can never take the place of getting the job done with nobody left to run his mouth off. Too bad, because they really were good people. First though, Julian decided how and when to take care of Aguilar. Maybe, just maybe, he might need them. In that case, he needed a good idea of how to handle them afterward. He saw problems popping up already. This was going to be a special case and required extra caution, even if it meant killing his helpers. Not a thought that he liked, but if his guesses were right about the police, there would be hell to pay. Plus, a big reward would tempt the most trusted allies. Lupe and Sixto? Good people — damn good. But they'd sell their mothers and sisters for a few thousand dollars. No doubt about it, because Lupe actually did it. He sold his niece to a pimp when she was twelve years old, because her mother was dead and she didn't have anybody else to take care of her. He got a few hundred Yankee dollars and sold his niece into a whore house. He'd sell out anybody for a good price, and there'd be a hell of a price on this. Lupe? Sixto? Yeah, no doubt about it. They'd turn him in.

"Oh, well," he said to himself as he slept on the clean sheets, "I'll have to keep all the money for myself. Life's a bitch."

Julian Espino Gatica was born in Mexico City. His earliest memories were that of a street urchin. No home or family. No brothers or sisters or aunts or uncles. No grandparent. No person to give him food or a bed to sleep in on cold nights. No person to take him to church or school. No one to give him a name. He never learned how he got his name, but older boys told it to him and he accepted it. It was much later in life that he learned the significance of his name; six letters and six letters and six letters, six sixty-six, so he decided to live up to his namesake.

Julian learned to beg for money from business people, to sell Chiclets to tourists, to wipe windshields for pennies or pesos. He learned to survive on his own, never allowing himself to think about the hardships. In fact, he never considered them hardships at all. It was just life as it was lived — nothing more and nothing less. The older boys showed him how to live, how to get food and maybe a little money, how to watch out for *la policia*, who to trust besides his own little ragtag group, and when backed into a corner, how to take care of himself.

Julian didn't cry as some of the other boys did when there wasn't enough food or when another gang invaded their domain of alleys and gutters and stole what little they possessed. Never in his memory could he recall crying. Early on, very early on, he decided that whatever happened to him, he learned from it and did not make the same mistake twice. If it was a fight he lost, he licked his wounds and carried a bigger stick. If there was no money to be made selling gum or washing windshields, he just as easily snatched a purse or a wallet. Maybe even took the hubcaps from a tourist's car. What the hell, they were afraid of him anyway, and were glad to see him get away and leave them alone. No, things were not bad at all. Learn from today, and get on with tomorrow. It was that simple.

Julian wasn't always happy, but he was street smart and knew how to cope — somehow to get along. He did not always have enough to eat, but things weren't all that bad. Whenever he started to feel sorry for himself, he could always find someone much weaker — someone afraid of his own shadow; someone afraid to take a purse or afraid of *la policia*. He looked with disgust at them and was glad he was his own person. He was never weak and got whatever it was he wanted. Long before it became a company logo, it was his way of life — no fear! He slept under the bridges or in empty buildings. He stole scrap lumber or sheet metal and cardboard to build a shanty. He survived. If somebody stole his shanty or tore it down, he built a better one. No one stopped him.

"Things could be a lot worse," he said to himself. Julian not only survived, but prospered. He learned first from the older boys, then young men, and later from businessmen. There were times people did not turn to the police or courts for vengeance for what they deemed was a wrongdoing against them. They went to an alternative source. They went to the streets to find that one person who gave them their justice — always for a price. Nevertheless, justice was theirs.

A daughter impregnated by a scoundrel bastard — beat him to a pulp so no woman would ever again want to look at him. A partner in an unsavory business deal won't pay his debts, then burn everything he owns — his house, his business, his car, destroy everything. Teach the dirty bastard a lesson. Even a priest. He wouldn't perform a marriage for a divorced man, so burn him out. Burn the church to the ground and let the uppity, holy priest see what it is like to be without his bride. Now the son-of-a-bitch will know what it is like to find somebody who has power over him. Let his phony god come and rebuild his church. Teach him what it's like to have power over people. This was real power. Julian's reputation grew as a person who was hired to carry out business where others failed. He was without scruples. He did whatever he was paid to do — no questions asked!

By the time he turned twenty, Julian outgrew the market for his talents as a local thug. He did not have political motives, but knew that his talents could bring a good price for the right job. He traveled to Puerto Rico to learn and to work with the *Macheteros*. They became his introduction to an education of bombings and political murders. They didn't have money to pay him, but he learned from them so he could sell his talents later.

From the *Macheteros*, he went to Peru with the *Sendero Luminoso*, the Shining Path. From them, he refined his talent of murder, and added the art of kidnapping to his list of marketable skills. Julian's reputation and willingness to attack, his lack of fear, and his dependability to complete a job crept across the lands and oceans, through the jungles and the mountains, through the nether world of the underground armies. Julian Espino Gatica was the one person for the most difficult assignments. What he lacked in a formal education he more than made up for in his indescribable skills. He learned languages in South America, in Iran and Afghanistan, in Israel and Egypt. He wore a suit and tie, a peasant's ragged bits of clothing, a police or military uniform. He blended in like a cup of water being poured into a river, never being noticed, but nevertheless, there.

Kidnapping, he said, was the one most lucrative skill he possessed. The skills of a kidnapper are simple, but effective. Anybody will say anything or pay any amount if they are in the hands of the right kidnapper. The kidnapper's unlimited strength is found in the very weaknesses of the kidnapped person. Take full advantage of the human emotions! Isolation, helplessness, intimidation, fear, degradation, hope, and of course, pain.

Julian traveled the world for ten years at the behest of the highest bidder. From Peru to Bolivia, from Guatemala to Argentina, to the Far East and beyond. Someone, somewhere, always paid for his services. It was in the jungles of Central America where he received the name for which he was most widely known — *Matagente*, the one who kills people.

Padre Ricardo Ruiz was the voice of the people, the voice of the *campesinos*. He spoke out against trials without due process, forced labor, unfair labor practices, and the slavery of the people for the benefit of the rich. He argued against the government for land reform and for health care.

His voice needed to be silenced.

One night the good *padre* sat on the hard board that served as a chair in his cabin. His dinner was to be a small piece of goat cheese, a tortilla, and an orange. It was a simple meal for a simple man.

The priest made the sign of the cross and asked God's blessing on his food. He was thankful for the few possessions he owned and for the miserly food he ate. He sought only to serve God's people. "I am in your hands, my Father," he prayed. He was taking a bite of the cheese as he heard the door squeak. He did not move from his bench or even turn his head to see who came into his humble abode.

"I know who you are," he said. "I know why you are here, so be about your business, but first, I ask you, hear me out."

The priest turned to face Julian. "The people have seen you with the army. They know your name and what you do." His voice was rich with compassion; a voice of love and forgiveness. "They say your name is *Matagente*, the son of the Prince of Darkness."

Julian exploded in anger. "Even as you are about to die," he screamed, "you still lie. I am not the son of a prince. I am no more than your darkest hour, and I take you to the gates of hell."

Matagente reached into his belt as he stepped toward the priest. Slowly, he pulled a small handgun from beneath his shirt and placed it to the priest's forehead. Father Ruiz bowed his head in prayer.

"Do not fear me," the priests said, "but fear the One who sent me." The quiet of the jungle night was shattered as the single shot echoed though the valley.

*

Guzman eased the boat out beyond the breakwater and slowed the engine to an idle. The smooth swells slipped passed the big fishing boat, gracefully rolling it from side to side. Guzman sat at the helm while Gatica sat in the sun on a bench aft, drinking a lukewarm beer. Guzman turned his seat around and spoke to Gatica. "Well, what is it going to be?"

"I'm going to blow him to pieces, that's what I'm going to do," Julian said with a smile. "I'll blow him sky high." He chuckled to himself as he threw the empty beer bottle overboard. He leaned forward and opened the ice chest for another one, rolled it slowly over his sweating brow, and sat back. "I'll blow him up, don Guzman. I think that is best. The way I see it, what with terrorists blowing up half the world," he paused and looked far over the horizon. "I'll blow him up, just like the Seventeen November group from Greece, or the Dev Sol group from Turkey. I'll find a cause like they did after the Gulf War. Those assholes tossed bombs everywhere just so they could get famous. He is so involved in politics that this is our only hope to try to disguise it. Personally, I don't think the blind will work very long, but we must give it a try. There are a couple of mosques in Tucson where he lives. I can call the newspaper with some bullshit. You know, claim some group did it for freedom against a big capitalist. Blame it on the sand niggers." Gatica snickered as he tossed another empty beer bottle into the swells.

"Now," Gatica said politely, "I need detailed information on him. His address, his habits, where he works, what he drives, when he moves around, where he goes, everything. There will only be one chance, and I can't screw it up."

"*Amigo*, like I told you before, I am a rich man. I have someone inside his house all the time. I'll get you whatever you need."

The two men spent the rest of the hot, humid afternoon bobbing in the Gulf of California, fishing, drinking beer, and talking casually about the demise of Aguilar. It was strange, once the decision was made, how easy it was to discuss what they now called "the transaction." It was nothing personal, just business.

The waters took on a deep translucent glow as the afternoon sun reached out and threw its long arms of red and yellow into the sky for one last burst of brightness. For that one millisecond before it was gone, there was a green flash on the horizon. Then, darkness swallowed the land and sea.

"*Bueno*," Guzman said. He smiled as he spun the boat around back toward the dock. "I'll get you what you need to know, and see you here the day after tomorrow. From then on, it's up to you."

CHAPTER 2

"Damn," Tony Castaneda grumbled as the sun crested the mountains, hurling its rays across the desert floor and into the bedroom window. Six o'clock on a Sunday morning is not an especially good time to get up, but once he was awake, he was up for the day.

"Crap," he grunted, shuffling across the bedroom floor, reaching for the shutters to close out the invading sun. Tony scooted his bare feet across the Saltillo tile floor toward the bathroom, rubbing his face and eyes awake. "Why didn't I shut those shutters before we went to bed?" he thought, turning on the tap, waiting for the water to get hot. He glanced at himself in the mirror. Proud, but not vain of how he looked. His waist was trim — well, almost trim. Other than a little love handle, he was still in good shape. The muscles of his stomach were firm, but not quite like they were when he was younger. If he searched, he could find a gray hair or two. Just enough to be able to say he was aging with grace, but still a fairly solid thirty-two-year-old.

The water was hot. Tony splashed it on his face, shook his can of shaving lather, and filled his hand with the foamy stuff. He looked over his shoulder into the bedroom where Muncie still slept. Muncie gave birth to their two boys, Matthew and Mark, but she was still slim and beautiful. There was barely a stretch mark on her stomach.

She was more beautiful now than when they married nine years ago. She could sleep through a monsoon, but if one of the boys coughed, she was up and into their bedroom in a flash.

He loved to watch her while she slept. She looked like one of those models for mattresses. He never met anyone else like her. Twice since they met he slept with other women. The first was Mary Lindquist, his tutor for English for Report Writing. They studied too late one night. One thing led to another and it happened. There was no love — no real passion. It was just two people who were together and did it. Linda Lewis was the only other woman he ever met who was bound and determined to marry him. She was an animal in bed, but a classless bitch. One time with her was more than enough. No one could replace Muncie, and since their marriage, he was true to her.

He looked at her long legs, crooked slightly at the knees; her gown crumpled high on her thighs, exposing a glimpse of her hips; her short dark hair tousled in a sexy, casual look. "Ow," he said softly as he nicked his throat and suppressed an oath. Tony finished his shave. His heart picked up speed and he trembled. He pulled the towel from the rack, and dried his face as he stepped toward the foot of the bed. He went to his knees and carefully grasped her ankles in his hands, lifting her feet to his lips.

"Mmm," she murmured, scooting farther down toward him. Tony stroked her toes with his lips, then with his tongue. "I love you, Tony. I want you, *mi amigo*. I need you."

Tony lifted himself onto the foot of the bed and caressed her ankles, then up her calves and stroked delicate little circles on her thighs. Gently, he raised her gown, put his lips to the small of her back and kissed her.

"I want you," she urged. Tony stretched his body over her. She wiggled and squirmed gently. "I love you," she whispered.

Their bodies flowed in unison. Her breathing became labored.

Afterwards, they lay together for a few minutes before Tony relaxed and rolled onto the bed beside her. Muncie shifted around, facing him and taking his hand to her breast. He held her for a moment, then leaned forward and kissed her ever so lightly. "Let's get wet." He rolled over her and sat on the side of the bed, then took her hand and helped her up. With his free hand, he unlocked the patio door and led the way outside to the swimming pool.

"It looks cold," Muncie laughed, standing there, nearly naked in the early morning sun, her arms wrapped around herself in a form of modesty. She touched her toe into the water. "It is cold. Please don't throw me in."

Tony stepped behind her, wrapped his arms around her, and held her close to him. Muncie turned her head and he put his lips to her ear, kissing and touching her, watching as goose bumps formed on her legs. Gradually, he loosened his arms and slipped his fingers down to the hem of her gown, lifted it slowly up and over her head, then tossed it onto a chair. Once again he wrapped his arms around her waist and held her close to him. They swayed to and fro to the love of the silent music in their hearts. The morning sun grew brighter, reflecting off the blue water of the pool.

"Tony, I'm getting hot."

He leaned over her shoulder and held her tightly to him. "Shall we?" he said as he leaned farther forward and pitched them into the cool water.

*

Detective Antonio Castaneda loved being a cop, but it was times like this that made his life seem perfect. Muncie was a good wife, smart as they come, a great lover, a wonderful mother, and somebody who could play and tease, giving as well as being the brunt of a joke. On top of it all, she was a good friend.

Tony beamed when he thought of their two boys. Seven-year-old Matthew already was adept at kicking the soccer ball through the house without breaking the lamps. He was in the first grade at Rolling Hills Elementary School, and was definitely a teachers' pet with black hair and bright eyes that melted ladies hearts. Mark was two, and a case of the "terrible twos." Markey, as they called him, couldn't resist grabbing anything that was in reach. He continually tested Muncie with how far he could go before she would bring him down to earth with her firm but loving discipline. Mark was a mirror image of Tony when he was a little boy, except for his hair, which had his mother's curliness.

Tony and Muncie had purchased an acre of desert land near the Spanish Trail and designed and built their house with the help of Tony's extended family. It took two years from the time they made the down payment on the lot before they started construction, and another two years before it was close enough for them to call it "nearly done," so they could move into their home. Even then, much was left to be done, and it was another full year before they had their official housewarming party. Tony invited his friends from the department and all of his aunts, uncles, cousins, and, of course, his parents and brothers and sisters. Muncie invited all of their new neighbors, her friends from the university, and the other parents with whom she shared carpooling adventures for the last several years. The party started at seven o'clock and the last guest left at two o'clock in the morning, except for Sergeant Ransom, who was partied out and slept on the chaise lounge on the patio.

*

Muncie looked at the clock through the kitchen window. It was nearly eight o'clock and if they were going to get to church on time, they had to climb out of the pool, get the boys up, feed and dress them, and get themselves ready. Whatever else might be happening, Sunday was a family day. It was also the day that Tony and Muncie would talk to the boys about their families, just as his parents and grandparents talked to him. The fast-paced life of television and video games robbed young people of their cultural heritage. They wanted their children to know their family, and to be close to one another and to their many cousins, aunts, uncles, and their grandparents. Everything they did aroused a story about "the old days," when "we" were kids. The boys were quick learners, and often asked to hear some of their favorite stories about the beach or the days in the cotton fields or the mines.

Tony's dad was a laborer most of his life, chopping cotton as a youngster in the Avra Valley, greasing wheels on the machinery in the copper mines as a young man, and finally, opening his own little restaurant on the south side, the Irvington Road Tortilla Factory. He worked long hours almost every day, and was a true believer in family values. He passed on to his children his work ethic and devotion to his family. He was proud of his children, and of what they accomplished. Two sons owned a construction company, one son managed a convenience store, one son became a detective, and two daughters were married and became the first to present him with grandchildren.

Elizabeth Califano came from an entirely different background, and it seemed to her that only a miracle brought her and Tony together. Her parents divorced before she was born. Her mother, Doris, struggled to make ends meet. They lived in a small flat over a dry-cleaning shop in the Bronx, but as life would have it, those who work the hardest get the worst deals. On a bright summer afternoon, two neighborhood thugs walked boldly into the cleaners and pulled out a cheap Saturday Night Special and demanded what little money the cash register held. Mrs. Califano hesitated for a moment, but that was too long for the amateur robbers. In a split second, there was a little pop and a spit of fire from the gun. Doris may have felt a quick sting before she slumped to the floor dead. Elizabeth was only two years old.

The New York Department of Social Services located Elizabeth's only known family member, a grandmother, living out her retirement years in an apartment in Miami Beach. It was there that Elizabeth was raised. She went to elementary school and high school, and did maid work for the little old ladies in the apartment house — the "blue hairs," as she and her friends called them. There was seldom time to do the things girls love so much to do, to paint their toenails and talk on the phone, to date, to dance, to play in the surf on a quiet evening. Maybe even have a boyfriend and make love under the moon. It would be so intimate. Lie on the beach and look at the stars. Listen to the rolling crash of the surf as her lover took her to the heights of the heavens, then gently lowered her back to Earth. That's what she wanted to do. To have a lover, a husband who adored her, go to school, have babies, and die with her children and grandchildren standing at her bedside. Just like in the movies.

Her grandmother often told her, "Honey, you have a good mind, but sometimes your head is in the stars. Be practical. This is the real world. Get a good job, work hard and save your money. Get a husband," she commanded. "Marry a good Italian boy and have some babies." Grandma was so practical. She didn't know anything about love, or books, or life.

But Elizabeth didn't want to do as so many of her friends did. They worked their jobs at Katz's Department Store selling cosmetics, stocking shelves, trying on shoes in their spare time, but going nowhere. What little spare time she found at night, she walked on the beach gazing at the millions of stars, twinkling, beckoning to her. "There is so much to learn," she said to herself. "They're not just decorations. Its life itself — life we have never seen. There's a whole new world out there, and I'm going to be part of it."

Elizabeth worked hard at school and even harder in the little old ladies' apartments, scrubbing toilets and sinks, washing their laundry, changing their bed sheets, and listening to their venomous gossip. She was on the honor role every semester and spent what hours she was not committed to school and work to browsing the library books and the Internet on her true love, the love for what lay beyond the hand of man — the stars and planets, the cosmos, the black holes and beyond. "The other life out there?" she wondered. Like her future husband, Elizabeth developed a strong work ethic, and saw her first dividend when she was awarded a scholarship to the University of Arizona.

Her first semester at the university passed quickly as she settled into campus life. It was after Christmas break. She hurried to the astronomy building, late for a meeting with her professor when she had a chance encounter that changed her life. She was lugging her books and a science project and was about to drop everything into the street when a complete stranger ran up from behind as she teetered on the curb. "Here, let me help," he said with a smile she would never forget. He took her books as she balanced her science project in the little box she carried.

"Yikes, thanks," she said.

"C'mon, let me get you there," he said, nodding toward the stairs.

Thus started the friendship that carried them on through school. Love grew quickly for Elizabeth Califano and Antonio Castaneda. They met in the library to study, then went to a coffee shop on Sixth Street to talk about anything, so long as they were together. It was in their favorite coffee shop, Einstein's, where he nicknamed her Muncie, to describe her beautiful cheeks. It was there, one year later where he asked her to marry him.

Tony graduated Magna Cum Laude with a degree in Public Administration, and Muncie with a degree in Astronomy. Six months later, they were married in a small ceremony at St. Margaret's Catholic Church. Elizabeth became a teaching assistant in the Astronomy Department while she worked toward her master's degree. Tony followed his dream and joined the Tucson Police Department.

"Stay with me, lover. Someday I'm going to be *El Jefe*, the chief," he said. His voice and the look on his face told her he was dead serious about this.

*

Tony and Muncie sat on the edge of the pool, dangling their feet in the water as the sun dried them off. "Come on, we need to get clicking if we're going to get the boys up and to church," Tony said as he hopped up and headed toward the door.

The day passed quickly. They went to church, ate breakfast at the Pancake House, and hurried home to get ready to go to the mountains. Later that night as they crawled into bed Tony briefly mentioned that they hadn't read the paper or listened to the news all day, and it was nice. There was no crime, war, or car wrecks. It was just a fun day and not a worry in the world.

*

Julian sat in the back of the stolen van, carefully wrapping duct tape around his shoes so he would not leave any legible footprints. A paper bag of PETN explosives lay on the floor beside him. Lupe drove and Sixto sat in the right front. No one spoke. Each knew his job. They drove quickly and quietly through the city, each with his own thoughts.

Less than three hours ago they crossed the border and picked up a car belonging to Lupe's uncle. He left it for them in the parking lot at the grocery store near the international border crossing. Rather than take the direct route to Tucson and take the chance of being questioned at a Border Patrol checkpoint, they took the roundabout route through Patagonia. Although it took nearly an hour longer to reach their destination, it was considerably safer than dealing with the Highway Patrol and Border Patrol. They drove into Tucson from the east and went directly to Movies 16 where the parking lot was filled with a good supply of available cars and trucks for their use. Lupe was an expert car thief, and except for a chance encounter with a city police officer two years earlier, was never arrested. That time it was just plain dumb luck on the cop's part, and Lupe ended up serving six months of a four year sentence in prison.

Sixto and Lupe climbed out of the car at the theater parking lot and quickly found a suitable van. In less than a minute, it was running and heading out of the lot. By the time the owner left the movie, they would be finished with the van and have ditched it in another parking lot. Just to throw the cops off, they would leave behind a couple of empty beer cans and a cigarette with lipstick on it. They brought these simple props from a Nogales bar, certain to make the cops think some kids were joyriding and partying. No big deal. Just a simple case of a stolen and recovered van like the other dozen or so that were stolen every day.

Julian left the eastside theater and drove Lupe's car to their pre-arranged meeting place at the Tucson Mall on the northwest side of the city. Lupe and Sixto followed in the van, carefully observing traffic laws. They couldn't afford to get a ticket now. Julian got out of the car, carrying an innocent looking paper bag, being careful to lock the doors. The van stopped nearby. Julian slid the side door open and climbed in. By this time, the sun was setting and darkness was falling over the valley. Lupe carefully guided the van the remaining few miles into the foothills. In an hour, maybe longer, it would be over. Julian looked at his watch. Antonio Aguilar's maid promised Guzman that she would stall dinner so it would be totally dark before the family finished. She didn't know the reason why she should delay the meal, but she knew her family was still in Mexico and at Guzman's will and mercy, or lack thereof. That was all she needed to know.

Julian sat quietly in the rear of the van, looking at Sixto and

Lupe. He felt a twinge of remorse for what he was about to do, but there was no other way. Lupe was a good helper and be missed, but unfortunately, he was expendable. Sixto was the same. He was good at getting explosives and using them, but there was danger in so many knowing the circumstances of Aguilar's death. Julian bit his lip in frustration. He didn't like killing his helpers, but he was committed. There was no turning back.

Lupe parked the van on a deserted trail or, more appropriately, a lover's lane. It would be safe there for a while. They quietly and quickly walked the short distance to a small ravine, about three or four feet deep near the house, and assembled the explosives into two sets of charges. The charges were set to go off almost simultaneously, one under the driver's seat and the other under the gas tank.

Aguilar's Mercedes was parked in the curved driveway in front of the house. A porch light was on, but where they were hidden was in almost total darkness. Lupe stayed behind while Julian and Sixto quietly slipped through the desert scrub brush the remaining few yards to the car. They scooted beneath it and Julian taped the explosives in place with his duct tape while Sixto held them firmly against the undercarriage and the gas tank. If all went well, the explosion would be fatal, but just in case it wasn't, the ensuing fire would finish the work.

In less than three minutes, the two men were back in the ravine. The first part of their work was done. Julian looked at his watch. It was a few minutes before nine. It was just a matter of time before someone, maybe Guzman himself, would call Aguilar on the telephone to come to a meeting. The call would come from a pay phone so the cops wouldn't be able to backtrack it to anyone. Aguilar would go, that was sure. When he got in the car, Sixto would finish the job. It was so simple, just flip a switch and it would be over. There would be a lot of noise and bright light and confusion, and in the midst of it, Julian and his friends would leave. In another hour or so they will be safely back in Mexico.

Julian looked at his watch again, and then at Lupe. "Head back to the van," he whispered. "When it goes off, start up slow and easy and head down the road. We'll meet you right over there." He pointed toward a side road a couple of hundred yards from where they hid.

Several minutes passed after Lupe left. The desert was quiet. In the valley below, the lights and sounds of the city seemed surreal; the residents were oblivious to the three men. Looking out across the city, everything looked as bright and peaceful as Christmas. Lights twinkled. A pleasant cool breeze blew, thousands of people went about their business, children did their homework, mothers did the dishes, and softball games at Santa Rita Park were played as usual. But in the tranquility and peace of the foothills, the three of them plotted a man's death. Sixto looked at his watch and grimaced. "What's up, *ese*? This is taking too long."

He became impatient and so was Julian, but they waited. Guzman promised a phone call, and it would happen. They would just have to wait it out.

"Shut up!" Julian whispered harshly. "Just shut up and wait. You have to be ready when he gets in, and don't worry about anything else."

In the glow of the city lights, Julian looked at his watch again. It was well after nine o'clock. Sweat ran down the back of his shirt. He caught himself wiping his brow. Every job scared him. His heart beat so hard against his shirt that he thought Sixto might be able to hear it. There was tightness in his stomach and arms and legs. He was tense, but that was okay. That was the only way to stay alive, but there was going to be hell to pay over this one. Too damn many people were involved. This kind could get screwed up fast.

He and Sixto saw it at the same time. The front door opened and voices came from the house. They looked at each other. Julian nodded and whispered, "That's him."

Arturo Aguilar walked nonchalantly from the house and opened the back door of the car as two little girls scampered from the house carrying what looked like overnight bags. "What the hell?" mumbled Sixto. "What's going on?" he whispered to Julian as the girls got into the back seat. Sixto crouched further down into the ravine, sweat pouring from his brow as he looked up at Julian who stared intently toward the car. "This ain't right, man," he said through parched lips.

"Shut up," commanded Julian softly. He looked at Sixto who held the switch box cupped in his hands. "When I say go, you go!"

Sixto closed his eyes and slid further down into a little ball. In the darkness, Julian could see his eyes open again, looking at him, pleading but not saying a word, terrified at what they were about to do. Julian stared, his eyes piercing the depths of Sixto's soul. Sixto took a deep breath and nodded. "Okay," he mumbled.

The front door of the house was still open. Aguilar walked back toward it, saying something to somebody inside. Julian heard some women talking, then saw a lady come out to the car. "Damn it, I can't believe this," he said to himself as she walked around the car. Aguilar followed her and opened the front passenger door for her. Julian watched them speak to each other for a few seconds, then she got in and he shut the door.

Sixto still crouched down in the ravine. Julian looked at him and put his finger to his lips. Julian looked back as Aguilar opened the driver's door and got in. The moment he sat down and shut the door, Julian ducked low in the ditch and nodded his head at Sixto.

The blast of noise and light tore through the quiet of the night. The light was like a thousand flashbulbs going off at the same time. It was a huge white flash, and then it was gone, replaced by the flicker and glow of light from the flames. The concussion rolled across the desert foothills and echoed off the low mountains to the west. Julian heard the tiny pieces of shrapnel from the car body and windows zing over their heads. They buried themselves in the bushes and cactus. Somewhere nearby, he heard the crash of what must have been at least one large part of the car body slam down into the ground. The two men did not stop to look at their handiwork. They jumped out of the ravine and trotted softly and quickly through the desert, taking only a moment to look over their shoulders. Julian was a little surprised. There was not enough of the car left to be recognized, and the fire was lapping around its remnants. He smiled grimly. It was good. It was his job, and he did what he needed to do. He expected a big explosion and fire, but this one was huge. Nothing was left. As for the wife and kids, that was too bad. It was Aguilar's fault for being such an asshole. He brought it on himself and his family, and couldn't blame anybody else. Aguilar would burn in hell, just as Julian promised.

Lupe carefully drove the stolen van back to the shopping center, signaling for every turn and staying just under the speed limit. There was no conversation among them, but Julian watched Sixto in the right front seat. He fidgeted, looked from side to side, and wiped his brow and occasionally his eyes. In the back, Julian unwrapped the duct tape from his shoes, rolled it into a ball and put it in the paper bag that he saved from Nogales. His eyes never left Sixto, except for an occasional glance at Lupe. But Lupe, too, was aware of Sixto's discomfort — or his guilt. That might be it. Maybe this was too much for him, what with Aguilar's old lady and the kids.

It only took a few minutes to get back to the shopping mall. Each of them used their handkerchiefs and wiped down the interior before they got out and walked to their car, leaving the empty beer cans and the cigarette on the floor. Lupe drove and Julian directed him to the shopping area near the front gate of the university. He pulled into a parking spot. Julian jumped out, took the paper bag and tossed it into a trash barrel as he walked by it on the way to the pay phones in the middle on the block. They were less than a mile from the Islamic Center. Just in case the cops or feds tracked back on the phone call to the newspaper, this would be the right neighborhood.

"Star-Citizen, how may I direct your call?" asked a polite feminine voice.

"I say this only once," said Julian in a forced, accented voice. "The freedom of Islam cannot be forgotten by the rich. We will strike until we are free. The United States of America cannot continue to support Jerusalem." He wiped off the phone as he hung it back on the receiver. He couldn't be too careful.

He walked back toward the car, mingling with students and visitors who hung around the burger joints, bars, and coffee shops. He wasn't in any hurry. Everything — well, almost everything was finished. The rest would wait until they were back in Mexico. He stopped at the walk-up window at Dinkies Dogs and bought three chili dogs and cokes before going back to the car. He was hungry and thirsty and knew the others felt the same way. He passed the bag of food and drinks through the window to Sixto, who was relaxed by this time. Julian figured that Lupe talked with him while Julian was on the phone, and Sixto was trying hard to calm himself down.

Julian climbed into the back seat again and Sixto handed him a chili dog and drink from the sack. "Drive, man. Drive," said

Julian as Lupe backed out of the parking spot. He ate ravenously. In an hour they would be completely safe. They could drive down the Interstate and leave the car in the parking lot and walk across the border. Julian's truck was parked a couple of blocks across the International crossing. From there, it would be only a short drive back to the adobe shacks where they would stay for a few days. Everything went perfect and according to plan.

*

Safely across the border at El Mercado, Julian ordered another stop to pick up some food and drinks, then headed for the old mine. Now, Sixto sat in the back of the truck drinking beer, while the others sat in the front, their conversation too soft and muffled to be heard in the bed of the truck.

"Well?" queried Julian as he glanced at Lupe and then nodded at Sixto.

"I'm sorry, man," Lupe said. "He fell apart and I think we can't trust him. What are we gonna do?" He tossed an empty beer can out the window. "He's our friend, ya know. We've done a lot together."

"I'll do it, but you might have to help. Just follow my lead and we'll get it over," Julian said as he stared into the blackness of the night.

"Man, this ain't good, and I don't like it. Ain't there another way?" Lupe looked at Julian. The glow of the headlights reflected on their faces. Julian saw the sweat running down Lupe's cheek. Neither of them liked it, but Julian knew it must be done.

"Not if we want to stay alive," he said. "Besides, we'll split his take. It's not our fault." Julian lit a cigarette and exhaled through his nose. It tasted good. He felt a twinge of nervousness running through his body. "It's just the way it is, that's all. Let's don't talk about it anymore."

*

They banged and slammed the truck up the road, finally bringing it to a halt in front of the old adobe shack.

"Let's have a beer," said Sixto as he jumped out of the back of the truck. He was smiling as he reached back in and grabbed two bags of groceries. "You guys want a beer?" He led the way into the shed, putting the bags on the old broken-down table while Julian fumbled in the darkness to light the lantern.

They finished a six pack without much discussion, not much more than simple bullshitting. Julian looked at his watch. "Let's hit it. We've been up all night. I'm tired."

He walked to the corner and sat down, leaning against the wall and pulling his boots off. Sixto and Lupe stretched out on the old cots where they slept the last few nights. Julian closed his eyes, but did not sleep. He only listened. His skin seemed to crawl on his bones. His heart pounded to the point he thought it might stop and he'd die and go to hell for what he did tonight. He committed many sins in his life, but never killed babies. Friends? Yeah, sometimes that was going to happen, but not babies. Go to hell? Guess so. If that's where you come from, that's where you go, so there was no sense worrying about it.

Sixto lay on the cot, his arm folded across his eyes — first the right arm, then the left. He tossed from one side to the other, tucking an old blanket under his head for a pillow before he got comfortable, then slowly began to relax. A few minutes passed before he breathed deeply, and then snored. Julian waited briefly before he moved. He opened his eyes and saw that Lupe was awake, watching him. Lupe would not move unless Julian told him what to do. Slowly, very slowly, Julian got up and went outside to the truck. Without opening the door, he reached through the open window and halfway crawled in until he could reach under the seat for his blackjack, his gun, and the roll of duct tape. He slipped the gun under his shirt and into his pocket. He returned to the shed without a sound and stood over the snoring Sixto. Without any hesitation, he swung the sap down solidly across the side of the sleeping man's head. The crack of the weighted leather against the skull made a loud pop as the bone shattered. Sixto made involuntary noises as he coughed and trembled.

"C'mon," bellowed Julian.

Lupe jumped up from his cot and Julian tossed the duct tape to him. In seconds, they wrapped the tape around Sixto's ankles, then pulled his hands behind him and taped them together. They dragged the unconscious man out the door and down the side of the canyon, bouncing him off the rocks and cactus. He was going to die anyway, so what the hell. They went about two hundred meters into the canyon, stumbling in the darkness as they went.

"Bullshit," said Julian. "This is far enough."

Lupe lit a cigarette and held the match for an extra few seconds as he looked at their friend, hogtied, helpless, and about to be dead. He turned his back as Julian bent down and fired a shot from his .22 into the back of Sixto's head. The sound echoed off the side of the canyon, then was lost. Lupe turned around and knelt beside his friend and made the sign of the cross. "Sorry, amigo. Sorry, but you got too weak."

Julian stood back and watched his friend crying softly over the body, then leaned forward and fired a shot into the back of Lupe's head.

"Yeah, I'm sorry, too," he muttered as he stumbled back up the canyon. He got only a few yards from the bodies of his friends before he stopped and vomited.

CHAPTER 3

Tony took his time as he headed toward the door to go to work. Matthew was valiantly trying to pour his cereal from the box with only fair success. Mark was sprawled on the floor trying to get his shoes tied. Neither of them were in a good enough mood for a hug, so Tony decided to tell them good-bye from a safe distance and not get in their way. He stopped at the front door for a long moment to hold Muncie in his arms and kiss her good-bye. "See you about five-thirty or so," he murmured, then walked to the carport.

Moments later, Tony guided his new City of Tucson undercover car through the neighborhood. By the luck of seniority, he passed along his old Pontiac to a younger cop in the squad and was assigned the only new car his unit would get this year. A new Saleen Mustang, bright red, with a CD sound system, AM and FM radio and an engine that loved to go fast and couldn't pass up a gas station. As Tony melted into the morning rush-hour traffic on

Broadway, he pushed a button under the driver's seat, and a drawer slipped open from beneath the seat exposing a multi-agency radio with the selector on the scramble frequency of the Attorney General's Major Crime Task Force. As he worked his way through the morning traffic, Tony glanced between his legs and inventoried the contents of the drawer: a Sig 9mm semi-automatic, a Tucson PD identification card, an AG identification card, and his badge. Tony learned a lesson early in his career. He showed up for work in the Patrol Division and fell in for inspection, only to be told by the not-too-friendly sergeant that his holster was nice and shiny, but would be a damn sight nicer if he remembered to put a gun in it. Ever since then he took a quick check as he left home in the morning, and again as he left work in the evening. The last thing a cop needs is to go to a gunfight with an empty gun, or worse yet, no gun at all.

The Task Force office was located in the Catalina Office Building in the center of downtown. It occupied the fourth and fifth floors, but was known to the other building occupants and the building owners as the America-Pacific Center, a computer hardware and software company that specialized in research and development of information systems for the international commodities markets. The cover organization was carefully developed to give the Task Force a feasible cover for the number of different people who came and went on weekends, holidays, and at other odd hours. Obviously, most of the people of the world were not on Mountain Standard Time, so the "information consultants" and others needed to work when their "clients" around the world were working. In reality, crime and criminals were a twenty-four hour job, and the Task Force investigators, crime analysts, secretaries, and technical clerks were always coming and going. This was a place where the lights never went out.

Tony wheeled the Mustang into his assigned parking slot on the third floor of the parking garage, popped his Dave Brubeck compact disc out, and took the elevator to the fifth floor. He glanced in the mirror as he walked down the hall. Muncie always dressed him right, with color coordinated Polo shirt and trousers, Cole Haan loafers, and a thin gold chain around his neck. When he opened the door to the outer office, he felt the tension in the air. Instead of her usual smile and "good morning," Angie, the receptionist, pointed her finger toward the briefing room door and said, "Its hit the fan this weekend. You better get your coffee and get to briefing. It's not going to be a fun day!"

Tony walked quickly to the coffee urn and filled his badly stained Fraternal Order of Police coffee mug with what might occasionally pass as a good cup of coffee, and headed for the briefing.

The squad called it the briefing room, but the sign on the door made it clear that this was a place where there was no nonsense.

EYES/EARS. NEED TO KNOW ONLY.

Sergeant Peter Ransom sat at his desk at the front of the room, shuffling papers, his face already tight with tension. Tony took his usual seat in the back corner and looked around as everyone found their seats. If the walls of this room could talk, they would tell stories about the state senator with a fetish for little boy's underwear, the president of the civic board who turned to the Mafia for financial backing to build a golf course that later went bankrupt, or of the chairman of the American Cultural League who ran a fleet of planes that brought cocaine and marijuana across the border through the Indian reservation and into the United States. The Task Force was one of the best kept secrets in law enforcement. It did not show up in anybody's budget, so it did not have politicians breathing down its throat. The state attorney general, William Markham, was elected on a hard law-and-order platform. He pledged an end to inter-agency bickering, and promised to bring law enforcement together to fight big-time criminals and corrupt officials.

During the same election, Markham's longtime friend and college roommate at Stanford, Morris Tinsdale, was elected as Tucson's mayor. Tinsdale also campaigned on a "get tough on crime" platform, and after their swearing-in ceremonies, the two began a series of meetings with Governor Spencer Wood, a retired navy pilot and former prisoner of war in Iraq. Wood was a strong legislative leader with a record of law-and-order bills. He pushed for faster use of the death penalty, life without parole for child molesters, and his favorite, a mandatory life sentence for selling drugs to a person under seventeen or within one thousand feet of a school. When the three men met, it was clear they had a single purpose: professional and ethical law enforcement aimed at ridding the state of some of its major offenders, many of whom were high-profile civic and business leaders. The greatest challenge was to implement the program without political influence. The potential targets of what they named the Attorney General's Task Force would most certainly be some of the biggest political contributors in the state. If the politicos could control the unit's purse strings, essentially, they could control or eliminate the Task Force. The only solution was to bleed money and personnel from other units, add some funds from seized drug money, and hope for the best. The unit started operating with a staff of two clerks from the police records division, and two investigators each from the Arizona Department of Public Safety, the Tucson Police Department, and the Pima County Sheriff's Department who were brought into the fold. Its first year of operation was a jumble of starts and stops, but slowly a satisfactory chain of command was developed, along with work styles that fit this unorthodox bureaucracy. The Task Force finished its first year by developing a case of fraud and extortion against Sammy "The Toad" Spliotro, an old time Mafioso and land developer.

Even reveling in the conviction of Spliotro, the Task Force remained in the background. After all the investigative work was done, the case was turned over to the Pima County Sheriff's Department Detective Division which actually made the arrest and took all of the public credit.

Markham, Tinsdale, and Wood liked what they created, and carefully but efficiently pumped money into the Task Force. By the third year, the Task Force grew to thirty-five people. Their commander was Captain Hector Martinez, a Tucson police officer of twenty-five years. There were no quotas of who would fill what position. Whenever there was an opening, the best person from any of the participating agencies would be picked. When cops were selected for the job, they considered it a plum assignment — the best of the best. The Attorney General's Task Force became the best-kept and least-kept secret, but was clearly a choice assignment for anyone. They liked to joke among themselves that they were La Tuna fisherman, meaning they liked to catch big crooks and send them to the federal prison in La Tuna.

After the Spliotro conviction came a quick series of arrests for land-fraud schemes, political kick-backs and income tax evasion. The time finally came to take the wraps off and let the Task Force stand on its own. With their track record, not even the dumbest or laziest legislator would try to subvert them.

So began the Attorney General's Task Force.

"All right, everybody, sit down! We've got work to do," barked Sergeant Ransom. "The captain and lieutenant will be here in a few minutes. For those of you who were in a vacuum this weekend, somebody blew away a family, and I do mean blew away. They're bringing in a couple of guys from homicide, and we're going to inherit the case. Pay attention! The pressure on this one is going to be unreal. We're really gonna have to hump it on this one."

The door of the briefing room opened and Captain Martinez and Lieutenant Jacobs followed two detectives from homicide. Tony didn't know the little one, but went to the academy with the heavyset one, Willie Barton. A cop's cop. Everybody liked Willie. He was a good patrol officer and never forgot his friends in uniform — the guys who got all the crap work but never the credit. When Willie was at a crime scene he always went out of his way to speak with the uniform officers, to be sincere about asking them about their family or asking them to help him. He was their friend, and they were his friends. Willie was a good detective and Tony hoped that someday Willie would get transferred to the Task Force. Willie and the little guy grabbed seats off to the side of the room. Willie caught Tony's eye and smiled. Tony nodded. He didn't know squat about what happened over the weekend, but from what Angie said, and the way Ransom acted, whoever got this assignment was going to be in the barrel. He heard it before, "Tough times baby, tough times."

Martinez strode to the front of the room and sat on the edge of Ransom's desk, looking like a man who carried the weight of the world on his shoulders. "Guys, ladies, I've asked Detectives Rooney and Barton to fill you in on their case, which, as of now, is our case." He nodded his head at Willie, who left his chair and walked to the front of the room, picking up a marker out of the tray of the whiteboard.

"Well," Barton said, "to make a short story even shorter, somebody blew up a family and killed them all. We don't know who or why. No real suspects to speak of, but the newspaper claims to have gotten a call from some kind of group, kind of like a terrorist group and something about the capitalist that forgot the Arabs, something like that. Anyhow, the FBI is going to look into that for us, but we think it is some kind of bullshit. Other than that, we don't have any suspects. No nothing. *Nada*! If you have any questions, Rooney and I probably can't answer them, but then, nobody else can either."

He pulled a chair around and sat, leaning over its back. "Anyway," he continued, "Rooney coordinated the crime scene technical investigation and I did the interviews. What there were of them. I'll let Andy tell you what he found so far, and for you guys that don't know him yet, this Andy Rooney doesn't tell dumb stories like why socks are called socks and not gloves. Andy, you're on."

Rooney got out of his chair slowly, like an old man who worked all night and was worn out. He walked in front of Willie, taking the marker out of the detective's hand, and went to the dry erase board. "Just a few notes for you," he said as he began scrawling on the board. "At about 9:20 Saturday night, forty-four year old Arturo Aguilar and his wife and two kids got in their car to go to a birthday party at Mrs. Aguilar's sister's house. They were in the driveway of their own house at 2440 Playa Del Sol, a two-acre estate with a house valued at about a half a mil, plus furnishings. Just as they were getting ready to leave, they left, just not in the direction they intended, but in more pieces than they intended. The DPS crime lab and ATF figure it was about twenty pounds of dynamite — maybe something else, but whatever it was, it did the job. About half of it was beneath the driver's seat, but not inside the car. It probably was taped on or with a magnet. The other half of it was under the gas tank. It was one hell of an explosion. So far, it looks like it was set off with a device triggered by somebody in a little arroyo that runs west to east about forty yards north of the house. We found where it looks like somebody probably spent quite a bit of time there. From the tracks, there were two of them — maybe three. It's hard to tell. We could make out the tracks going from the ditch up toward the house and car, but nothing real close because of the first responders who trounced around there. The tracks followed the arroyo down about sixty-five yards and then went north a quarter mile to Calle Ensenada. That's where we lost them."

Andy's notes looked like a Chinese fire drill, but he made his point and everybody understood it.

Willie got out of his chair and slid it out of the way to let Andy walk back to his seat. "Here's what we got so far. They have a live-in maid, a legal alien, named Marta Espinosa, who was at the house at the time but didn't see anything. She can't give us a whole lot now 'cause she's really rattled, but she can give us a fair idea of what was going on.

"Here is your roster of dead people." He hesitated for a second and caught his breath. "I can't believe I said that — roster! Shit. I never said that in my life. Let me start all over. Your victims are the owner of the house and car, Arturo Alfredo Aguilar. Let's see, he was about forty-four or forty-five years old. Next was his wife, Elaine. They were married eighteen years, and she was about thirty-seven years old. Next was their oldest daughter, Angelica." He paused and looked at his notes, then continued. "She was fourteen and went to junior high. Last, but not least, was their four-year-old. It was her birthday and they'd just celebrated a little party. You know, cake and ice cream and presents. That kind of stuff. Just the four of them and the maid. The party was after dinner, and they ate late because the oven was cooking slowly and Marta made the cake. Anyway," he continued, "they finished dinner around a quarter after eight, and then had their little party."

Willie sorted his notes again and continued his briefing. "Marta said that while they were eating, maybe about seven forty-five, she took a call from a Mr. Jones. She never heard of him before, but anyway this Jones wanted to talk to Art. In fact, she remembers the guy asking for Art because no one calls him that. So Aguilar took the call and talked to the guy for a couple of minutes and then went back to eating. The kids were supposed to spend the night with a cousin who lives on the east side of town. Mr. and Mrs. Aguilar were going to take them there and drop them off, but after the phone call, Marta heard him tell Elaine that he was going to have to meet somebody for a little business so he would drop them all off and take care of his business and then come back for her.

"Our guess is that whoever called did not expect Aguilar to be leaving the house for anything, so they set up some phony story to get him into the car. It was very unlikely they had any idea about the whole family going along. Anyhow," Willie snorted, "now you know just about everything we know."

Martinez moved to a chair at the side of the room, and as Willie finished, the captain got up and took a position at the front of the room. Commanding officers are supposed to have "command presence," and whoever wrote the book had Martinez in mind. He quit college after two years and joined the Marine Corps at the height of the Gulf war. He saw two tours of duty as an infantry sergeant and still looked like he could take on the world and whip its tail. He kept his short crew-cut, but now the black hair bore a scattering of gray. He chided people into betting him how many pushups he could do, and he almost always won. Martinez was Marine to the bone, and cop from head to toe.

"Ladies, gentlemen," he said. He made eye contact with everyone, slowly, to be sure he had their attention. He glared, but did not intimidate. Martinez wanted everyone to understand the gravity of these terrible deaths and to understand his confidence in his staff. Someone wiped out an entire family. Everyone in the room dealt with murders, but this one was different. This was extreme violence — tremendous overkill. Somebody out there was mean beyond belief and must be caught. They would have to bust their butts on this one, and the press would eat them alive if they didn't get an arrest — and soon. Phones rang in the chief's office; the public wanted to know what they were doing and if arrests were imminent. This was going to be a hard case with a lot of pressure.

Martinez began. "Yesterday the analysts worked their computers to find everything we could about the Aguilars, especially the old man, since we consider him to have been the primary target. Don't ask why. We just have to make some assumptions to get started and that seemed like as good a place as any. Here's what we know. Most of it comes from newspaper clippings, so take it for what it is worth. He is pretty well known in the big money circles and was the Hispanic Man of the Year two years ago, so that's probably why there was so much newsprint on him. Kind of a like a rags-to-riches guy."

Martinez opened his notebook and sat on the edge of Ransom's desk. "Arturo Alfredo Aguilar was born in Nogales, Sonora, Mexico. The dates aren't clear, but we think it was in February of 1964. He lived with his family in one of those little shacks on the hillside, but there was a fire when he was about seven or so."

The captain shifted his weight on the desk, rumpling Ransom's duty roster and car mileage sheets. The sergeant winced as the captain continued, oblivious to the sergeant's grimace. "His folks and brother and sister died, but he just happened to be sleeping by a door and got out. Afterward, he lived with some nuns, but somehow, he was adopted and immigrated to the United States.

"His education was pretty good, especially considering his background. He went to college at some school in Mexico and graduated with a degree in International Finance." The captain shook his head and turned the pages of his notebook before continuing. "The victim came back to the United States and became a citizen, worked at Banco Internacional on this side of the border, but left after two or three years."

Martinez contorted his mouth quizzically and shook his head as if in disbelief. "That's when he got really big, brokering deals on things going either way across the border, but there's no indication he was doing anything illegal. But," he said, "his business took off like crazy about the time of NAFTA.

"Now comes the big part." Martinez paused for effect, then slowly scanned his notebook. "This guy is big, and probably really pissed somebody off. He was on the President's Advisory Council on international trade, and had a lot of say-so on NAFTA. He was on the board of directors of just about everything this side of the Mississippi. He contributed like a crazy man to every politician, and knew his way around the governor's mansion." Martinez smiled as he continued, "Hell, he has even taken the mayor and city manager fishing in Mexico. He's on a first name basis with everybody, but they don't call him by his first name."

Martinez walked back to his chair. "Jacobs, you're on."

"Okay, listen up," barked Jacobs as he took a position standing at attention in front of the squad. "I'm going to keep a lot of this loose until things start to come together, so if I don't give you an assignment right now, I want you to pretty well clear your desk of whatever it is you're working so that when I need you, you'll be ready on a moment's notice. Here we go."

"Willie, we appreciate what you've done. Just cover everything in a supplement report and turn it in before you leave." Jacobs turned to Andy and smiled. "Andy, you've done a good job coordinating the technical investigation, so I'm going to keep you around, at least until you come to some sort of conclusion. What I want is for you to coordinate everything technical and scientific. Turn in a supplement everyday. Don't miss a damn thing. I want you and those crime lab people inspecting every cactus and looking up the asshole of every lizard within a hundred yards of that house. Don't miss anything."

Lieutenant Jacobs turned his attention to Detective Margo Lanier, a four-year veteran of the team and undoubtedly the best analyst to ever walk through the door. "Margo, you know what you've got to do. Every report. Every iota of information. Anything you get that is supposed to be fact: I want it confirmed with at least one other source. Better yet, try for two."

Jacobs was getting serious. Tony read his body language like an open book. "Every week," the lieutenant said, "I want to see a link analysis chart. Who knows who? Who goes where? What's everybody's common denominator? Somewhere in there is a link, and that's what you have to find."

"Finally, at least for starters," he said, "here's the interview team. Chico," he glanced at Chico Garza, "you'll lead the interviews. You can have Ann and Jimmy to help you."

Tony felt a breath of fresh air sweep over him. Chico was a thirty-year veteran who looked half his age, and was famous for getting people to tell the truth when they didn't want to say anything. Ann Deberg and Jimmy Lake were fairly new to the unit, but already built a track record of attacking like bulldogs. Things were off to a good start. Tony's old cases were stacked on his desk, and the last thing he needed was to get submerged by this monster.

Somehow or other, he thought as he headed back to the coffee pot, we're all going to end up in the middle of this friggin' thing. All of us are. This mother is too damned big for just a few detectives.

It was a common feeling among most detectives about bigtime cases. They looked glamorous on television and in the movies, but they were a living hell. They all saw their share of cops taking a beating in the press and in the courts. It started at the 1968 Chicago convention; moved on through the Vietnam War and the riots and demonstrations; carried over into riots in Detroit, Los Angeles, Miami and dozens of other cities; and was played out to its epitome in the Simpson and the Brown-Goldman trials. Of course, there were others but they were all the same. Beat the crap out of the cops, but make sure the attorneys get their fees — that's all that counted. Justice long ago was left in the wake. What about a good cop's career? Screw that son-of-a-bitch down the drain.

The chances of coming out on the top in this case were slim to zero and it hadn't even started yet. No, Tony was not chomping at the bit to take on this one, and he knew no one else was. They weren't afraid of being able to do it — they loved and lived for the challenge, but the rules of the game never changed. The villains were the cops until they proved themselves in the press.

"Tony?" It was Angie. "Some man is on the phone. Says he's your cousin and he needs to talk to you. He's really upset. Says it's something about the bomb case."

CHAPTER 4

Tony hung up the phone and exhaled long and hard. He caught himself mumbling an old saying that he picked up years ago from an old-timer shift lieutenant who came from some hick town in west Texas. "Sometimes you get the bear, and sometimes the bear gets you."

"Ho, Ho, Ho," the lieutenant said when he handed out some kind of crappy job, "I'm the bear, and I just got your ass." The bear just got Tony.

Tony went by Angie's desk and told her that he would be out for a few hours, but could be reached on his pager. He walked quickly to the elevator, and minutes later was pulling the Mustang into the mid-morning traffic. He slipped through the downtown streets and out onto the freeway to the Southside. Twenty minutes later he found Benny Osuna sitting at the bus stop on South 12th Avenue by the park. Benny was flopped across the bus bench, leaning his head across the backrest. Tony pulled up in front of him and tapped the horn. Benny must have nodded off, because he almost jumped out of his skin coming off the bench. "Holy crap," he snapped at Tony. "Man, you didn't have to do that. You scared the shit out of me."

"Sorry," said Tony as Benny opened the door and got in. "But the way you look, it's a wonder some uniformed cop didn't come along and bust you for being drunk."

"Well, I wish I was drunk or maybe even dead, 'cause I'm into all sorts of shit and don't know what to do." He looked around at Tony's new car and managed a smile. "But you must be doing okay. Look at this ride. What'd you do, screw the mayor's ugly sister or something?"

Tony accelerated and pulled into the nearly empty street, continuing south. "So where are we going?" he asked. "Tell me, cuz. What happened?"

"Oh, man, I'm in a jam and don't know what to do so I called you. Ya gotta help me, Tony, we're family. You gotta help me," he pleaded.

"I'll do what I can," Tony said, glancing briefly at Benny, "but you have to be straight with me."

"It's a long story," he said softly. "A really long and sad story and I'm scared." Benny pointed to a convenience store. "Let's stop here. I gotta get some beer."

Tony pulled in and Benny climbed out of the car, halfway smiling at Tony. "Man, you gotta get a bigger car or I won't be able to ride with you."

Minutes later he was back with a six-pack. He popped one for each of them as Tony pulled back onto the nearly deserted street. "Just head out of town," Benny said. "I don't want anybody to see us together. Just drive."

Tony turned out onto the freeway and headed east, away from

the city and anybody who might know them. They drove in silence, Tony sipping his beer while Benny chugged one and then a second.

"You gonna talk?" asked Tony.

"Yeah," replied Benny. His eyes were wet and tears slowly ran down his cheeks. "I'll talk as soon as I can, *primo*, just give me some time." He shook his head as he looked down at his beer and cried. He sniffled a little bit and then turned and looked out the window, away from Tony.

Freeway traffic was too heavy to be able to talk without having to watch for the big trucks, so they turned on the road back toward Saguaro National Monument, a lonesome road that curved and rolled through the foothills. They were miles from civilization when Tony found a turnout with an overlook of the city sprawled below them. He wheeled in and stopped. They sat in silence for a couple of moments before Tony spoke.

"Look at the city, Benny. When you're down there it looks so neat and clean, but when we get up here, we see how dirty it really is. That's what everybody is breathing and they think its nice fresh desert air." He turned in his seat and looked at his cousin. "See, Benny, everything isn't like what people think it really is." He took a deep breath, pausing for a moment for Benny to think. "Everything's dirty. Everything!"

They looked at each other for a while, then Tony continued. "Damn it, Benny, the whole world is screwed up and you're just now seeing it for what it really is. A screwed-up mess with a bunch of jerks running it." He smiled as he reached out and put his hand on his cousin's shoulder. "Welcome to the real world, *amigo*."

Benny got out and sat on a boulder at the edge of the overlook. He looked at the city, then turned to Tony as he got out of the car. "Okay, cousin. I'm ready if you're ready. Sit your ass down here.

I'm going to make you a hero, but you gotta keep me and my family alive." He looked deep into Tony's eyes. "You have to believe me, I didn't do anything wrong. I just walked into an ocean of pee and you're the lifeguard."

"You're on," said Tony. He leaned back across the boulder and looked gravely at Benny. "Let's do it." He tossed Benny another can of beer and opened one for himself.

Benny sipped the beer and set it at the side of the boulder in the shade, saving it for when his mouth would be dry — too dry to talk. "It was simple enough," he said, beginning to tell of the biggest crisis in his life. "I was just doing a pretty easy subcontracting job on a ranch the other side of Tubac, almost to Nogales. The guy who owns the place was having it updated, and little old me, hell, I'm just doing a little tile work. But I'll tell ya, looking back, I thought something was kind of weird."

He reached down for the beer and took a long swig before he continued. "I saw the owner only once and that was from a pretty long distance. He's a big Mexican dude. Nice clothes. Most of the time he was nowhere around, but man, he kept this really nice looking lady around. Her name is Sara. Man, I tell you. She's a looker!

"Anyway, they wanted a bunch of work done on their pool and patio wall, and I came in at the end to do the tile. Really nice stuff, they paid a bunch for it. I was about finished when the lady tells me that Reynaldo, I guess that's her old man's name, liked my work, so they wanted me to do a little work in the bathrooms and kitchen."

Benny reached down again for a drink and continued with his story. "But, *primo,* I thought then, this place is really weird. It's a big beautiful place, but no family things. I never saw anything in the house like family pictures or stuff ya see that women put in houses. It wasn't like a home, it was just a place. And the lady — Sara. I could tell she was a little weird, too. Like I would be doing my work and would see her just sitting around. Man, she didn't do a damn thing except be there. Anyway, after a little while I could tell she was lonesome, but I didn't do anything about it. She started coming around me and just talking."

Benny paused and looked over the city, shrouded in brown air. "She didn't talk about anything special, just ho-hum bullshit, you know, just talking to be talking. I told her about my family, and you, and everything. It was like she really liked to hear about a regular family. Man, I decided that she was just a hung-up rich bitch, but nice anyway. So, anyhow, a few days pass and I about got my job nearly done. She'd come around, maybe bring me a coke or something to drink, but honest man, I didn't even touch her. You know me. My wife would kill me if she thought I was farting around on her. I just did my work, but here's where I got in trouble."

Benny reached down for the beer that was getting warm and took a long swig. "If I would have gotten done in time, this shit wouldn't come around on me, but I got behind schedule. The friggin' kitchen tile was hard to set and it was a bitch to cut, so I got really behind." He stopped again and looked at Tony as if he was afraid to continue. "So I was behind and was supposed to be done by Friday and I wasn't, and I didn't get done Saturday either. So this guy from Belaire Construction calls me Saturday night, really pissed off, because he's the prime contractor. They're on his ass to get finished, and he's bitching me out to get done or I won't get paid. So, Sunday morning I get my ass out of bed and drive all the way down there just to do a little finish work, and this lady Sara is there alone. At least I figure she was alone, 'cause she looked like she saw a ghost or something, and really scared the shit out of me." Benny paused and took a long breath and exhaled. "She comes up to me and asked me if I was honest about you. You know, I kinda bullshitted her a little about my big city cousin cop hero, and I told her, 'Yeah, I was,' and she started to cry. Really hard crying and told me she was going to go to hell, but she wouldn't go alone. Damn it, she scared me. I thought she was going to kill me or something. But she calmed down and got us a little something to drink." Benny laughed. "Man, we didn't have no soda pop, but some really good hooch out of her old man's liquor cabinet. Shit man, you can't believe what she told me."

He reached down again for the warm beer and chugged, then twisted the can into a knot. "Sara tells me her old man is a big crook, big doper, big everything and he ordered that guy blown up. Says he's got friends in South America, Mexico, New York, Washington, everywhere, and he's really big and one mean son of a bitch. But whoever did it wasn't supposed to kill the whole family. That wasn't the way it was supposed to be."

Benny gave a half-hearted laugh. "She says she thought it was more or less okay to kill the guy 'cause he was a real bad ass, but she couldn't live with the idea that they killed his wife and kids. She says that made her realize that she was living a life of crap and she would do whatever was necessary to do to try to make it right."

He looked at Tony and shrugged his shoulders. "That's what she said. I didn't know what to do, but we talked about you. Anyhow, some way or other, she'll get in touch with you. She's got family in San Diego and goes to see them. Her folks are getting old and she has to look after them. She'll set something up with you, and man, I've got to get out of this mess." Benny looked at Tony with pleading eyes. "You gotta believe me man, I think this lady is telling the truth, and her old man will kill me and my family if he gets on to me. You gotta help me, Tony."

"I'll do it," Tony said softly to Benny in hopes of helping him calm down. "I'll take care of you and your family, so don't worry. C'mon. You can have the last beer while we drive and you can fill in all the gaps. I assume there is more."

"Yeah, there is," Benny said. "She told me how big and bad this dude is." He looked again at Tony as they pulled back onto the old highway. "He's really big, and really bad. He'll kill me, Tony."

*

It was mid-afternoon before Tony pulled back into the parking garage. Benny was as nervous as a whore in church, and he had every right to be. He was in a deep hole, and he was right. If Sara's old man was all the things that she made him out to be, he would kill Benny in a New York minute.

"Lieutenant, we need to talk," Tony said as he stuck his head into Jacobs' office. Tony shut the door behind him and sat down, shifting his weight to try to find a comfortable position. His heart pounded, and acid indigestion seared his chest. "How about a couple of your Rolaids? In fact, you might take some yourself, 'cause you're going to need them."

"Tony, if this is about the bombing, and it's as big as I think it is, why don't you just hold on to it for a few minutes. Let's get everybody together and we can all hear it at the same time."

"Fine, I'll make a head call and meet you in the briefing room in a couple of minutes."

Captain Martinez, Jacobs, Andy, and Margo were already in the room when Tony walked in. "Have a seat, Tony," said Martinez.

"Chico will be here in a second. I assume you've got news on the killings?"

"Yeah, sure do. It came and found me. I didn't stick my nose into somebody else's case."

The door opened and Chico walked in, looking like a tiger on the prowl. Tony screwed up and violated one of the basic rules of an investigation. Never go off and do something without touching base with the primary detective. At the very least, it is discourteous; and at the other end of the continuum, the lead investigator may already be doing something and you will screw it up. "Sorry I'm late. I was working on my murder case," he growled, throwing a sharp glance at Tony.

"Nobody's cutting in on your territory," said Jacobs. "Tony just happened to land in it, which he is going to tell us about. Right, Tony? It's your quarter, let's hear what you have."

The six cops sat around the sergeant's desk, using it as a sort of conference table. Tony sucked in his breath and began. "I've got a cousin, Benny Osuna. He's a first-class brick layer, tile setter, that kind of stuff. He called me here this morning and was scared shitless. I met him at a bus stop out on Twelfth Avenue and we drove around for a few hours while he calmed down. He actually started crying. That's how scared he is. Bottom line? He's got the inside story on the murders."

People began opening notebooks and shifting around in their chairs. The temperature in the room soared. It was stifling. Not a breath of fresh air. These are the kinds of things that you hope for, but even still, you're almost afraid to hear it. Tony thought he actually heard their hearts beating. All eyes fell on him as he picked up his story. "Benny is perfectly clean. He didn't have anything to do with the murders. He's just a hard working family man who happened to run into this mess, so he did the right thing and called me. However, our mister perfect citizen victim may be one of the biggest dope dealers in the state, if not in the whole USA.

"Benny is the subcontractor on a job at a ranch down near the border at Tubac. It's the Santa Rita Hereford Ranch, but it doesn't have any cattle on it. Benny doesn't know who owns the place. He is just under contract to Belaire Construction, which is doing some remodeling on the place. Benny came in after most of the work was done, and he put up a real long retaining wall around the patio and pool, and did the tile work on the pool. Then he did some tile work inside in the bathrooms and the bar and kitchen. But," Tony said, "most of the time he was working no one was there except this lady, probably about thirty or thirty-five years old named Sara. Benny doesn't think that she's the owner's wife. She's probably a live-in girl friend. You know," he said as he shrugged his shoulders, "a good looking chick for the dude to hang on his arm when he goes out to some big party or something.

"Benny said that he never got anything going with her, and I believe him, but she would come out and sit around and talk to him while he worked. She'd bring him cokes or a beer and they would talk. Benny said she was just lonesome, kind of a lost soul without a friend and he was somebody handy for her to visit with. You know, innocent chitchat. She's got lots of clothes and stuff, drives a new Expedition, but he never saw her talk with anybody except once he saw a pretty good sized Mexican guy named Reynaldo. He's the owner of the place."

Tony shifted in his chair, leaned back until the front wheels were off the floor, and balanced it with one foot. "Anyway, Benny got behind on his work. He was supposed to have everything done Friday, but he didn't. So, Saturday the primary contractor called him and told him he better get back there and finish up this weekend or he wouldn't get paid."

Tony got up and leaned against the wall. "Saturday he worked, and it was just like any other day, but Sunday was when it happened. He got down there about nine o'clock and just needed to do a little finish work. He was through most of it when Sara walked out. He said she looked like a ghost and it scared the shit out of him. He did some bragging about his cousin being a great cop, you know, a hero kind of guy."

Everyone smiled, and Tony gave a depreciating shrug. "She asked him if he was being honest about me and then to his astonishment and embarrassment, she started crying. Poor Benny didn't know what the heck to do, so he walked her back in the house and they had a couple of drinks — chug-a-lugged them, I think, from what Benny said. So he says, 'she looked me straight in the eye and said she knew everything about the bastards that killed the family. The old man probably had it coming, but killing the kids was wrong. It was a bad sin. The bastards who did it need to be killed themselves.'"

Tony glanced around the group, eyes resting on each face.

"So, she told him the story. Aguilar has run tons of cocaine and heroin into the states for years. He doesn't touch any of it, and never gets close to it, but he has contacts all over Mexico, South America, and in the big cities back east. He puts up a million bucks and makes two; he puts up two million and makes four. He's got lots of expenses, but lots of money. In the early years, other people could have cheated him, but he helped them and they helped him. Things went well for everybody, probably a little too well. Aguilar started getting bigger at some other people's expense. People he worked with for years. She knows because they would have their meetings at the ranch. It was kind of an Appalachia type thing. It got where they couldn't trust him, so they decided to do him."

Tony paused, framing his words carefully. "Sara told Benny

that killing Aguilar was business and she could accept that, but killing the kids was wrong. Bad wrong. An unforgivable sin, and if she didn't do something about it, then she would go to hell, too."

*

The afternoon hours slipped away quickly as the investigators discussed Tony's story. The shadows were long when Tony finally returned to his desk and haphazardly tossed things into drawers and file cabinets for the night. He was exhausted. Poor Benny was just trying to be a good guy. But he walked into one of the biggest murder cases in Arizona history. If anybody found out what he knew, they would take care of him in a hurry and he knew it.

"Damn, I'm tired," said Tony to no one in particular. "Guess I won't make it home by five-thirty." He shrugged his shoulders and pushed back from his desk. "I'm worn out."

The drive home was a good catharsis. He missed the going home rush hour, and traffic was smooth as he headed east on Sixth Street past the high school. The sunset glared into his rearview mirror, but felt good. Sunset was his favorite time of day. Let the day's troubles slide away and blend into the night. Relax. The Saleen Mustang knew the way home, so he just let it go. The captain's last words ran through his mind. "We don't have anything solid yet. Just information from a woman we don't know, and whose honesty and intent we don't know. She could be as honest as Moses or just a lying whore out to do somebody in. Time will tell."

At least Benny was smart enough to know that he needed to arrange a meeting between Tony and Sara. They talked about it and came up with an idea. She said she flew to San Diego about once a month to see her parents, and planned on going in a few days. Maybe they could work something out where Tony could meet her there.

*

Tuesday morning's briefing started out with Captain Martinez reviewing the incident between Benny and Sara before he turned the meeting over to Andy. "Tell them what you have come up with so far," he said, as Andy walked to the front of the room.

"People, even if we didn't have this story about Sara, I would still have a lot of questions about Aguilar." He pulled a crime lab report from his pocket and started going over it with his finger until he found what he was looking for.

"Keep in mind that right now everything is tentative, but it looks good from what we have seen so far. Basically, that Mercedes that blew sky high was not legitimate in the states. The lab says from what they have looked at, the emission controls and the window glass are not even close to meeting the minimum American safety standards. So then I asked the DPS auto theft unit in Phoenix to help us out. They checked with the motor vehicle department on the title and have pretty much decided that things are not right. They can't find any seller or former lien holder. The car just materialized out of nowhere. Now, our guy might be rich and famous, but he can't shit a Mercedes. What it looks like is that the car came illegally into the states. Someone made up a phony registration and/or paid some little clerk to dummy one up for them, and presto, they got themselves a legally licensed car."

*

Benny was more than a good bricklayer, he was an artist. Sure, he wore a blue collar, sweated like a pig, and his hands were rough as sandpaper, but he was blessed with brains and talent. He would never be famous like Picasso, but he was a brilliant artist nevertheless. He told Sara to call him Tuesday, but not from the ranch. Just too big of a chance that even if she was home alone, somebody as big as the people she ran with would have a tap on the phone. Benny spent a sleepless Monday night and didn't have any jobs for Tuesday, so he stayed around the house, listening for the phone. He didn't say anything to his wife and she went to work at the mall, so he was alone, just waiting for the phone to ring. Tony gave him some ideas on how to handle it, but it would be up to Benny to arrange things.

When the phone rang, his mouth went dry. His heart pounded. It was ten o'clock and the sun was not yet making the day miserable, but sweat was pouring from his brow.

"I can only talk a minute," Sara said. "I'm at the grocery store in Nogales picking up some things. I'm going to see my folks this weekend. Have your cousin there. I'll call you Saturday morning." Sara paused and caught her breath. "Have him in San Diego at a phone number and I'll call him. He and I will set things up, and you're out of the deal. I never want us to talk to each other after that. You're a sweet guy, Benny, but forget everything you ever saw or heard. Just forget it!"

*

Friday morning Tony walked casually off the plane and into the crowded terminal at Lindberg Field, blending in with the thousands of other weekenders dumping their money into the San Diego economy. Jacobs faxed Tony's picture ahead to the San Diego police, and he took only a few steps into the crushing mob before he felt a hand take his right elbow. "Tony Castenada?"

He spun only partially around and came face-to-face with a young, boyish looking detective cupping his police identification in his hand. "Hi, welcome to God's country," the young man said with a wide grin. "I'm Eric Molina." He guided them down the concourse.

The two detectives talked quietly about nothing in particular as they made their way out of the terminal and found Eric's unmarked Ford sedan in the parking garage. Tony looked at his watch as they drove away, only eleven-fifteen California time, and the streets and highways were already crowded with beach-goers. Eric worked his way through traffic, finally coming to a halt at the rear of a small strip shopping center just off Interstate Five.

"This is our cover joint," he said as he unlocked the back door, quickly pecking in the numbers on the alarm keypad. Tony looked around the nearly empty storefront, barren except for half a dozen telephones spread out in three small offices in the back. Each phone was rigged with an automatic recorder and pen register, picking up the numbers and address of any incoming calls. To protect themselves from crooks that did the same thing, they ran their outgoing calls through a blue box. Anyone with caller ID or a pen register who tried to trace the call back would get a fictitious name, number and address, picked at random by the computer. They were virtually untraceable. Their humble little storefront was a far cry from the Arizona Attorney General's Task Force office, but Tony assumed it met their needs — a safe house where they could come and go.

Eric gave Tony a phone number, what he called a "cool number," a safe number for Benny to give to Sara. A number she or whomever else might get it would not be able to identify or link to cops anywhere.

"These things aren't perfect," he said, grimacing as he laid out note pads and an extra set of earphones and a tape recorder so he could listen as Tony talked on the phone. "Nine out of ten ain't bad," he laughed, "and it just screwed up yesterday, so the odds are it'll work fine today."

When or if she called, the recorder would automatically come on, and the pen register would identify the address and subscriber's name where the call originated. That was the way it was supposed to work, and it did. At precisely two o'clock, the phone rang. Eric quickly held his hand out, blocking Tony from picking it up too soon. They watched the pen register, and on the third ring it showed the call coming from the Gold Coast Inn. It was Sara. They were off to a good start. Tony answered and introduced himself to her.

"I know who you are," she said softly, "and I need to see you now."

Tony listened to her giving directions on how to get to the motel, then he jumped in asking her questions, not giving her time to think or to take charge of the conversation.

What room are you in? She hesitated. Was anybody else there? How long had she been there? Who else knew she was there? Could he see the room from the parking lot? Did she have a gun? Did she have the room bugged?

He didn't expect her to be totally honest on all of these, but at least it gave him a feel for how she acted, and gave Eric a little gut feeling on how carefully they would have to handle her. She may have come forward, but he knew a cop could never trust a snitch or whatever he might call them officially — confidential informant, cooperating individual, C.I., or just plain snitch. They were all the same. You must play your cards carefully, holding them close to your chest. As they say, "You gotta know when to hold 'em, and you gotta know when to fold 'em." Always be in charge! Bottom line, never forget that the snitch is dirty and he, or in this case, she has a reason for doing whatever it is that she is doing. They can turn in the blink of an eye, and many have done it before. Just be damn careful."

*

Tony watched the surveillance team members take their positions before he pulled into the parking lot of the Gold Coast Inn on Mission Boulevard. Four members of the San Diego police intelligence unit stationed themselves where one of them would always have visual contact with the door of her room. The others covered Tony's borrowed undercover car and the parking lot exits. Nobody came or went without them knowing it.

In the next block, inside a shabby, rusted-out surveillance van in a grocery store parking lot, Detective Eric Molina adjusted his ear phones. He listened as Tony adjusted the body bug under his belt. He got out of the car, and walked up the stairway. Eric and Tony tested the bug earlier and it worked fine, but both of them knew the wires came unplugged easily. If that happened, it would be up to Tony to remember what she said. Everything would be totally dependent on him, and all of Eric's tape recorders wouldn't be worth zilch.

"So far, so good," Eric spoke quietly into the radio to the other cops on the surveillance team as Tony knocked on the door. "I can hear him fine, just hope she doesn't take his pants off him."

"Come in," said Sara, opening the door. Tony stepped past her and she gently closed the door behind him.

"Have a seat," she said, pointing to the standard motel chairs and table. "I've got some cokes if you want one.

Sara was not just "a looker" as Benny described her; she was nothing short of beautiful. Tony caught himself staring as he pulled out a chair to be seated. She was unquestionably the most beautiful woman he ever met. His mind raced back to the days when he walked a foot-beat downtown. That one hung over the bar at the old Legal Tender, a dive of drunken Indians and derelicts, but she hung there. Spanish Gypsy, a copy of an old Vargas painting. She was a piece of absolute elegance in the stench of spilled beer and urine. Here she was in real life, a woman who could not possibly have been the model for a decades-old painting, but if there is such a thing as reincarnation, then this was she. Long, silky black hair flowed down over her shoulders. She didn't smile, but simply presented herself. No wonder Guzman was taken by her. She was wearing jeans and a cotton blouse with the top two buttons undone, not making a point of being sexy or trying to turn him on, just being herself. A beautiful, elegant woman. Hard to believe that such a gorgeous creature could possibly be wrapped up in a sleazy deal of murder, drugs, and who knows what else.

"We need to talk," she said, sitting across from Tony. "I've lived some good times. God knows I've eaten in the best restaurants, dressed in silk gowns and worn gold and diamonds like they grow on trees. I've been treated like a lady," she said as she glanced at her reflection in the mirror. "My man has treated me right, but what happened to those kids did me in."

She paused and looked around the little motel room, trying to bring herself to continue. She brushed her hair back and looked down at her feet. "I never had kids of my own, so I can't say I know what it's like to lose a child. But, damn it," she said, shaking her head in disgust, "you don't kill little kids. They're innocent. They're not responsible for what somebody else did." She paused, breathing deeply. "The kids were the last straw. I can't take it anymore. I just can't. I just can't take it anymore."

They sat is silence for a few moments, Sara with her face in her hands, breathing deeply, catching her breath. Finally, she looked at Tony, her eyes red with tears. "I have to do what I have to do. I'm a whore and I know it. A real high-dollar whore," she said with a pitiful laugh. "My mother would die if she knew the truth about me, but starting now, I'm going to do what has to be done. Will you help me?" she asked, her voice almost pleading.

"You know I will, Sara. That's why I'm here." Tony reached out across the table, taking her hands, consoling her, holding her hands in his as she relaxed. "We'll work this out together. Trust me and I'll take care of you. That's a promise."

She moved her chair closer to Tony. Tears rolled down her cheeks. She leaned her elbows on the table, nearly face-to-face with the young detective. Her voice was as soft and gentle as an innocent little girl. "In a way, I've thought about this for a long time, and I know what I have to do. I'm no saint, but for the first time in years, I'm going to do the right thing. I'm not going to go to jail for someone else, and I'm sure not going to hell for them."

"Then, let's talk," Tony said with a reassuring smile. "And how about one of those cokes?"

Sara scooted her chair back and went to the bathroom sink, retrieving a coke for each of them from the ice she dumped on them earlier. "Where do I start?" Once again, she sat almost face to face with Tony. He felt her warm breath on his face, the sweet scent of her perfume lightly floating out to him.

"How about, in the beginning," Tony said with a light laugh. "Just like in the Bible, and just as truthful," he added.

Sara sipped her drink, wetting her dry, parched lips with her tongue. She looked away from Tony as she went through the same story related to Benny. She talked slowly, as if visualizing everything in her mind's eye as she spoke. She seemed to be concerned that she didn't omit anything. At the same time, he sensed that she was being very careful not to fabricate the facts she didn't know. Tony listened intently, not interrupting, but letting the conversation, or more realistically, the monologue, flow freely from her. He watched carefully, trying to detect signs of hesitation, signs of deception, any indication that she made it up as she went along, but the signs weren't there. He was convinced she was telling the truth, and her monologue was the first time in years, maybe the first time ever, that she could completely rid herself of the guilt that was buried so deeply in her heart and soul. It was as though he was her priest and she was in the confessional asking forgiveness for her sins.

"I was born in Cananea, Mexico, but my parents immigrated to the United States when I was an infant. They were typical Mexican immigrants, and worked hard at making a decent life in America. They saved their money and eventually opened a small neighborhood grocery store in Chula Vista, just across the border from Tijuana. It didn't take them long to become leaders of the neighborhood. They knew what it was like to be poor, and they sold food on credit to all sorts of people, many of whom could never repay, but would always try. They gave money to their little church and my mother, Rosa, took every Saturday morning off from the store to go to the church to clean and dust. Twice a month after Sunday mass, she would take the altar linens home to wash and iron them."

She sipped her coke. "After high school, I went to work at the Miramar Inn, an exclusive hotel on Mission Bay. I started as a housekeeper, but I quickly advanced from the drudgery of housekeeping to the lobby with the title of Concierge." She paused, smiling a deprecating smile. "I was a hit with the hotel owners and their free-spending guests. I seemed to have an innate ability to understand the guests and match their desire for food and fun with the nicer attractions and restaurants in the San Diego area."

The coke rested between her palms, apparently forgotten.

"Seven years ago I arranged a weekend cruise for Reynaldo Guzman and his wife, and that was the beginning of my 'new life.' Mrs. Guzman was being treated for cancer at the UCLA Medical Center, and her husband took her out for a long weekend of pleasure and beauty along the coast. Just two months after that joyful weekend with her husband, Teresa Guzman died.

"Reynaldo became a regular customer at the Miramar, and five months after his wife's death, he asked me for a date, a dinner cruise on the bay, dancing at the Hilton, and finally, walking on the beach at La Jolla. It was dawn before I got back to my apartment. It was a night of regal splendor, and was the beginning of my introduction to the life of money and violence." Her lips twisted, marring her beauty.

"I accepted Reynaldo's offer to manage his house near Tubac," she said. "My role was clear-cut and simple: to be seen on his arm when he needed me, to sleep with him when he was passionate, and to keep his house ready to receive his important business associates. This was a new life for me. I embraced it eagerly. I shed all remnants of my life as a poor Mexican, a peon working in the hotel, taking care of rich people. I traveled with Reynaldo, and I was waited on by 'those people'. I thought I had a new freedom, money and clothes. I drove whatever kind of car I wanted. I was important and made clerks hurry to wait on me. That's the way it worked out. My life exceeded anything I imagined — more than I ever dreamed about. It was too good to be true."

She drew a deep breath. Tony waited, not wanting to interrupt the flow of her words. "I've never been a part of Reynaldo's life or business other than to be there when he beckoned me. Nevertheless, as the months turned into years, I was introduced to important people who would visit the ranch. I picked up bits and pieces of conversations that were carried on behind closed doors. I shared pillow talk with Reynaldo whenever he had a bad day or an unusually good day."

According to Sara, Reynaldo was a shrewd businessman, even when working in the legitimate market, but his shrewdness turned to greed as he saw the profit margin on a few kilos of cocaine. His first big deal was a simple coke deal, moving a load from Nogales to Phoenix. Of course, he never got close to it, but arranged for its movement from a warehouse into a truckload of frozen shrimp that joined the hundreds of other trucks that cross the border each day. Just nine hours after leaving the warehouse, he nearly doubled his money, even after he paid all of his expenses.

Reynaldo graduated from the school of hard knocks, but he possessed an uncanny ability to be self-taught. He was good with almost anything he started, and his mental prowess was matched by his personal charm. It was said that he could sell refrigerators to Eskimos and talk a lion out of its fresh kill. Reynaldo didn't have to go to school, he could teach it.

He started working on the loading docks of the produce-import trucking lines when he was only fourteen years old. By the time he was eighteen, he managed a shift of drivers and loaders during his summer vacation. After college and when he was in his mid-twenties, he talked several doctors in Arizona and California into backing his investment plan to start his own business, Greater America Imports. The holier-than-thou doctors looked the other way while their profits piled up. They declared little income and he laundered the rest of it for them. Everybody made a ton of money. No questions. No problems.

"That weekend," she said. She looked up at Tony. "The weekend Benny finished his job. That's when I was positive what Reynaldo did, and I was equally positive about what I must do."

"Is there anything else?" Tony asked.

"What else do you want? I've told you who and why."

"Okay." Tony said. "I believe you, but I've got to have something to take back to my bosses before they'll let me go very far on this case. Let me tell you how the system works." He looked at her with the gentlest appearance he could muster. "We'll treat you like a confidential informant — very confidential. But first, you have to give me something. Something nobody else knows, something I can independently verify." He tossed her a smile. "Then you change from being a confidential informant to being a reliable, confidential informant," he said with a strong emphasis on reliable. "And that's about the difference of one to a hundred. There are lots of informants, but very few are reliable. That means that you're trustworthy, you're on our side."

"I'm not now?" she fired back.

"Those are the rules of the game," Tony replied. "I didn't make them up, but those are the rules we have to play with."

Sara looked at her watch. "We've been at this for a long time. I've got to take my dad to the drug store. I don't like the way you're treating me. Maybe this is all wrong." She shook her head in disgust.

"Damn it! Screw this whole thing. What are we going to do?" She looked sorrowfully at Tony, tears streaming from her eyes.

"Damn it — damn it! Can't you take what I've told you and arrest him?"

"Don't let it end like this Sara," Tony said, taking her hands in his. "You are almost there. Don't stop now. For your sake, get this over."

Sara pushed back from the table, pulling her hands from his grip. "When will this ever stop? When?"

"Get it out of your system," Tony said, coaching her to tell whatever it was he could use to validate her truthfulness.

Sara picked her purse up from the bed and walked toward the bathroom. "Be gone when I come out," she said. "Please, be gone, and take this with you."

She took a deep breath and let it out slowly, calming herself. "Philip Oper, a German-Mexican. Everybody thought he was a big trucker in Sonora, and they were right. He was big and rich. But you know what? He shipped more heroin into Arizona than just about anybody else, but he cut into some guy's territory."

She paused for effect as she looked directly at Tony, then continued, "And now he's gone. Not a trace. Reynaldo owns his trucking company, and no more little Philip. He's gone without a trace."

She smiled as she finished, "Even his wife and kids didn't try to do anything about it. They know what happened but Reynaldo took care of them, and that's how our system works," she emphasized the word "our," as though mimicking Tony. She stepped partway into the bathroom, then turned to Tony. "One month from today I'll be back here to check on my folks. I'll call the same number and we'll go from there."

"Good," Tony replied, "and you'll never regret what happened today. I promise!" He smiled as he got up, "That will give me some time to check out your dead German friend. But, here," he said as he scribbled a phone number on a scrap of paper. "Don't call that number again. Use this one! It's mine in Tucson. Call me here," he said as he handed the paper to her. "It's a private number and untraceable. If I'm not there, my voice mail will come on and you can leave a message for me and I'll find you someway or other." He smiled and his voice softened. "You just be damned careful when you call so that nobody can hear you or is tapping your line. You gotta watch yourself, you hear?" He turned and headed to the door, hearing the click of the bathroom door shutting behind him.

*

To the surveillance team outside the motel, the afternoon droned on. Other than Eric, listening to the conversation in room 204 of the Gold Coast Inn, they didn't know what was going on. It was a long, boring afternoon. They took turns doing what they called "the eyeball", taking turns watching the motel room door so they could go get coffee, stretch their legs, and let their eyes relax. Every once in a while Eric would comment that she was on a roll. Otherwise, they struggled with the boredom.

Eric kept the tape recorders and mini-recorder running, taking in every word she said. If they could verify what she said, she was, as they would say, "a dynamite snitch."

As the sun started its fall into the ocean, Eric barked over the radio. "Heads up everybody. Sounds like its over. They're setting up how they can contact each other again and he's heading out. Unit One, make sure you're in position to get some good pictures of her if she comes out while there is enough light. Everybody remember, don't tail her, just let her go. Get a license number if you can, but don't blow anything."

"Okay folks, it's over for now," Tony said as he walked down the stairs toward his car. "Everything went great, hope you copied it. In fact, hope you copy me now."

Tony drove the undercover Geo onto Mission Blvd. and headed north toward La Jolla. "I assume you can copy me," he said. "I want to be safe and make sure I'm not being followed by any bad guys. Sure would be surprised if she was setting us up for something, but no sense taking chances. I'll drive the long way around and meet you back at your office." He accelerated out of range of the body bug.

*

Thirty minutes later Tony pulled off the freeway and into the rear parking lot of the safe-house. "Did you guys think I was lost?"

"No way," said Eric. "We guaranteed your boss we'd cover your ass." He nodded toward a tan Suburban pulling into the lot. "You were covered all the way."

Tony smiled as two detectives hopped out of the Suburban. The driver was laughing. "Hey, my friend, you drive like an old lady."

The next hour was spent filling out surveillance reports and property inventory control forms for the reel-to-reel tapes and the mini-tapes. Sipping coffee, Tony watched everyone go about the routine tasks — those things they talk about in the newspapers about cops having to spend all their time doing paperwork and not doing police work. "This was real police work," he thought. Finally, they were boxing up the tapes. Tony gave Eric a thump on the shoulder. "If things pan out, we'll fry somebody's ass on this thing."

The team said their good-byes as they headed toward the door. They were cops, but it was the weekend and they wanted to get away from the zoo and enjoy what was left of Saturday night. Eric finished cleaning off his desk, leaned back, and blew a puff of smoke from his Marlboro toward the NO SMOKING sign.

"Tony, I'm going to pick up my girlfriend in about an hour. Why don't I get you to your motel and check-in and we'll pick you up for dinner and some drinks? We go to a neat jazz joint in the gaslight district. Great food and drinks, and jazz better than New Orleans. Well, almost better," he laughed.

Seeing Tony hesitate, Eric shook his head. "Don't give me any shit. We'll pick you up in one hour."

Eric was right. Good company, a couple of good drinks, shrimp and corn-on-the-cob, and some great jazz. It was midnight before Eric and his lover, Sonya, dropped Tony off at the motel. "Tony, you take care," said Eric. "You're really into something big. You watch your ass and play your cards right 'cause you're into some bad ass people."

With that, they shook hands and Tony watched as his new friends pulled into traffic.

*

It was Sunday at noon when Tony settled back into his seat and looked out the window of the plane. He saw the recruits in Marine boot camp "They'll have better days," he thought as the plane pulled away from the gate. What kinds of days were ahead for Sara? he wondered. Oh, well, it was no longer his concern. It was up to the Task Force to decide what to do with the information he got from her. Minutes later he was thrust back into his seat as the plane roared down the runway, past the jogging recruits and the Coast Guard helicopters parked on the tarmac. Slowly they lifted off the runway and away from Sara and her life. Tony looked out the window at the cigar-shaped submarines with their tall sails, berthed close to each other like fish in a school.

The plane rolled to the right and Tony's last view before they slipped into the clouds was the thousands of white crosses in the military cemetery on Point Loma. Then San Diego was behind him.

CHAPTER 5

Tony walked off the jetway and to the luggage carousel, looking for Sgt. Ransom. He was surprised when he saw Muncie, all but lost in the throng of people milling about, trying to find relatives and friends — greeting, hugging, and slinging their luggage through the mob. He couldn't help but smile as he saw her on her tip-toes, craning her neck, trying to find him. A warm rush flowed over him. "God, she's so beautiful," he thought. How could I ever start to compare her with that witch, Sara? She said it herself; she was nothing more than a high-dollar whore. He worked his way through the crowd as Muncie saw him and started waving. He reached out and put his arm around her waist and pulled her close to him.

"I love you, Tony," she whispered. "I called Ransom and told him to enjoy his weekend and that I would take care of you," she said, giving him a peck on the cheek

They grabbed his bag from the carousel and walked to the

parking lot. The boys were at his parents' house and were going to spend the night there. "I told your mom that I wanted to be with you, so she volunteered to keep them. I want us to be together." She frowned. "All week you've been too busy, and I want to be with you. Today is our time," she emphasized. "I've planned something just for you and me," she said as they got in the van.

"Where're we going?" Tony asked.

"I'm the navigator and you're the pilot, so you just go where I tell you," Muncie said with a smile. "You drive. Be a good boy and do everything you're told."

"Everything?"

"Unless you're a chicken." Muncie threw her head back, letting the wind from the open window blow her hair free and loose. "Yeah, everything," she said as she leaned back in the seat, scooting her skirt above her knees. 'Think you're man enough to handle it?'

"Golly, Miss Muncie, I'll sure enough try to live up to yer expectations," he joked.

Minutes later they were on the interstate heading out of town. Tony's mind bounced back and forth between Muncie and Benny. It was only days ago that they drove out this way while Benny cried and emptied his fear onto Tony, looking for someone to bail him out of the mess in which he so innocently found himself. But today was their day, and the hell with Benny and everything else. The rest of the world could go get screwed.

Muncie planned their interlude well. A few miles out of town, they turned on to the Patagonia highway, south — away from where he and Benny went and were quickly deep into the rolling foothills of the Santa Rita Mountains.

"Hey, babe, give me a hint," Tony said as he reached out, grabbing her knee and twisting her around in her seat so she was facing him.

"Remember the first time we saw each other?" said Muncie softly. "Without clothes? That's where I want to go, and that's where we're going. I've missed you badly, Tony. I don't like the dirty people you have to work with. They scare me and I don't want anything to happen to you." She paused for a moment and then leaned over the console and rested her head on his shoulder. "I don't want anything to happen to us."

The miles slipped quickly beneath their wheels. Tony's heart pounded and his skin tingled as he remembered the first time they explored each other. They hiked in the foothills and found a little stream nestled beneath some cottonwood trees. The sun was warm, and they took off their shoes and socks to wade, but the thrill of nature overcame them, and they made love. It was a long time ago, but the memories never faded away.

Muncie was the first to see the turnoff on the old ranch road. "There it is, my little sugar baby," she squealed with a laugh as she wrapped her arms around his neck, gently taking his ear between her teeth and tugging ever so slightly. "You didn't think I could find it, did you?"

Tony pulled off the highway. Muncie jumped out and swung the gate open. "I'll never forget this place," she said when she climbed back into the van. Tony drove slowly over the rough road, past the prickly pear and the creosote bushes, his heart still racing as he remembered their first time together. Twenty minutes ticked by before they crept over a little ridge and saw the trees and creek.

"We're here," said Tony. "Looks just like the old days."

Tony guided the van over rocks and stumps, scraping the undercarriage on the brush and an occasional boulder. In the distance, a herd of Angus cattle stopped chewing to watch the van rumble over the brush and stumps as it approached the creek. Tony pulled the van to a stop on a small rise. "Look at it, babe. It looks just like it was yesterday. It hasn't changed a bit," he whispered.

"I love it," said Muncie with a smile as she swung the door open. "I dream about this place. It'll always be special to me."

Muncie slid the side door open and pulled out an old wicker picnic basket while Tony strolled the twenty yards down to the stream.

"Come help me," she said as she pulled the Playboy ice chest out of the van. "I've got ham, cheese, chips, and two six packs of Dos Equis. We are going to eat and make love, or visa versa, and you get to decide which is first."

Muncie pulled a sheet from the basket and tossed it to Tony. As he spread it beneath the cottonwood tree, she laid out what she called her "gourmet" picnic. The minutes slipped quickly away as they sat quietly eating their sandwiches and sipping their ice cold Mexican beer. "Tell me about San Diego," she said suddenly. "Was it a girl?"

"Yeah, but why? That doesn't make any difference does it?"

"No, I guess not," she said. She looked sorrowfully at Tony. "But I've got bad vibes. I don't know why, I just do." She tossed her sandwich wrapper back in the basket and looked back at him. "Was she pretty?"

"C'mon! Damn it, Muncie, don't talk like that."

"Tony, you're such a nice guy, but sometimes you're as I as they come. There's something about this case I don't like and I don't know why. Just call it a woman's intuition." She sat in silence for a few seconds with her thoughts, looking out at the distant peaks. Purple shadows drifted over the sides of the canyons, and the tall range grass swooped back and forth under the gentle breeze. They could have been a million miles from nowhere. It was so peaceful and quiet.

"Damn it," she said. "I wasn't going to say anything about this, but it's on my mind and I can't get rid of it. I'm sorry. Forget it."

"It's been a long time," Tony said. He leaned back on the sheet, resting on his elbows as he watched two buzzards riding the thermals aloft. They slipped along the crest of a grassy hill, their silent, long black wings nearly brushing against the deep grass. With a gust of wind, they disappeared over the crest of the ridge and were gone. "It's been a long week," he said meekly. "I'm sorry I've ignored you guys."

"Nevertheless, today is just for you and me." With that Muncie put her empty beer can on a rock and walked down to the stream. She kicked off her sandals and stepped into the ankle-deep water. She carefully waded through the rocky stream until she stood on a sandbar in midstream. She kept her back to Tony as she unbuttoned her blouse and dropped it at her bare feet.

Tony's heart raced as Muncie reached around and unhooked her bra. She was a thing of grace and beauty. She carefully put her bra on top of her blouse and turned to him. Neither of them spoke as their eyes were locked into each other. They neither smiled nor gave any outward emotion of what they felt for each other. Muncie paused for a few moments, letting him take in this private and intimate pleasure as she stood there silently, without word or motion, beckoning him. Her delicate little breasts glistened in the late afternoon sun; the warm breeze bathed them in its freshness. She slowly unbuttoned her skirt and allowed it to fall to the ground around her feet. She kicked free from it, tossing it part way into the stream. Tony watched silently as she slipped her fingers beneath her panties and guided them over her hips. They slipped down her slender legs, falling to her feet. Tony caught himself moistening his lips.

She stood on the sandbar, naked. She used her toes to scoot her panties aside, letting them drift into the water. Tony's heart pounded as he got up and walked to the edge of the creek. He felt like a virgin on his first date. His fingers trembled and he couldn't take his eyes off her. It was more exciting now than it was years ago — that first time they came to this spot.

The shadows grew long, and in the distance they heard the first lonesome howl of a coyote. Tony watched her face as he undressed, not hurriedly, not without poise, but slowly, watching her every movement. Her breasts rose and fell as she breathed, while her hair flowed in the wind.

She couldn't have pleased him more. He was everything she could ever want in a husband. His disarming smile, his wit and humor, his love. Deep, tender love. He loved her and the boys with unlimited depth and zeal. But he, only he, could explore the depths of what made things so special between them.

The sun had long set over the mountains before either of them thought about the need to start getting dressed and packing up the leftovers of their food and drinks. The afternoon was everything she hoped for and more.

*

Tony crawled out of the Saleen Mustang and walked down the hall toward the office, running his mind over all the events of the past week: the reel-to-reel tapes and the mini-tape back-ups were in his brief case which he tossed on this desk.

"Good to see you, Tony." It was Angie, as she hurried to catch the phones that signaled the beginning of another busy work day. "How was San Diego?" she blurted as she reached her desk.

"Yes sir, he's right here. I'll tell him," she said to the caller.

Angie turned her eyes toward Tony. "The captain wants all of you in the room in fifteen minutes to hear about your trip."

Tony got his usual cup of coffee before pulling his chair out and sitting down at his desk. Seconds later he turned the combination locks on the briefcase, popped it open and removed the tapes and evidence sheets. It was still hard for him to believe how much happened in just one short week. He was curious how the boss wanted it handled from here on. "I guess I will find out in a couple of minutes," Tony thought to himself. He scooted away from his desk and walked into the briefing room. Most of the group was already there, shuffling papers, turning in vehicle reports, and otherwise getting things in order for another week. Ransom was in his usual position at the desk, busy being busy, totally unaware of what was going on around him.

Martinez and Jacobs walked through the door and strode to the front of the room. They went through the Monday morning rituals of most detectives: reading briefing sheets, sick leave logs, vacation requests, and the all-important vehicle mileage logs. Martinez finally turned his attention to Tony. "Okay, traveling man, you're on."

With that, Tony went to the front, sat on the edge of Ransom's desk and began the story of San Diego and Sara Hurtado, the mistress of Reynaldo Miguel Guzman.

The hours passed quickly as Tony went over her tales of bribery, smuggling, murder and high finance that reached the halls of government in Arizona and throughout the world.

Late in the morning, Martinez sent Ransom out for sandwiches and drinks. Everyone else sat mesmerized by how much information that came from just one person deep inside the tangled world of a major crime organization.

"One person," the captain said. "All it takes is one person, and look at this. Right here under our noses all the time." He shook his head in amazement at Sara's tale. "I can't believe this, but I guess I do," he said as he looked at Tony. "Now what?"

"I get started on Oper. Anybody ever hear of him?" Tony looked around the room as each one shook their head. No! No one knew him, but that was no surprise, since they never heard of any of these guys. People pushing millions and millions of dollars worth of dope right under their noses, and here they sat, ignorant of the whole damned thing.

"Okay, everybody," Martinez said as Ransom returned with their fresh deli sandwiches. "Let's do Oper."

*

Tony was surprised at how easy it was. Sara was right and told the truth. The Federal Drug Enforcement Agency had an old record on Philip Oper from an informant, but never verified anything. Supposedly, Oper was heavily involved in the cocaine traffic crossing the border into Mexico from Central America, but they never linked him to anything. That information was five years old, and the confidential informant dropped out of sight — maybe even was killed before they could get any deeper in the case. Anyhow, something must have happened to Oper, because he, too, dropped out of sight. Rumor was he left his wife and ran off with a new girlfriend to South America. From there on, nobody heard of him. DEA was busy enough with other things to do, so they dropped him like a hot potato. There was more dope than they could handle now, so why worry about him? But, sure enough, his old trucking company, Linea Pacifica, was now owned by an American, Reynaldo Guzman.

CHAPTER 6

The Task Force discreet communication room was unlike the San Diego storefront with its sparse office and little phone bank — nothing like that here. It was a soundproof room with more than a dozen private telephone cubbyholes, each about twice the size of a public phone booth, equipped with a tape recorder, note pads, pens, pencils, extra phone jacks, headsets, comfortable secretarial chairs, fold-down table tops that were stored in the wall, and all the connections that were needed if they would be running a court-ordered telephone wiretap. Everything was first class — color coordinated, modern, and comfortable. And, much like the San Diego system, a blue box that would randomly select phony names, addresses, and phone numbers if anyone else was trying to track a call into or out of the Task Force.

Every detective controlled at least one phone that was his own "cool" phone. Standard policy said no one answered anyone else's phone in the communication center. Detectives gave out their numbers only in special circumstances, and only to very special people. Usually, the numbers were given to informants who could call in without fear that anyone other than "their" cop would answer the phone. The system was considered foolproof, and so Tony was comfortable giving his number to Sara.

Along with the number, he gave her strict instructions. Never call from the ranch; never use the same pay phone more than once; always delete the outbound calls on her cell phone, and never call if she thought anyone was watching her. Sara lived by her wits and was smart enough to use the phone with great discretion. Of course, she was to memorize the number because they could never take the chance of it being found by the wrong person.

*

Tony was waiting for the call, doing busy work catching up on some of his old cases. Doing back-up work for other detectives. In general, killing time but still trying to be useful to somebody. Finally, after more than a week, it came.

"This number actually works!" Relief was evident in her voice when Tony answered the phone.

"Of course. You don't think I'd scam you?" he joked.

"I'm not sure of anything right now," she answered, a catch in her voice.

"Where are you?"

"I'm in Green Valley, getting a flat tire fixed. This is the first time I've felt safe enough to call you. My dad called the ranch because Mom is getting what he calls "loose in the head." We've seen it coming on for the last two years, but yesterday Mama got lost in her own neighborhood. From the symptoms, we think she has Alzheimer's disease, so I have to go back to San Diego."

Tony interrupted her rapid flow of words. "What does Reynaldo say about that?"

"Reynaldo says it's all right. I will fly to San Diego Saturday." Silence for a heartbeat. "At times like this, I really love him. He can be extremely nice and considerate of my family, even though he never had kids and never speaks of his parents. I learned early in our relationship not to ask questions. When he wants me to know something, he tells me. His family was something he has never talked about. But when I need to see my parents or to do something for them, Reynaldo is a kind and caring person. Tony, how a person can be so decent, and be the same person who could order a murder without the slightest twinge of hesitation? I don't understand."

"Neither do I," he told her. "But nothing surprises me anymore. I guess that comes from staying in this business so long."

"Do you want to meet me in San Diego?" she asked.

"Sure." He thought a moment. He didn't like the idea of going to a motel room of her selection like the first time they met. He remembered a place where he, Muncie, and the kids went when they visited San Diego on vacation. "Tell you what. Let's meet at Crystal Pier. Sunday at noon. That okay with you?"

Sara agreed and Tony felt relieved. They could blend in with the thousands of tourists roaming the boardwalk and pier. It was a perfect place to talk, and most of all, it was a place where the San Diego cops could keep a good surveillance on them. For the first time since the murders, Tony felt comfortable with how the case was coming together. It was almost textbook perfect.

*

"*Déjà vu,*" Tony said as he walked off the plane and found Molina waiting at the top of the concourse. The two young men walked casually through the airport and found Eric's car in the parking garage. They slipped smoothly into the Saturday evening traffic, coming out across from the airport and turned abruptly into a motel parking lot. "Couldn't get any closer, huh?" laughed Eric as he pulled up in front of the office. "Five minutes from the airport and about fifteen minutes from the pier."

He pointed to the same worn-out, tired looking Geo that Tony used on the previous trip. "There's your hotrod. All gassed and ready. We took the liberty of wiring it so if you guys end up driving around and get too far from our body bug, we can still hear you."

Tony thanked Eric and climbed out. "You sure you don't want to come with us tonight?" Eric hollered as Tony closed the door. "Saturday night, you know. Party time."

"No thanks," Tony replied. "It's been a long day and I'm pooped. You single guys can have it, 'cause I hear my pillow singing my name. I'm going to call my wife and sack out. See you a little before noon tomorrow." He waved and turned toward the motel office.

*

Tony left his room at the Motel 6 early Sunday morning and drove the couple of miles to the beach. It was only ten o'clock, but he was in the mood to enjoy some of the sights and smells of the ocean. A far cry from Arizona's burning desert. Besides, he knew the Sunday beach goers would be flocking into all of the parking places and he wanted to get one without having to park a mile from the pier.

With a little luck, he found a spot just a block from the beach. He was dressed as any other casual visitor might be for a weekend stroll on the boardwalk: a San Diego Padres sweat shirt, shorts and running shoes, topped off with a well-worn baseball cap that shaded his eyes. He grabbed a cup of coffee from Starbucks at the foot of the pier, and walked slowly south on the boardwalk. He was always amazed at the conglomeration of lifestyles at the beach. He and Muncie came here a dozen or more times, but the street-freaks and tourists never changed. Got older maybe, but basically, things never changed. Two fifty-year-old hippies with dirty, bare feet sat on the seawall playing chess. Nearby, a black man in his twenties, who looked like he hadn't seen a shower in years, was playing a flute while a snake was winding itself around his neck. And of course, there were droves of tourists taking in the sights, falling off their bogie-boards, eating a Big Olaf, or chugging a cold beer while they watched the bikini-clad girls hop around as they played volley-ball.

Tony walked for nearly an hour, and then headed back toward the pier. Rather than walk back on the boardwalk, he hopped over the seawall and walked down to the water's edge. The sand was hard-packed from the tide. He picked up his pace and broke into a steady jog, joining the masses of people doing their ritual run on the beach. Twenty minutes later, panting and sweating, he reached the pilings beneath the pier. He slowed to a brisk walk while he caught his breath, then walked back across the beach to the boardwalk. It was eleven-thirty. By the time he got to the entry of the pier, he saw Eric Molina waving him over to the van in the alley.

"Dude, we were starting to wonder where the hell you could be," said Eric. He was irritated that Tony didn't check-in with them before he took his time on the beach.

"Sorry," said Tony sincerely. A few minutes later he was wired up and ready to go.

"Just remember," said Eric, "we don't want to do a car chase in this traffic, so you just stay around here. It's okay if you guys go into a café or something, but stay out of a car if you can."

With that, Tony climbed out of the van and walked onto the pier. He walked past an old Filipino couple doing the required underhand cast as they worked to catch enough fish to feed their family for the week. He stopped for a few minutes and was impressed with how good they were. Every couple of minutes one of them would pull in a fish. They weren't very big, but Tony guessed that if you caught enough of them you could eat your fill. A little farther out he watched a teenage couple role a marijuana cigarette and try to light it. He couldn't help but laugh quietly. They thought they were so damned cool, but they looked like two babies playing with a new toy. Every time they tried to light it, the wind blew out the match. Finally, just as the young girl got it lit and was handing it to the boy, the wind snatched it from her fingers and blew it into the sea. A little justice!

Tony walked to the end of the pier and leaned on the rail and watched the surfers. They looked totally at home lying on their boards nearly a quarter of a mile from the beach, rolling over the small waves, but watching for the big one — the one that would give them a thrilling ride to the beach, or would throw them beneath its awesome power and pound them into the sand.

Tony checked his watch. It was ten after twelve. She was late. "Women," he said to himself. "Never on time."

It was nearly twelve-thirty when he saw her walking toward him. She was wearing white shorts and a white blouse and sandals. Her black hair was pulled back into a bun, her face glistening in the sun. Tony reminisced how beautiful she was. Men have killed for less. He was glad to be here with her. There was something about her that made him feel special — to be able to share her innermost thoughts — to be the one who will guide her to a new life. She was special and she made him feel special. He almost forgot what he was going to do. He just enjoyed being with her.

"Sorry," she said. "I haven't been to the beach in a long time and didn't plan on all of this traffic."

"No problem," Tony said as he took her hand and started walking with her to the little fish and chips stand on the pier. "Let's get something to drink."

Tony ordered Diet Cokes and they walked back toward the end of the pier. He wiped the sand and grit off an old bench, and they sat down, leaning against the side of the abandoned bait house, protected from the wind. Tony popped their Cokes open as he watched her gazing out over the surf, watching the innocence of families and young couples enjoying their weekend.

"I would gladly give a million bucks to trade places with them," she said. She stood up and walked to the rail. She leaned over the old, white-washed rail, looking down into the churning surf, then turned and looked at him. Tears, ever so gently, flowed from her eyes.

"You've got to help me, Tony," she whispered against the wind. "You're the only chance there is for me to get the rest of my life straight."

Eric and the other people on the surveillance team watched through their binoculars and listened over the body bug. Today everybody wore earpieces because they didn't know how much walking around Sara and Tony would do. This way, wherever they went, somebody would be able to keep an eye on them and listen to the conversation. Eric held down his usual position in the van, recording the conversation and sipping his Royal Crown.

It was a beautiful California afternoon, just the kind the Chamber of Commerce advertises. Everybody was content as Tony and Sara talked. They spent nearly an hour at the end of the pier talking about her parents, their store, her stay at their house last night, and about his lumpy bed at the motel before going to the boardwalk and finding a quiet table on the deck at the Seawolf Bar and Grill. Obviously, Sara didn't think about a surveillance team recording their conversation. She constantly veered off and steered the conversation away from what they needed her to talk about. It was becoming clear to everyone that she enjoyed Tony's company, and if he wasn't careful she would take the whole thing astray and screw it up. Tony was also aware of how hard it was to keep her doing what they called "time on task," that is — he continually guided her back to what they needed to talk about. In the back of his mind, he knew he was enjoying every minute he shared with her.

It was almost two o'clock and Sara hadn't eaten anything and was starved. Tony ordered a burger and beer while Sara opted for a seafood salad and glass of wine. Their conversation during the meal was strictly polite chitchat. The tables were much too close together to have any discussion about drugs and murder, so they talked about the weather, the sun and the surf, the crowds and the traffic, and the prices on the menu and even managed a little laugh at them. Sara was melancholy and Tony knew she was badly troubled. It was a lot more than just Rosa's illness: the whole thing, the deaths of four people, how her life was passing by and she couldn't undo what she did with her life. All the money in the world couldn't buy back the years that she spent with Reynaldo. What a waste and she knew it.

They finished their food and went back to the boardwalk. Sara pointed the way to a small park up the boardwalk from the pier. Ten minutes later they sat under a palm tree watching the surf. Tony thought to himself how passersby might think of them as lovers on a getaway weekend from the kids. They could never guess that such a perfect looking couple was talking about murder, drugs, and all the filth of society.

"You just talk," said Tony as he sat on the grass and leaned back against a palm tree. Sara, too, sat on the grass and leaned back, tucking her head into the crook of his shoulder. "I don't know if I want to talk anymore," she said. "This is too perfect and I don't want to mess it up." She watched for a few minutes as the surfers slipped down the face of the breakers, gracefully "hanging ten" as they headed toward the beach.

"Okay, I guess," she said as she tilted her head up, looking into his eyes. Their lips nearly touched before she turned away and began talking. "It is just like the Mafia, so organized and corrupt. They corrupt everything they touch. Rey never sat down and talked business with me, but I'm not blind or deaf. I knew what was going on. Sometimes he met with one or two guys. When there were just a few, they talked in the library. I never eavesdropped, but I'd be in and out with food or drinks or if they needed something. I knew what they were talking about."

Sara leaned forward and rested her chin on her knees. "They never used those magic words. You know, heroin or cocaine, but I knew what they talked about." She turned and looked at him, "They never said 'murder,' they would just say that someone had to go, and that would be that."

She leaned back against him again and stared at the sea as she spoke. "Sometimes there would be money, lots of it. Sometimes it would be in cardboard boxes, there would be so much of it. Sometimes it would be there before somebody came and it would be gone when they left, sometimes just the opposite. More money than you could count."

She gave a soft laugh as she continued, "And the big meetings, wow, they were something else. I know about how the Mafia held that big meeting at Appalachia, well Rey has something like that once or twice a year. Nine, ten, maybe a dozen people. They were in the dining room, but I never went in while they were there. Sometimes somebody would come out and I might get them some food or something, but I never went in. They control everything, and if they can't?" She paused and looked up at him, "They would take care of it. It would be that simple."

"Tell me a name," said Tony. "You were right on the spot about Oper. What about some of the people that came to the house. Any name, that's what I need," he said.

"Isn't that stupid?" she replied. "Honestly Tony, I can't because I don't know. I know Aguilar because they were friends for years." Sara sat up straight and looked over her shoulder at Tony. "You must believe me. I don't know the others. They came and went, but Rey never talked real business to me. You don't know him, but I do. He's very private, and frankly, I never wanted to know. Maybe that's how I absolved my sins 'cause I didn't know."

She leaned back, again finding comfort in his warmth, breathing deeply, enjoying the fresh salt air. "Sounds like the Nazis, doesn't it? I didn't know. I was just taking orders, so I'm not guilty."

Tony wrapped his arm around her and held her. She was so weak. Her hair was so soft against his cheek. Her body so warm. The scent of her perfume. Amarige!

Amarige! Muncie's perfume. Until this very moment he was

always faithful, but the temptation was there like never before. Her helplessness and beauty overwhelmed him. He wanted to be with Sara, if but for a minute, but in the back of his mind ran the poem that Muncie said to him so many times. Something about love is a spring that never runs dry.

"Oh, yeah, before I forget it," she said, snapping him back to her attention. "NAFTA, wow, that's when money really flowed." She laughed out loud. "Good for everybody, they said. And it was. Damn, Tony," she said as she sat forward and looked at him. "Did the government know what they were doing with that and all the other junk that was going on about then?"

"Why? What do you mean?"

"I'm sorry Tony, but are cops dumb as hell? NAFTA! Think about it. Almost overnight the number of produce and fish trucks coming across the border nearly doubled." She shook her head in disbelief. "And at the same time you cut way back on the number of inspectors at the border. That's part of a conversation I heard one night. That night Aguilar was at the house. They were laughing and having a good time. Seventy-five percent, that's what they were talking about. Their chances of having a truck caught dropped by seventy-five percent. It wasn't long after that when I figured out that they had a big falling out. I heard Rey in the library one night and he was having a fit. Something about Arturo starting up a new deal or going off on his own to the mid-west. I think he bought a house or something, but I'm not sure. There was so much I didn't know," she said softly. "Rey would just be gone without a word. Sometimes for a day; sometimes for a week. Never a word. Gone. That's all. I'd get so lonely. Sometimes I would be so lonesome I would cry myself to sleep. Then he would come back and make everything okay. Give me a coat or buy me a new car or we'd go to New York and see a show." She looked again at Tony. "He'd treat me right and I would pretend that everything was fine, but it wasn't, was it?" she asked.

"You're right there," he replied. "It wasn't."

He took her hands in his and held her for a minute before he spoke. "Can you take me in Sara?" he said seriously. "Take me into the organization?"

"We were made for each other," she said with a smile. "We think alike, Tony. That means something."

"Huh? What are you talking about?"

"You're not going to believe this, but that is exactly what I was thinking. Listen, my cousin Freddy lives here. He's an all right guy, but never amounted to anything. Some days he helps my dad around the store, ya know, that kind of guy. Just there. A few months ago I asked Rey about letting Freddy work in the business, and he said it would be okay."

They were still holding hands, and she looked down at their clasped, interlocking fingers. "Maybe God planned this for us, Tony. Maybe so. You and Freddy could pass for twins. We'd have to be smarter than Rey and his friends, but yeah, I can take you in."

She stood up, extending her hand to help him get up and they started walking toward her car. "What about me when it's over?" she asked. "What will happen?'

Tony took one last look at the beach before they turned away and started down a side street toward her car. "Nothing too much," he replied. "It'll be kind of anti-climatic after all you have been through. We'll put you in federal protection — a new name, new everything." He put his arm around her waist and held her as they walked. "It'll be like you never existed and you'll disappear to wherever you want to live. Maybe San Francisco or New York."

"Those places are too cold and damp," she whispered. "I don't want to go there, can't it be someplace warm?"

"Sure," replied Tony. He kicked an empty beer can off the sidewalk and into the gutter. She looked mournfully at the can wallowing in the grime. Was it symbolic of her and what was going to happen when the cops were done? Would they throw her away like an old can?

*

They walked hand-in-hand the three blocks to her rented Lincoln Town Car, each with their own thoughts. Hardly a word was spoken. They stood for a few minutes saying their good-byes, then she got in and Tony closed the door. Sara pushed the power button and lowered the window.

"Come here," she said. Tony leaned over and stuck his head in the car, expecting her to say something about Reynaldo. Sara reached her hand behind his dark hair and eased him toward her. They stopped only inches away from each other, feeling the other's breath float against their lips, then she pressed her mouth against his and held him tightly. Tony caught his breath and then reached his arms around her. Her tongue slipped between his lips as he stroked her cheeks. Slowly, she leaned away from him.

"Tony, where were you a few years ago?" Then she started the car and drove away.

*

"Wow, man, you're gonna have to watch your ass," commented Eric as he stowed the electronics in the locker at the substation. "I'll make sure the last couple of minutes get erased, but you better be cool."

Tony was mad at himself. A major rule on any investigation is that you never let yourself become emotionally involved with anybody, especially not with a snitch. He couldn't believe he let her kiss him, much less believe that he enjoyed it and kissed her back. This was his second mistake. The first was not telling Chico about Benny, and now this. He was being careless.

"She caught me off guard. That'll never happen again, sorry," mumbled Tony as he signed the property control sheets for the tapes.

From this, he learned a lesson. However well prepared you are, and however much you are on guard, you can never let your guard down. Never, never let yourself feel good about a snitch. This time everything came out okay, but what about the next? He marked this one up to a learning experience never to be repeated.

*

It was dark before the plane backed out from the ramp and taxied away from the terminal. Tony looked out the window, but tonight there would be no jogging recruits or view of the big navy base. He leaned back in his seat and closed his eyes. He felt the power surge as the jet roared down the runway. He started a silent count to himself. Just as he counted to forty-five he felt the rotation as the plane lifted its nose and headed him back to Tucson.

How, he wondered, could such a beautiful and smart woman

get so deep into such a mess? Then he answered his own question. Greed! Pure and simple greed. That's what drives all of them.

The flight home was uneventful as it is supposed to be. Just enough time for a glass of juice and some peanuts. Typical airline snacks, but something to do while he thought back over his afternoon with Sara. They put together a rough idea of how they would pull it off, but it would be full of risks. Lots of them. This would not be a simple "in and out" case. It could drag on for months, and that's a long time to be undercover, especially day and night. He would have to be sharp, no doubt about it. Was it too dangerous? No, probably not, but he would have to be on his toes. He never went this far undercover before and it wouldn't be easy, but nobody ever said life was easy. There would be a lot of preparation and back-up, but it could be done.

He was going to bring down Reynaldo Guzman, of that there was no doubt. The frosting on top of the cake was that he could spend some time with Sara — beautiful, beautiful Sara.

CHAPTER 7

Monday morning started out like every other Monday morning in the briefing room — bureaucratic mumbo-jumbo to get out of the way before they got down to the business. Once again, Tony spent the morning going over his second meeting with Sara, covering everything but the final good-bye, and then opened it up for discussion on the general plan he and Sara developed. Not that it was a very detailed plan, because it wasn't, but at least it was an idea until somebody came up with something better. He sketched out for them about her cousin, Freddy, and how Reynaldo already gave his blessing to bring him into the fold to work. Sara and Reynaldo never discussed exactly what his job would be, but he would have a job doing something. They would figure out what he could do and go from there. Except, instead of Freddy, it would be Tony.

He did a lot of two and three day undercover jobs in the past, and figured this wouldn't be drastically different in how he would carry on, except for one big point — this might go on for a long, long time. Nobody liked it, but when challenged to come up with anything better, everyone fell quiet. They didn't like the ball game, but were stumped for anything better. So far, the Task Force came up with a big zero. There was nothing other than Sara's story. Aguilar, Guzman, their businesses. Nothing! On the face of it, everybody and everything appeared to be one-hundred percent legitimate.

By noon, they exhausted the discussion so they broke for lunch. Chico invited Tony for lunch at the Downtowner, a favorite place for the yuppies, lawyers and secretaries who worked around the courthouse. They filled their plates from the buffet and found a table in the corner where they could talk. Chico scooted around with his back to the wall and Tony sat across from him. They ate in silence, picking through their salads like two men who came face to face with the day of reckoning.

"I don't like it a bit," Chico finally blurted out through a mouth full of lettuce. "Not one damn bit."

"I guess I don't either," Tony responded somberly. "I just don't see any other way of pulling it off. All of your interviews, the lab work, ATF, nothing is bringing us any closer to that son of a bitch. If we don't get him this way, that scumbag will skate. He'll get away clean."

Tony flipped the few remaining lettuce leaves with his fork, looking deeply into the salad dish for some answers. "Look at it," he finally blurted out. "You guys have talked to everybody who has been even remotely connected with him. They all say the same thing. Aguilar was a saint — a business giant, a civic leader, a top notch guy, a family man. You haven't found diddly about his connections to anybody doing crap."

"What about the car?" Chico fired back.

"Yeah, sure. The car. That doesn't do squat to tie him to dope or anything else. Look at it, Chico." Tony put his fork down in disgust. "How many people have you talked to?"

Chico looked forlornly across the table. "Sixty-one," he said. "Sixty-one people who will go to the wall about what a great guy he was. Bankers, neighbors, lawyers. Hell, even the bishop. They all say the same thing: the guy was a living saint. I tell you this, though," Chico said with a grin. "He was a Jekyll and Hyde, but we can't prove it with what we've got so far." Chico shook his head in disgust, "And, that Rey guy. Shit! He's just the same: a white knight in shining armor."

They finished their coffee in silence, each with his own thoughts. Without thinking about how Tony would take it, Chico blurted out what was on his mind, "Dead man walking, that's what it is. Damn it, I don't like this covert thing. These people are too unknown to us. We don't know zilch about them, except, of course, that they'll murder anybody who gets in their way."

He gazed seriously at Tony. They were friends for a long time and worked lots of cases together, but this one was different. This was a horse of a different color. These were bad people who would drop a guy in his tracks, cop or not.

"C'mon, let's go," said Tony. "Lunch is on me." With that he dropped a ten and three ones on the table and pushed his chair back.

*

The next three days were ones of awkward silence for Tony. Captain Martinez would tell him only that they were evaluating all of the evidence and would decide in a few days on which way to go. Tony spent those days doing busy work around the office, killing time but accomplishing little.

Muncie read his body language and silence as signs of frustration, worry or maybe even something else, but she was not able to pull anything out of him. She only knew the basics of what he was working on, and found herself getting irritated with his silence. He worked hard cases before and went undercover, but he was never like this. Was it the girl? It must be. For the first time in their years together, she felt at a loss about what was happening to him, and indirectly to her and the boys. As they lay in bed Wednesday night, she sat up and threw the sheets back in anger.

"Damn you, Tony. You can't keep this up. Something is going on and it's happening to all of us. You haven't said a decent word to anybody around this house all week." She jumped out of bed, pulling the sheet up and wrapped it around her.

"Damn you, Tony. If you want to keep your stinking secrets, then you just do it," she screamed as she walked out of the bedroom, slamming the door behind her.

Tony lay in bed, looking up at the ceiling fan as it slowly spun in its never-ending little circle. That's me, he thought. Just going around in circles and not going anywhere. He rolled over and sat on the edge of the bed, holding his head in his hands. The house was silent except for the soft hum of the fan. Tony's thoughts were hazy as the hour grew late. He knew she was right. "For better or worse," that's what the priest said when he married them, and now they were heading into the worst.

He must have dozed off, because all of a sudden he was aware that he was lying across the bed. He looked at the clock and saw that it was nearly four o'clock. He crawled out of bed and went down the hall. He found Muncie asleep on the couch in the living room, curled up into a little knot with the sheet wrapped around her.

"Honey, wake up," he said softly. "We need to talk."

Muncie opened her eyes and looked at him for a second, then reached her arms out and pulled him onto the couch with her. They curled up, arms and legs wrapped around each other, each feeling the warmth of the other's body, smelling the unique scent that comes that only a wife and husband know. After a while, Tony said he wanted some coffee. He slipped off the couch and walked into the kitchen. Muncie followed, dropping the sheet on the floor as she walked. She stepped behind Tony as he stood at the sink and wrapped her arms around him.

"I'm sorry," he said. He reached his hand around behind her and grabbed around her waist. While the coffee dripped in the Mr. Coffee, they sat curled around each other on the family room sofa.

"It's a long story," said Tony. "We're not sure we will do it, but in all likelihood we will," he said. "It'll be a long-term deep undercover and I'm it."

Then Tony revealed the plan to Muncie. He filled in what she did not know about what they learned from Sara, and how they were stymied from making any headway against Reynaldo Guzman. With nothing else looking promising, the only apparent alternative they possessed was to put someone deep undercover and try to penetrate his operation. It looked like the only one who fit the bill for the operation was Tony. He told her the plan, leaving out the details of Reynaldo's long and stormy violent life, other than this murder that went afoul and took so many lives.

Rosa, Sara's mother was sick and not going to get better. Sara's father, Frank, wanted to sell the grocery store and move back to Mexico where things were a slower pace, and there were brothers and sisters and a few aunts and uncles who could help care for

Rosa through her final years. Frank knew all along about Sara and Reynaldo, and how they lived in what he called, "not in God's way." He didn't know exactly how Reynaldo made his money, but assumed that he was a *"narco grandisimo."*

After the bombing, Sara and Frank spent that first weekend talking about her and how she might safely breakout from Guzman. They talked about Tony, but they also talked about Freddy, her cousin who sometimes helped around the store. Freddy and Tony were about the same age, and in many ways even looked alike. After Sara's first meeting with Tony, she told Frank about the similarities. It was then she hatched the idea of what could be the beginning of the end for Reynaldo Guzman.

It would also mark the beginning of the end of her life of royal splendor.

Reynaldo knew a little bit about Freddy, but never met him or saw a picture of him. He only knew there was a nephew who worked at the store once in a while, but nothing more. With the store closed, Freddy would need a job and Sara could help him. All she needed to do was have Reynaldo put him to work. Freddy was arrested three or four times for minor offenses, but never been convicted of anything. He was strong, smart, and a good worker. He was perfect for Reynaldo.

For Tony to assume the persona of Freddy, he needed to go undercover and might go weeks or even months without seeing his family. If he didn't do this, Reynaldo Guzman would go free.

*

It was midmorning Friday when Sergeant Ransom came to Tony's desk. "C'mon," he said. "We need to get up to the chief's office."

They walked to the parking garage and got in Ransom's van and quickly drove the five blocks to the police station. Ransom pulled his van into a visitor's parking spot and walked around to the rear entrance where the chief's private elevator waited.

When they walked in Chief Biggers' office, his secretary pointed toward the conference room. "Everybody is in there, just go on in," she said politely. Ransom opened the door and led the way in. He grabbed a seat off to the side and scooted away from the conference table. Tony looked around the room, taking a second to size up the power in the room. Chief Biggers sat at the head of the table. The Sheriff was at his right, and the Attorney General to his left. Farther down the table sat Martinez and Jacobs and four people Tony didn't know.

Biggers got out of his chair and stepped toward Tony, reaching out his hand. "Good to see you, detective," he said. "There are a few folks here that you don't know. Let me introduce you."

They went around the table shaking hands. First was Anthony Allbright, a former CIA agent who spent the last twenty-five years planting listening devices and hidden cameras in some of the most secret places in the world: embassies, executive offices, bedrooms, cars, you name it. Next was Alice Chambers, a very tall and athletic looking prosecutor from the U.S. Attorney's Office. Since her graduation from the University of Texas law school, she was assigned to the organized crime task force in New York City. She served on the prosecution team that convicted fourteen Mafioso members, including John Gotti.

The third person looked like a twin of Frankenstein. He was Delbert Moore, a retired FBI agent who spent most of his career doing undercover work in the Mafia. He was on the same team as Alice Chambers. His role was strictly that of advisor. As they say, "been there, done that." He could be critical in giving advice on the simple things that tend to catch someone off guard and blow the operation. The last person was Sonya Reynolds. She was hired two months ago by the County Attorney from the Los Angeles County Attorney's office where she specialized in organized crime. She was at the top in Los Angeles, but finally burned out on the traffic and smog, and gave it up for the Arizona desert. Between them, they would guide Tony as he penetrated the Guzman operation which was now dubbed Operation Shamash, for the sun god patron of justice.

"I want to thank all of you for being here today," Biggers said as he began the meeting. "I think this case is probably a little too big to be handled just by us. The Sheriff and I have talked it over with the County Attorney, and he agrees. Between us, we've decided to take this thing federal and state," he said, pausing to look around at everyone. "We're going to take it to the County Attorney for the murder, and to the feds for the drug conspiracy and importation," With that, the chief sat back, nodding to the federal prosecutor.

"Thank you, Chief," Alice Chambers said with a strong voice of authority. "My office has reviewed all of the evidence that was gathered so far, and concluded that this case is a prime candidate for a deep undercover operation." She glanced across the conference room to Allbright and Moore. "We think these two men are experts in their fields, and can be a big help. Tony," she said with a smile he interpreted as being condescending, "We have all the faith in the world in you, but you're going to need some help on this one. I've looked over your case logs, and you've got your stuff together, but this one means going really deep. Deeper," she said with a nod of her head, "than anything you ever did, but all of us will be there to support you and give you whatever help you need."

Chambers paused, and Sonya Reynolds jumped in with what Tony saw as her opportunity not to be outdone by her counterpart. "Chain of command," she said in her own tone of authority, "is of the utmost importance." She quickly scanned all the faces in the room and continued, "The murder will precede the drug crimes, and we'll go for a death sentence on this one. If it was ever deserved, this is it." She paused, giving everyone time to be impressed with her ability to take charge. "Captain," she said with a glare at Martinez, "how will you work out the reporting so that both prosecutorial offices can stay on top of this so there are no slip-ups and everything gets covered?"

"No problem," he replied with a shrug. "Every document goes to both prosecutors the same day its cut. Our crime analyst will give me and you," he said with a nod to the attorneys, "a weekly update on the overall case status. On top of that, we'll do a daily briefing on any breaking issue. Bottom line," he said with his own authoritative voice, "nobody gets left out, and everybody has an equal say in how things are going. But," he said sternly, "I run my division, and I call the final shot. Because of that, we will not accept any challenge." He looked at the chief and continued, "The Chief and I will stay real close to this thing. We think we can use these other guys' expertise and experience," he said with a nod to Allbright and Moore, "and we'll pull this thing off and slam dunk it! Clean and neat!"

Finally, the chief suggested that they break for lunch and meet back in the conference room at one-thirty. Martinez invited Tony to be his guest, and they drove to a little Mexican restaurant in South Tucson for real Mexican food. The captain was far from being his militaristic self, and even ordered beers for them to chase down the spicy salsa.

"What do you think so far?" queried Martinez as he scooped salsa on a chip.

"Don't really have a feel so far," said Tony softly as though he was deep in thought. Then he continued. "To tell you the truth, Captain, I don't have a good feeling about it." He looked about the room, and then leaned forward to speak directly to his boss. "It's not feeling right, and we all know that these kinds of things have to have a feel about them."

Tony took a deep breath and let it all out. He was calm and professional, but he did not approve of all the new faces. "Let me take this thing one bit at a time," he said politely. "First, these folks are an unknown quantity to us. Maybe they did great things somewhere else, but none of us know them. We don't know how they work. Yeah, sure," he said sarcastically, "maybe they were the greatest thing since sliced bread in New York or California, but I'm putting my butt on the line for complete strangers. I don't know a thing about them, Captain. Don't you see?"

"I hear you, Tony." Martinez's voice was smooth and calming. "But, these are the best people in the country as far as I'm concerned. The Chief and I talked long and hard on this thing. I assure you," he said with a genuine smile, "if you, I, or the chief get at all uncomfortable with how things are going, we'll pull you out. That's a promise! No hesitation. We won't let you go down the drain for these assholes."

"Okay, but second, what about Moore and Allbright? The Task Force can work this guy, or is there something we aren't being told? Is that one guy really a former CIA agent, or is he still one and is getting into our case to make sure we don't get too far? We have all heard of that happening before, and who is to say it isn't happening here? The other guy," Tony said with a little smirk on his face, "he looks like he lost too many fights and like maybe he has lost his mind."

"I've checked them out, and the County Attorney did, too. These guys are top notch. We can trust them."

"Yeah, with my life." Tony replied sarcastically.

It was nearly one-thirty before they reached the rear entrance to the station and headed up the elevator. Tony chewed mints to hide his beer breath, and Martinez sucked on an unlit cigar. As they walked into the chief's reception area, their eyes met and they both broke out in a quiet laugh. Tony felt like they were two kids hiding their breath from their dad.

Ransom, Jacobs, Moore and Allbright were already there, pulled back into the corner waiting for the bosses. Minutes later, the chief led the entourage into the room.

"Good afternoon, everyone," he said as he pulled up his chair at the head of the table. "Let's get down to business. It's a go! Tony, from now on, you be ready on the drop of a dime to get it in action."

He paused a second, and then said, "If you will excuse me, I've got things to get done. I'll leave this up to you people to put it in gear and get it going." With that, he and the sheriff shoved away from the table and left the room.

Without a moment's hesitation, Alice Chambers stood up and walked to the front of the room. She did not leave a question in anybody's mind as to who ran this investigation. She is the boss! Alice didn't reach the head of the table before Sonya quietly got up and took a seat just off to the side from Alice. Anyone with a macho problem would not fit in here, but they knew that these two women were at the head of the class. If Tony was the quarterback, Alice and Sonya were the coaches. They called the shots.

"Okay, I want you to pay attention. We're not going through

this twice," Alice said as she and Sonya started pulling sheets of paper and envelopes of all sizes from their briefcases.

"Here's how we're going to get Tony into position. But Tony, once you are there it's going to be up to you," Alice remarked as she took her position in the chief's chair.

The attorneys laid out three certified letters for Tony. There was one each from the U.S. Attorney, the Arizona Attorney General and the California Attorney General. The letters authorized Tony to violate without fear of prosecution any state or federal laws that would have to be violated to protect his identity, or to further the cause of the undercover investigation. The only exceptions were that he could not commit murder or cause severe injury to anyone. Tony read the letters and tossed a glance to Martinez. The captain gave a nod, so Tony pulled a pen from his pocket and signed each of the letters.

Captain Martinez then pulled a letter from his suit pocket and slid it across the table to Tony. This was another signed and certified letter from the chief which authorized Tony to violate departmental policy in accordance with the letters from the Attorneys General. Tony felt the perspiration run down his back as he slowly read the letter, and then read it again. Once again he looked to Martinez who gave him a smile and a nod. Tony took a deep breath and signed the bottom of the letter. He pushed the four letters back across the table to Alice Chambers. Without a glance or a smile, she picked them up and put them in her briefcase.

"I'll have copies made for you this afternoon," she said curtly.

Tony didn't notice that Anthony Allbright had two boxes beneath the table that were not there this morning. Anthony bent down and picked them up and placed them carefully on the desk.

"We're going to cover your ass with these things," he said, smiling. "These are my toys, so you be sure to take care of them."

The next hour was taken by Allbright as he explained how the surveillance equipment worked. They knew it would be too dangerous for Tony to carry a body bug around with him, so they weren't even going to try that. Their real concern, explained Allbright, was that Guzman's people might want to check out Tony's apartment when he wasn't there. Not that they would find anything, but it was still important to know if Guzman's people were digging around in Tony's place when he was gone.

"What we've done," explained Allbright, "is to give you the equipment to put in your place when you move in." All of the equipment turns on whenever anyone comes into a room where the microphones and cameras are set up. If no one is in the room for more than five minutes, the equipment automatically shuts itself down. Everything was automatic, except for a master override switch if Tony wanted to shut things off for his own privacy.

Allbright carefully went over the equipment with Tony. There was a nineteen-inch television set with a camera lens beneath the speaker on one side, and a microphone behind the speaker on the other side. The TV set needed to be set up in the living room, facing the front door. As soon as anyone came in, the camera and microphone would be activated. Next was an electric razor that would be kept in the bathroom. It didn't have a camera, but was equipped with a speaker that would turn on when anyone came within five feet of it. For the bedroom, there was an AM/FM radio. Like the TV, it had a tiny lens and a microphone.

"Then there's the kitchen," grinned Anthony. "Just like every other little homemaker, you need a radio. It's like the one in your bedroom. We've got you covered if anybody checks you out. And of course," he continued as he reached into his magic bag of tricks, "this is your Global Positioning Satellite device. We'll attach this beneath your ride so we'll track you wherever you go."

"Last, but not least," he said as he picked up an electric can opener. "Sometime, you might want some privacy. Just push the off/on switch far to the right and you shut everything off. By damn, though, you better remember to turn it back on before you leave."

Tony looked on in amazement. The Task Force was an elite unit with lots of toys and gizmos, but he never saw such an array as this. These were the things from a James Bond movie. He was impressed to say the least, but at the same time kept a clear and focused mind. They were just that — toys. However he did depended on his own skills, intuition and drive to survive. Everything else was nothing more than back-up equipment.

As Anthony carefully packed his toys back into the boxes, Delbert put his briefcase on the table and popped it open. "We've got you covered, too," he said with a grin. "Here ya go," he said as he slid an envelope across the table to Tony.

Tony ripped the envelope open and dumped its contents onto the table. Carefully, he picked up each item and examined it. There was a California driver's license in the name of Frederico Ochoa, but with Tony's picture on it. Next was a social security card, badly weathered and worn, also in the name of Ochoa. The third item was an Arizona driver's license, again in the name of Ochoa. This one was newer than the other items.

"You have to remember," said Delbert. "You don't get that until you supposedly move to Arizona, so it's got to be new."

"A few other tidbits," smirked the former FBI agent. "These people you're after are good, so we're going to cover you more than we normally would. We have done this a few times before," he said as he tossed a sheet of paper to Tony,

"A school district just east of San Diego lets us do this a little. You've got a whole high school transcript there. You went to Desert View High School and dropped out during your sophomore year. Take a look at your classes. Memorize this shit, then shred it before somebody else sees it."

"Next," he said as he gave Tony a last document from his briefcase. "This is a made up bullshit family heritage, but everything is covered if they go to check you out. Memorize this too, then hit the shredder."

Alice Chambers nodded to Sonya, giving her the go-ahead for the next part. "We have already arranged to work with the DEA and FBI on this case," she said. "Everybody thinks he's worth the effort, so we have pooled our money and we are going to buy the grocery store. Besides that, Immigration and Naturalization was looking for a cover place to do some work, so they'll actually run the store. We expect to buy them out within the next three or four weeks, so you better get ready to go," she said without a hint of feeling.

"We've put a lot of money in this thing, so you better not blow it," she said. She then began a droning monologue about the quality of the support staff he would have behind him, and of their numerous successes. She switched gears and droned on about how she and Alice were looking forward to adding another feather to their caps with the indictment of Guzman and his hangers-on and how this could be a crowning achievement for both of them. Finally, she looked directly at Tony. "Detective, one thing we must have between us is honesty, and to be totally truthful with you, you were not our choice for this assignment. You're too young and green. You are a rookie to the big leagues, but we are in too far now to try to make any changes so we're stuck with you. All I can say is the United States government is investing a lot of money in this thing and you better not screw it up. Is that understood?" she barked.

Tony leaped from his chair, knocking it over as he bellowed at her, "Look here, you bitch, I'm putting my life on the line out there. Don't you ever talk to me like that again!"

He looked back and saw his chair lying on its side, and reached to set it upright. The sweat poured from his brow and his heart raged. "Son of a bitch," he mumbled as he sat back down.

Martinez reached over and patted Tony's shoulder. "Hang on, buddy," he said with a smile.

Delbert Moore, who spent his career undercover, got up and sat on the edge of the table and smiled. "Sorry we did that," he said, "but it was planned."

Sonya quickly walked around the table and put her arms around Tony. "I'm sorry," she said. "It needed to be done, and we drew straws at lunch and I lost. Besides that, these jerks made me buy lunch."

"I'm sorry," she said as she returned to her seat.

"It was me," Moore said with a smile. "You've done undercover work, but never anything like this. These people are going to test you before they trust you. Sometimes you can smell it coming and you'll do okay. But," he said sternly, "where they will get you is when you don't see it coming. You have to be ready for anything at anytime or your ass is grass," he said without a smile. "And, you never did smell this coming. Look, those people are sharp, and you will be out there alone. Sure, we're there for back-up, but help can be a long way away. All we wanted to do today was create a bit of awareness on your part. You have got one hell of a good track record, but you're going up against the best there is. Be ready for these assholes, 'cause when you least expect it, they'll catch you." He paused for a second, then continued, "You slipped up here and that's okay, but you can't do it with them. They don't give out second chances."

Tony couldn't help but take count. Strike three. Maybe they were right. Maybe he wasn't ready for the big leagues. Maybe he was only a good Class AAA player.

"Just a few more things," said the captain. "Here's seven hundred dollars in old used bills that will let you do the necessities to get settled. Just don't spend any of it until you are there. You're going to have to rent something, pay some utilities, and that kind of stuff."

"Here," said Ransom. "are the keys to a cool 2002 Dodge pickup. Just what you always wanted. Got California plates and even some fringe around the windshield. You're going to fit in all right," he said with a smile.

"Okay everybody," said Chambers, re-establishing her place as boss. "It's been a hard day. Let's all call it done and head home."

"Tony," she said with a smile, "hang loose the best you can. Enjoy the next couple of weeks while this comes together. Relax. Have a beer. Take a swim and enjoy yourself, because once you get into this thing it may be a long time before you can cool your heels. The captain tells me you like to hike. Go do it, and have fun."

She smiled at Tony as she closed her briefcase and headed for the door. "You'll do great," she said with a tone of real sincerity. "You're *numero uno*, and we're with you to the bitter end."

CHAPTER 8

If the government said they could do it in three or four weeks, it was a safe bet that they wouldn't. Not surprisingly, they didn't. Tony spent his days in the office working with Margo on the computer. They were a good team. He had that thing, whatever you call it, the "feel" or the "instinct," and she was the analytical mind. If anyone ever thought boys were better than girls in math and that girls leaned toward the social graces and arts, they didn't know Margo. Nobody was a match for her, but she and Tony complimented each other, playing to the other's strength, and still having time for a little dry humor when they ran into a brick wall.

Margo could spend her life on her terminal and enjoy every minute of it.

"Is this thing your life?" Tony asked cautiously as they were coming to the end of another workday.

Margo looked blankly at him. He caught her from left field. "Why? What do you mean? Aren't you getting a little personal?"

"Sorry, didn't mean anything." He flashed his disarming smile. "You know. It's just that you're always here or doing your gourmet cooking at home. You're almost always by yourself. Don't you get lonely? Damn," he said as he shook his head, realizing how he came across to her. "I'm not trying to make a pass at you. I really like you as a good friend and I've learned a lot from you, but there's more to life than this place."

"Tony." She sat up straight in her chair, looking like a school teacher about to lecture her fifth graders. "To start with, my personal life is none of your business, but I happen to like it the way it is. It's uncomplicated. I'm thirty-two years old, make about fifty-three thousand dollars a year, have my own place, and know where I'm going. So don't start feeling sorry for me. And no, I'm not a lesbian!" She paused and tilted her head and looked at him with a grin. "Is that what you thought?" She laughed. "Tony, some days you're a complete horse's rear end, and today is one of 'em. I like guys, but I like myself, too. I like my work. However, sorry to say, just about any guy I date has a one track mind and thinks I should be grateful as hell."

She grinned as she continued, "Girls have feelings, too. Sure, we get passionate, but we have more self-control than you perennially horny dudes. Besides that, I have this thing about STDs and don't plan on getting any of it." She got up from her chair and started shutting things down for the night. "And, last but not least, somewhere in the back of my mind I keep hearing mama say to me to be good."

She slammed a couple of drawers closed and announced her retirement for the night. "Don't stay up late worrying about me."

Tony watched her leave. He started toward his own desk, ready to wrap it up and call it a day, when he heard a voice behind him. It was Anthony Allbright, one of the new guys.

"Tony? Got a minute? Sorry we haven't spoken in a while, but I'd like to touch base with you if you have time."

"Sure. What's on your mind?"

"I've got an idea about what you're thinking. You know — what's with these outsiders? I understand, but I'd like to visit with you. It's free advice, but if you say no, then that's it. I won't bug you any more."

"Sorry if I've come across like that. Sure. Let's get a drink somewhere, then I need to head for the house. How's La Bodega? Down the block on Meyer."

"See you there in ten minutes," Anthony said.

*

Tony waited at the door, giving his eyes time to adjust to the darkened bar. Young lawyers, secretaries hot to become Mrs. Young lawyers, bankers, and an assortment of downtown upper crust mingled together, most with a similar purpose. Wash away the day, and with a little luck, score.

Tony spotted Allbright at a table at the far end of the bar, squeezed in the corner with a slick brunette bumming a cigarette from him. As Tony slipped through the crowd, Allbright gave her a soft whack on her fanny and sent the eager little slut on her way.

"Five more minutes, and I could've gotten laid," Allbright quipped.

Tony pulled up a chair just in time to look down the front of the cocktail waitress. She leaned close, leaving little to the imagination.

"Want anything?" she asked.

"Yeah," Tony growled. "But, I'll wait 'til I get home. How about a scotch and water?"

"You're cute," she smirked, spinning on her heel. She glanced back over her shoulder. "But not irreplaceable."

They watched her slink her way toward the bar. Allbright shot a quick grin at Tony. "I think she'd be double trouble for any guy, but that's not why we're here, is it?"

"Frankly, no. Tell me why you guys were brought in? I don't mean any offense, but I'm a little puzzled by all this. We've handled some major league players before without any sweat. I don't see why anyone should feel it necessary to give us help if we don't need it."

Allbright watched as the waitress brought their drinks, dipping slowly in front of him with her back to Tony. After she left, he laughed. "I think you may have pissed her off. Anyway, let's talk business, okay?"

He leaned across the table, his nose only inches from Tony's. "I can tell you what I know, but don't get me wrong. I think you're as sharp as they come. It's just that we've been deep undercover for weeks and months at a time. I'm shooting straight with you. It's a whole different world than any undercover job you've done before."

He hesitated and looked around the bar. "You're going to have your eyes opened like you never imagined. This isn't something where you get back to the office at night and go over things with your boss. You are in deep — and alone. More alone than you will ever guess. You have to be able to make fast decisions. Ya gotta be flexible, on your toes twenty-four hours a day. Can't trust a soul — nobody. Everybody is a rat. You have to remember that. Don't trust any guy, and trust a woman even less."

Allbright waved down the waitress and ordered another round.

"That may sound a little chauvinistic, but it's true. It's your life. Tony, I'm not here to be a know-it-all. What I can do for you is to let you learn from my success, and from my mistakes. Sure as hell, there were a couple."

"So, tell me. What was your worst mistake? And, if you had it to do over, how would you do it?" Tony asked.

"Fair enough. Play hardball, don't you?" He tossed a twenty on the table, and nodded to the waitress. "Worst mistake? Easy, I screwed up, literally, and a friend got killed. We were in Belize, and I let us get separated. I knew better, but son-of-a bitch, she was good looking. A couple of hours later I found our car in the parking lot, and my friend was shot in the head. Not that there is any corruption, or anything like that. But, get this. They called it a suicide, but there wasn't a gun found anywhere around there.

So you take that, and you quickly figure out that the good guys you were working with are actually the bad guys." Allbright chugged his drink. "Hell, you can't tell the players without a program."

"Sorry. I didn't realize. How long ago was that?"

"Fifteen years, but I think about it every day."

"What about you best success?"

"Ain't any best of anything. Just lots of things I was hired to do, and I got them done. Some were scary. A few were kind of funny, but they all were important to the people who hired us. Every one of them."

He chugged the last drop from his drink. "Getting late, my man. You've got a wife and kids and need to get home, but we need to talk from time to time. I'm no hero, but I can share this with you. I've worked with some of the best people in the world on both sides of the ocean. Plus, I've worked with some of the most wicked people the devil ever created. So, for you, all I can say is this, you're going into the devil's den. Be prepared to be caught unprepared, if that makes sense. There's not a whole lot that I haven't seen, so take advantage of it. There's no value in having to learn it on your own when the bad guys are breathing down your neck."

"Fair enough. How about lunch tomorrow?"

"You're on."

*

The next morning found Margo at her drafting table, playing lines and circles with her link-analysis, trying to match up who was running with whom — who fit in innocently, and who else seemed to slide in and out where they weren't expected. Who was a major player, and who was a walk-on? That's what she must figure out.

"Margo?" Captain Martinez walked into her office, carrying his morning cup of coffee. "Got a couple guys here I want you to meet."

Margo looked beyond him as two dapper young men in three piece suits followed him into her inner sanctum. Hurriedly, she flipped a dustcover over her analysis chart and extended her hand to the strangers. "Hi, I'm Margo Lanier."

"I'm Jerry West from the Rocky Mountain Information Network, but you probably call it RMIN like everybody else," the first replied as he shook hands with her.

"And I'm Darren Fielding with Interpol," the second man said. He, too, extended his hand.

"Interpol?" Margo inquired, a strong note of curiosity in her voice.

"Yes ma'am, glad to meet you, Miss Lanier," he said with a slight British accent. "May we be seated?" he asked. He reached for a chair and pulled it to him.

"Yeah, why don't we all have a seat," Martinez remarked as he shuffled chairs around.

"Margo, I've been talking to the folks at RMIN and they hooked me up with Interpol." He looked at the two new players on the team, then back to Margo. "They did some background on our case and who we have working it, and they have decided to jump in on our side," he said with a smile.

"Well, we don't exactly 'jump in,'" West said. "But," he said with a big grin, "we can turn some of our resources over for your use for this specific case, and this case only."

"Right," Fielding said, joining the conversation. "We are pretty impressed with what you've got going, and since it is not only local, but interstate and international as well, we have things you can use."

Margo was caught off guard, even bewildered. She looked at her new colleagues. "What might that be?" she asked politely.

"Let me show you," Fielding volunteered. "It's easier to show you than to explain it. As they say, a picture is worth a thousand words. May I?" He got up and went to her computer.

"Sure, why not," she said with a shrug.

Fielding flicked on her modem with a few rapid-fire keystrokes, then sat back and watched the screen as it raced through a series of password approvals, then came to a halt with a website titled INTERPOL CONFIDENTIAL–ENTER CODE NOW.

"May I, sir?" West said as he leaned over the keyboard.

"Be my guest." Fielding scooted back as West pecked in a twelve digit code and watched the screen race through another series of password approvals, then stop at another website. This one was titled INTERPOL AUTHORIZED-PRESS ENTER.

West turned to Lanier. "Enter any of your credit card numbers or your full name."

He smiled as he watched her dig through her wallet until she retrieved one of her cards. Slowly, ever so slowly as if not sure she really wanted to do this, she entered the numbers, then tapped on the ENTER key. The computer hummed, flashing through a series of screens faster than she could read them, then went through a series of INFORMATION PROCESSING screens, then came to a halt. Margo was dumbfounded. INQUIRY COMPLETE, flashed across the screen. The entire history for the credit card number she entered — dates, locations, items charged, amounts, payment record, and last but not least, her credit rating.

"I'll be damned." Her voice was barely audible. "Every cotton-picking thing I've ever used this card for," she said, shaking her head in amazement. She pulled up a chair to get a closer look at how often and where she used the card. "Everything," she repeated. "I'll be damned. I didn't know you could do this. You don't mean to tell me that we can get this information on our suspects, do you?"

"Yes, ma'am. You sure can," West said as he handed her his business card. "There's your password on the back. If you ever get stuck, give me a call and I'll work you through it. And the first seven numbers of your password are the DSL connection."

"Love computers, don't we?" He laughed, scooting his chair away from the table. "Need to be on our way, but call if we can bail you out."

Margo walked to the door with them, smiling to herself. Interpol and RMIN. The gods were looking kindly on her today.

Her new "toy" as she called it opened up a whole new world

to her, delving into the financial history of all of the people and companies that may have been involved in any way with this case. She spent hours on the computer with her password to their files, seemingly going nowhere, and then give her soft victory chant, "Bingo, Buster!"

Tony was as surprised as Margo at what she dug up. On six different dates in the last eighteen months, Guzman and Aguilar stayed at the Hotel Playa del Sol in Mexico City. Twice they were at the Hotel Dormir in San Miguelito, Panama. They always arrived on Friday and stayed over until the following Monday. Guzman usually traveled on American Airlines, while Aguilar traveled a roundabout route on Aero Mexico that took him through Miami going and returning.

Other than lunch, it was another routine, if not boring day. Tony and Allbright took a long lunch, talking about some of his exploits — things that went wrong, others that went surprisingly well. By the time they finished, Tony was glad to have Allbright in his corner. He was a wealth of knowledge. He was blessed with the "feel" for things that money can't buy. Tony felt guilty for having doubts about the outsiders. They were smart and their heads were on straight. His job would be better, if not easier, because of them.

It was nearly five o'clock when Margo called Tony on the intercom. "Can you come here for a few minutes?"

Tony looked at his watch and screwed his lips, "It's too late in the day to start anything new," he mumbled as he pushed his chair around and got up.

"Look at this," Margo said as Tony strolled in, "something's happening. They have changed their routines totally." She hit the print button, and her laser printer went to work spilling out all of their charges of the last five months.

"See what I mean?"

It took Tony a minute to see what she already saw, and then it jumped out at him. "Yeah, you're right," he whispered, staring at the printout. Everything that turned up from their charges almost always showed Guzman and Aguilar in the same place at the same time, except for a few dates that they couldn't account for, but that was to be expected. Otherwise, these two stuck together like glue until about five months ago. Guzman's records showed his regular trips to Mexico and Panama, but what leaped out were some trips he did not take before. He made four trips to Colombia in a seven week period. Twice to Bogotá, once to Cali and once to Medillin, but none with Aguilar.

"I'll be damned," said Tony. The weekend of the explosion and murders, Reynaldo Guzman was out of the country. His credit cards didn't have any local charges, but the airline ticket was all they needed for now. He left Friday morning on his usual frequent flier, American Airlines to Dallas, then caught a connection to Mexico City and on to Medillin. Like a creature of habit, he headed for home on Monday. There was no way of knowing where he stayed or who he saw, but the fact that he was in the cocaine capital of the world was enough to charge Tony's and Margo's batteries to keep digging.

"Now look at this," said Margo. She handed over Aguilar's credit card charges. Over this five-month period, Aguilar was nowhere near Guzman.

"See what we've got?"

Tony leaned back in his chair and put his feet on her work table while he stared at the printout. After a few minutes of silence, he got up and stretched. He walked to the window, deep in thought. For a few minutes, he stood there and watched the going home rush hour getting started on the downtown streets. He laughed softly as the crowds spilled out of the buildings. "Isn't this town ever going to get some freeways?"

"Well, what do you think about these guys?" she asked with a smile.

"It's like Sara said," replied Tony. He picked up the printouts for a second time. "They split. Guzman went farther south, and Aguilar went north. Just that simple. We don't know why, but we know it happened."

"Take a look at this." Margo pointed to six different dates and charges. "He's all over Missouri, Illinois and New Jersey, but look at Missouri. Four different nights in Springfield. I don't have any idea what's there, but he was up to something. Then he's got a car rental from Avis and some gas charges in Blue Eye, Missouri."

They looked at each other and laughed. "Blue Eye?" asked Tony.

Margo got out of her chair and kicked off her shoes. "It's after five. I'm on my own time, so the hell with company grooming standards," she laughed. She pulled open a closet door and searched the shelves for a few minutes, and then said with another little laugh, "Here you are."

She tossed Tony her freebie insurance company road atlas. "See if you can find it," she said, plopping down in a chair and putting her feet on a desk.

Tony flipped through the pages, and then took a deep breath and exhaled. "I'm tired," he said as he found the Missouri page. He studied the page for a few seconds, and then put his finger on the map. "Here it is, downtown Blue Eye." He spun the book around, and showed it to Margo. "Right across the lake from Branson. Real hillbilly country I'd say. What do you think Margo? Where's this taking us?"

"I don't have any idea, but I'm bushed and going home."

*

Allbright drafted Moore to be his shadow, and they started almost daily visits to Tony's desk. When they couldn't catch him there, they made a point of having lunch with him. Tony gradually developed a comfortable feeling about his new partners. Sure, they came from a different background than his, but their hearts were in the right place. They would do anything for him — absolutely anything. His success was theirs. They would travel to the ends of the earth. They saw the "worstest and the bestest," as they described it. They were a wealth of knowledge, and that's why they were brought in for support. They knew their business inside and out. Besides, Tony decided, they were damned good people — maybe a little strange to those who didn't know them, but he did. "Righteous troops," is how he described them to Martinez. They had their act together. He finally realized they were a major asset to the investigation, and equally important, they became good friends.

When he wasn't getting an up close and personal education from Allbright and Moore, Tony worked with other cops on the Task Force as they set up surveillance on one of the city's leading Asian-Americans. Too often, he turned up in the company of suspected smugglers who ran goods both ways across the border. Levis and typewriters going down, and heroin coming back. Nobody could come close to pinning anything on him, but he kept strange company. "Intelligence gathering," is how they classified their activity. Maybe they would never bust him, but if they did, they would nail him to the cross.

Near the end of the week, Captain Martinez called another one of the endless meetings of the Aguilar murder case investigators.

Years of experience taught him the importance of communication. Everyone must know what was happening if they were going to hold up their end of the job. He never considered briefings as a waste of time. Just the contrary, he considered them vital to a good investigation. Everyone gathered in the briefing room with their coffee, settling down in their usual chairs. Every player was important.

Tony went over the progress, or better yet, the lack of progress, they were making. They weren't going anywhere very fast, but the Feds were making progress, bit by bit, on getting their money together to buy the store in Chula Vista. "And," he went on, "everything else for our undercover operation is on hold until they get it. Otherwise, Freddy has no need for another job, and I stay put right here in the office going in circles."

He looked over at the captain and gave a shrug of his shoulders before going back to his seat.

"What about your girl, Sara?" came a voice from the side. Tony looked and saw Chico smiling. "Well, what about her? Is she keeping you updated, or what's going on?"

"Same ol', same ol'," Tony replied with a sickly smile. "She's doing her thing, keeping her old man happy. Otherwise, nothing has changed. He pretty much keeps her in the dark about what he's up to. She calls me every few days to see what's up with us, but nothing more than that."

He looked back at the captain. "I think she's starting to wonder if we really want to do this thing. She's not used to working with the government, and can't figure out why we are so slow."

"Have her hang in," Martinez commanded. "We're doing the best we can; she just needs to be ready when we are."

Martinez shifted his glance to Chico. "And?" he queried.

"*Nada por nada*," Chico said, mimicking Tony's shrug of his shoulders. "We've talked to everybody we can find who might have anything. Zip! A big friggin' zip. These guys are the best we've ever run into. Legit and otherwise, they cover their tracks. All of us have busted our butts, and there ain't anything there that anyone will talk about. Honestly, I don't think anybody knows a damned thing about him other than his above board business that was squeaky clean. Jimmy and Ann got tied up in court but should be here in a few minutes. I've got their notes." He held up a notepad, "I would rather wait for them so I don't mix things up. Besides that, I'm not sure I can read their Greek."

"Margo?" Martinez asked. "What's up?"

"Sir," she said as she got up and walked to the front of the room. "These guys are good, but crooked as a dog's hind leg. Let me show you." She unrolled a roll of butcher paper across Ransom's desk, letting it drape down to the floor on both ends. "Look at this," she said, pointing with her finger at the maze of lines, squares, and circles. "There is a name of a person inside each circle; the name in a square is a business; and, the lines show the connection of each person or business to any other person or business. It seems like there are a lot of players on the periphery, and they would likely be mid-level or upper mid-level distributors. We've got way too many people involved to track it any lower down the distribution system now, but given more time or staff, I would love to do it." She smiled at the captain.

"Dream on," he replied. "But, go on. Where are you getting with this mess?"

"Okay, look," she said as she traced along a line up to the box marked GAI. "That's Greater America Imports, and as you can see," she ran her finger along another line leading out from GAI, "it's like the hub. Everything leads into or out of it. Now, let's follow this line." She traced a line from GAI to another square with the letters SM. "That is Smallwood Flowers on East Broadway here in Tucson. Now, interestingly enough, Smallwood is owned by a fellow named Blaise Underwood. Take a look at this." She pulled a legal size notepad from beneath the butcher paper. "Blaise was arrested in Miami, Florida in 2000, and guess what for?" She looked at Martinez.

"Let me guess," he said. "Drugs?"

"You win a teddy bear," she said with a grin. "He did three years time and two more on parole. Technically, he is clean. Nevertheless, we think it is more than coincidence that he has a flower shop here and is connected with GAI. See here," she said as she pointed out a circle with the name "Sherlock" inscribed in it. "We don't know who this is for sure, so we call him this until we are positive, but by dumb luck one of the guys saw a GAI truck out on Broadway, so he did a loose surveillance on it. It went straight to the flower shop and was there for a few minutes, and then the guy left. He wasn't seen carrying anything in or out, so it could have been no more than a legitimate stop. You know, ordering flowers for his wife or girlfriend. But," she said with strong emphasis, "the guys started putting the shop on a loose surveillance, and that same truck has been there four times in the last eight days.

"He may be in love, but not that much. We've got to think the place is a cover for something — most likely dope. All of these people or businesses are connected with Greater America Imports — probably many of them legal, but we've got to think a few of them are like the flower shop. Plus, that does not count all the long haul trucks that leave the GAI shipping docks in Nogales everyday heading out all over the place. Captain," she said respectfully, "this thing is the biggest I have ever seen. It's huge!"

"Andy?" Martinez said as Margo completed her report.

"Okay, sir," Rooney said as he walked to the front of the room.

"All the lab work is done, for whatever good it does us. The explosive was PETN, not an everyday explosive, but something very popular with professional assassins 'cause it is very effective, as we have seen. And," he said with a disgusted expression, "the autopsies are finally complete, lab work and all. Each of the victims died immediately from massive trauma. No one burned to death. Hell, they never knew what hit them. One minute they were getting in the car, and the next they were meeting their maker. For better or worse! No traces of drugs or alcohol in any of the bodies. Just to be safe," he said as he referred to his notebook, "we did a positive match with dental records and some X-rays for positive identification. All I can say is the bodies were who we thought they were all along."

"What about the PETN?" Martinez asked.

"The Feds are working on it, trying to track it down, but no luck so far. I'll tell you, sir, my own idea. It's that this hit was a first class professional job, but the wife and kids were accidental hits. We're never going to track the PETN. I'll bet my paycheck that stuff came into the country just for this job. It got used, and that's it."

"What about an update on any evidence from around the crime scene?" Martinez asked.

"Well," Andy turned pages in his notebook. "Physical evidence in the arroyo near the house showed that at least two, maybe even three people were there. One wore size nine Nike basketball shoes, and the other wore a size nine vibram sole boot. From the depth of the footprints in the sand and in the harder ground between the arroyo and the house, as well as the distance between footprints, the crime lab guys were estimating that both of the people were less than six feet tall, and probably no taller than five feet-seven. Each of them weighed about one hundred and fifty pounds. Or, as a typical police report might read, 'two males, average height and average weight.' There was no clear evidence of a third person, but there were enough smudges on the ground to indicate a strong likelihood of there being a third person. My guess is that there was a number three, but he kept his shoes bagged with something to cover his tracks. Simple, but effective."

"Something else we have been working on," Andy said as he opened a legal size brown envelope, "is at the ranch itself. The power company security director let us hook up a hidden camera on one of their poles in the right-a-way along the highway. It's disguised as a transformer, and the lens is focused on the turnoff from the highway to the ranch. Here," he said as he passed around several black and white photos, "is what we're getting off it. As you can see, not much detail on the occupants of the vehicles, but we're gathering a few license numbers and giving them to Margo. So far, there isn't much to show for it, though. Most of the traffic is vehicles registered to Guzman, but a few are guys that we think are just laborers doing jobs around the place. One though," he said as he held the picture up for everyone to see, "looks impressive. This Lincoln Town Car is registered to Goldfarb Realty in Scottsdale, and, of course, we all knew Stanley Goldfarb when he was busted a few years ago in the savings and loan scam. So, who knows what he was doing at the ranch? We can show one of Guzman's Chevy pick up trucks getting there just a few minutes before this Town Car, and it's real hard to positively identify the driver, but the photo lab says it's about 99 percent chance to be Guzman. Who knows what the hell they're up to? But, it probably isn't any good."

Jimmy and Ann walked in as Andy was finishing his report. "Sorry, sir," Jimmy said as he looked at the captain. "We got stuck in court and couldn't get loose 'til now."

Chico tossed the notepad to him as he walked to the front of the room. Jimmy walked slowly, thumbing through his notes as he walked. He sat on the edge of Ransom's desk, crunching the sergeant's papers as he scooted back on the desk. Everyone but Ransom got the humor of it as Jimmy looked over his shoulder at the sergeant. "Oh shit, Sarge, I'm sorry."

Sgt. Ransom was what they called "critical mess", taken from the nuclear theory of "critical mass." He looked like he slept in his clothes, his desk was a jumble of scraps and stacks, and he usually wore samples of yesterday's food on his tie. But they couldn't get along without him. He was the one who held everything together with his finger on every button. If you needed anything, Ransom could get it. So he was their "critical mess."

Jimmy reviewed what little they learned from their interviews. Aguilar did not have any known enemies and was a leader in civic affairs. He banked at Southern Arizona Bank and Trust for his personal business, but kept his business accounts with First Interstate America. Two accountants went over his transactions and didn't find anything unusual for a person at that level of income. If he received dirty money, he laundered it and hid it offshore, which was a good possibility.

"Same ol', same ol'," he said. "Captain, these guys, Aguilar and Guzman, come up clean with everybody we talk to. If I didn't know better, I would say we are barking up the wrong tree."

He glanced at Tony, then continued. "Without going undercover, we're getting zilch on this thing."

It was late morning and they all looked to be near total exasperation. They knew what they had, where they wanted to go, and how to get there, but things were going interminably slow — past the point of frustration. All but Martinez, who maintained his cool, command presence.

The quiet was broken by a soft knock on the door as Angie stuck her head in. "Margo?" she said as she handed over a three page fax. It was from RMIN, the Rocky Mountain Information Network. Margo was overwhelmed by the amount of work and was falling behind. They said they would help if they could, so, not being timid, she asked them. She stood silently, reading as all eyes watched her every reaction.

"Listen to this. A contact from the banking clearinghouse guided RMIN to Borderland Federal Savings Bank where Guzman ran one of his business accounts. From there, they were able to identify two hundred-six people who drew paychecks from Greater America Imports over the last year. They were only able so far to find five of them in credit card records, but one looked like what they called, 'a keeper.'"

Margo read a little more, then summarized it. "Mary Elizabeth Martin is the comptroller of Greater America where she earns about sixty thousand dollars a year in legitimate income. What came as a surprise to RMIN from her credit cards was how and where she traveled. No less than once a month she was flying first class to Miami, but always spends the night in Dallas and stays at the airport hotel. Three times in the last five months, she went on from Miami to the Grand Caymans, but never stayed overnight. Now, listen to this," she said with an outward show of satisfaction. "In the two weeks before the murders, she went to Springfield and rented a car. To everyone's surprise, she even charged gas and food at a convenience store in Blue Eye, Missouri."

"Interesting. Very interesting," she said, folding the fax and putting it in with her legal pad. "Of course, we don't yet know what she's been up to with her trips. The two guys could have been working something together but got into each other's way," she said with some hesitation. "Or, Martin could have been working with Aguilar and spying on Guzman," she said with a frown on her face. "Or, she was loyal to Guzman, but was tracking Aguilar to see what he was up to. Who knows? All we can say for sure is that one or both of them were working to get something started in the Midwest and northeast."

Shortly before they broke for lunch, Alice, who sat quietly in the back of the room alongside Sonya, got up and went directly to the front. She pushed the sergeant's papers aside and sat on the edge of his desk. Tony couldn't help but notice her long beautiful legs as she crossed them, unaware that all of the men in the room were watching her every move.

"Okay people," she said sternly. She looked around the room, disappointment registering on her face. "What we've been able to come up with so far is interesting. Period! Nothing more! Crooks? Probably so," she said without a hint of pleasure in her voice. "But we're not getting very far or very fast. We need a lot more," She looked to Sonya, who got up from her chair and stood politely beside the sergeant's desk.

"We know you've worked your butts off on this thing," said Sonya, "but from a prosecutorial point of view, the bottom line is we don't have anything." She leaned against the desk and looked directly at Tony. "It's all up to you, Tony. If we're going to get him, you have to get the inside story for us. From where we sit, we're just missing too much. And," she continued, "what intelligence we do have is really indicating that these guys were big time dope dealers. I don't have to remind you that what we are actually here to do is to break a murder case. Now, we may have to do a dope case to get to the murder, but be careful that you don't let yourself get sidetracked."

As everyone sat there in silence, Angie knocked on the door and stuck her head in the room. "Margo, sorry to bother you again" she said. "It's for you. It's the State Police in Missouri. I figured you would want it now."

As Margo headed to her desk, Martinez leaned his chair back against the wall. "Listen up," he said. "Don't get rattled by the newspaper crap on this thing like was in this morning's paper. They're anxious to see some drama, you know, handcuffs, some defiant asshole standing up to the microphone to proclaim his client's innocence, or some jerk telling the world what a screwed up or corrupt job we did. The press is starting to give the chief hell, and we think they're going to get pretty crappy real quick. Easier to say than do, but I encourage all of you to just pass it off and go on with your work. We'll do things to our beat, not theirs. They want pictures, and blood and guts. You know your job; stay with it and stay away from any reporters who might run into you."

He got up and started toward the front of the room. "I'm not the only one to fight in a war and come back here and get into another one, but I'll tell you this." He cleared his throat and stood stiff, at attention, the Marine coming out in him. "We didn't get whipped over there 'cause we fought the war the way it was supposed to be fought, not how the press would have liked it. And, damn straight, they'd like to call the shots here too. You do your job the right way and we'll come out fine, but I'm warning you, the press is going to get after this thing hard, so beware." He pointed to Jimmy. "They get one word from you." Then he pointed to Andy. "And one from you, and before we know it, they've got a story. Just keep your cool, okay?"

The door opened and Margo nearly ran back in with a smile across her face. She stepped back to the front of the room and stood politely beside Ransom's desk. "A few good things," she smiled hugely. "It was the Missouri State Police Intelligence Unit, and by damn, another bingo."

Margo summarized her scribbled notes. "The state troopers took down four hundred kilos of cocaine, a big load by anybody's standards, but huge in Missouri. It was nothing more than a stroke of luck, but about four months ago a trooper was heading home in his patrol car shortly after midnight. He was assigned to Highway 65 south of Springfield to the Arkansas line. He lived south of Branson on a small farm near the little village of Blue Eye. As he drove along a narrow winding road, his headlights picked up a trailer truck parked on the soft muddy shoulder. It was leaning so far to the right the trooper thought it might turn over. He stopped his patrol car on the pavement, turned on the overhead lights, and started to open his door. It happened so fast that he wasn't sure exactly what happened, but he saw a blur when someone jumped out of the truck and ran into the woods. Just as the person disappeared into a thicket, the trooper saw a flash of fire and heard a gun go off. Nobody got hit, but the shooter got away."

"The truck turned out to have been reported stolen two years earlier from a construction site in Alabama. It was loaded with paper and cardboard that looked like it was heading for a recycling plant, but in the middle of the load was the cocaine. Apparently, the driver stopped because the radiator sprang a leak and it overheated.

"But," said Margo with a hint of cockiness, "RMIN talked to the Missouri troopers, and they put together a few things, and guess what? Another bingo. Arturo Aguilar bought a three hundred and twenty acre farm less than ten miles from where the truck was found.

"I hear what the attorneys are saying," she said seriously, "but the murders probably came over a dope deal gone bad, or something like that, and that's the road we have to take right now. Aguilar bought the farm two weeks before he got taken out. We know what they were up to, now we have to prove it."

She looked at Tony and smiled, then turned to Captain Martinez. "Not bad," she said. "Now we just need to put it all together, and that's going to be Tony."

"You're right," said Martinez. He shoved his chair around and faced the group. "Now I've got news. Immigration tells me they've about closed the deal and they take over the store next week — two weeks tops. Tony," he said. Martinez looked into the detective's eyes, "get in contact with Sara and put it in gear. It's your play."

CHAPTER 9

Sara called Tony as soon as the sale of her parents' grocery store went through. "It's a done deal, *Cajunga*,"

"What? Who is this?"

"What do you mean, 'who is this?' Do lots of girls call you on this line?"

"Sara? I didn't recognize your voice. And what's with the *Cajunga* thing?"

"That's the new nickname I've given you. It means that you're the big guy — the guy in charge."

Sara told him she was thrilled to get her parent's store behind them and to get on with things, and that her parents would walk away with enough money to retire. They wouldn't live high-class, but they would be more than comfortable living on the Mexican economy. Tony never heard her so happy, and it made him realize how serious she was over these many weeks they spoke with each other. He could never trade his life and family for her, but she was something special in his life. Someone that comes along once in a lifetime. He would never forget her. He truly really met the Spanish Gypsy. Everyone has a dream and they never expect it to come true, but his did. Just too late — much too late.

"She sounds like a whole new person," he said to Chico and Allbright when they went over the details of his final arrangements for his move. Even more important, his new persona, Freddy. "I was really having doubts about her for a while. I figured she was a totally screwed up person, but now I've decided that maybe everything will work out for her in the end. I think she has her head on straight and things will work out okay for her in the long run. Hope so, anyway."

"Maybe so, maybe not," commented Allbright as he leaned over his desk and looked at Tony. "Just remember, she was a bitch, is a bitch, and always will be a bitch," he said slowly, letting each of the words sink in. "You may think she has made the switch, but don't bet on it. Don't put your life in her hands."

He stared at Tony as if his gaze could drive the message home. "She tells us that she doesn't really know anything, that she doesn't have anything solid that she can testify about. Well, how do we know that? How do we know she's not trying to pad her own bank account? Tell me why we should believe her! Why don't we give her a grand jury subpoena and drag her butt in there and make her tell us everything she knows? Why not? Then, if she really doesn't know anything, we kiss her good-bye and set her up in witness protection"

"I'll tell you why," said Tony, looking straight at Allbright, his face tense. "Because before she came along, we didn't have a thing. Nothing. Zilch. We didn't have jack-shit. We never heard of these guys, and they've been running dope right under our noses." He paused and caught his breath. "There was nothing in the world to make her come to us with this thing. She's handed it to us on a silver platter, but it's up to us to put all the pieces together. Besides, sometimes we simply have to start believing somebody, and that might be pretty hard for us. We're not used to dealing with an honest person. So far we haven't even come close to catching her in a lie, and I've sure tried. Whether you like it or not, maybe she's telling the truth because of her conscience. Something we don't see much of anymore. Maybe, just maybe, we've run into somebody who's going to do something for nothing. Just straighten out her own life, and go on from there."

They sat there in awkward silence before Chico spoke up. "Look guys," he said with a grin on his face, trying to ease the tension, "I don't know whether she's a bitch or a switch-hitter, but its chow time and my joint needs energy for some action tonight." He grabbed his crotch and gave it a squeeze. "C'mon, it's my turn to treat you dorks for lunch."

"Fucking A straight," laughed Anthony. He made his point, for better or worse, and Tony could take it or leave it.

*

Tony spent the next few days waiting for Sara's phone call letting him know that she was again settled in at the ranch. It would take her a few days, maybe even a few weeks to get things straight with Reynaldo for Freddy to go to work on the loading docks or doing something in the business. The detectives did not let the time go to waste. Anthony worked like a man possessed as he adjusted, tuned and refined the surveillance equipment. To his own surprise, he was able to borrow some sophisticated devices from the Federal Law Enforcement Training Center in Glynco, Georgia. Nobody had money like the Feds, and they were able to transfer military and defense technology to what they referred to as the "civil authorities."

He reacted like a fourth grader at Christmas time as he unwrapped a box that was shipped overnight express. They promised him that they came up with just the right technology he needed for Tony. He couldn't help but beam and chuckle when he laid it out on his worktable. "No shit, you guys. Come take a look at this stuff," he hollered to whoever was within listening distance.

Chico, Ann and Sergeant Ransom were across the hall going over their notes when they heard Allbright celebrating with his toys. "Okay, little boy," said Ann. She and the others walked into Anthony's room. "Show me your new toy," she said with a grin as she tickled him, almost causing him to drop a camera.

"Damn it, lady, be careful," said Allbright. He put the camera back in a box. "Look at this. You're looking at nearly a hundred thousand bucks worth of technology." Anthony gave them what he called the two-bit tour of the new equipment, saving the in-depth explanation for the whole squad, especially for Tony.

Time was starting to get short and they wouldn't have many more of these investigative updates before Tony went in. "Okay everybody," said Chambers as she passed by Allbright's office. "Let's do it!" She gave the thumbs up signal and headed back to the briefing room.

Chambers started meetings every day with the investigative team so she was always on top of where they were and where they were going. She walked only part way through the rear door to the briefing room door when she saw Allbright balancing two large boxes as he came in the other door. "Holy hell, Allbright. Have you robbed Radio Shack?"

He laid it out on the sergeant's desk, covering every inch of the desktop with electronic wizardry of every size and shape. He wanted to get their attention and hold it, and he promptly succeeded.

Chambers pulled a stool up to the head of the desk as Sonya came and leaned over her back to look at Allbright's new additions to the investigation. Chambers opened her purse and pulled out a pack of Virginia Slims. She tapped one out of the pack and into her hand. With a quick flick of her fingers, she put it to her lips and lit up. She spun her Zippo lighter between her fingers for a few seconds, then tossed it back into her purse. She inhaled deeply, and then said, "Now you know. My big secret's out of the bag. Would somebody take that No Smoking sign and throw it in the trash?"

She looked at Anthony and smiled at him. "You're on."

Anthony Allbright spent most of the afternoon going over the equipment — more technological support than any of them ever worked with. A television set that was a two-way audio/visual system that connected Tony's apartment with the Task Force office. There were listening devices placed in key places in his apartment so every sound, every voice, every spoken word would be picked up. Everything was in place so Tony's support staff could keep tabs on him, and equally important, keep tabs on anybody who was slipping into his apartment to do their own background on him before they allowed him into the "other" side of Greater America Imports.

"Here's a little piece that I really like," Allbright beamed as he pulled a suitcase out of a box and onto the tabletop. "It's a normal suitcase with one exception. We've swapped out the handle grip with one of our own. Look at this," he said proudly as he twisted the handle and it came off in his hand. "What we have here is an electronic sweeper so Tony can sweep his place if he's got any reason to think somebody may have planted a bug there — that is, somebody beside us. This little critter has a direction finder in the antenna that will lead him right to anybody else's bug. Of course, he will have to shut off all of our stuff first, but then it'll take him just a few seconds to find their bug. Now what he does with it when he finds it is something else, but at least he'll know somebody besides us is watching him."

Allbright shifted gears from showing off the gadgets to going into the electronic background and circuitry of the various pieces. He loved his "toys" as he called them, and could talk endlessly about them — non-stop for hours if they would let him. He talked like an engineer in a language nobody else understood, but caught himself when he saw people dozing or daydreaming. He was a likable person, but not everyone shared his passion for circuitry and all of the other engineering background of his gizmos. He was good at what he did, but he could put a lamp to sleep with one of his monologues. Once he started talking, he never knew when to shut up. Today was one of those days.

"Now before you all flake out on me, there's one more piece I gotta show you. This is the thing that will really bring it all together for us. I know you've all been waiting for this," he said. People shifted around in their seats, rousing themselves from his hypnotic, droning voice. He held up a two-inch dish that looked like a smaller version of the kind people put on their roofs for satellite television. "This, my friends, is the crown jewel." He walked around the room so they could get a close-up view of the tiny dish. "Don't touch it." he barked as Jimmy reached out for it. Allbright completed a trip around the room before he spoke another word.

"You're the first non-secret classified people ever to see this. You should be proud," he beamed.

"Okay, okay," snapped Chambers. "We're impressed, now get to the point."

"All right," he said, wearing his hurt feelings on his sleeve from her short rebuke. "This is like military over-the-horizon radar that the troops use in war, except we're the troops and we're in the war."

Allbright explained as best he could in a non-engineering monotone what the new system would do for them. They already had everything else to wire the apartment for sight and sound, but its power output was too limited. At best, their equipment was good for about six hundred yards. Anything farther than that would probably not be able to transmit or receive. Chico previously assigned Ann and Jimmy to research rental property that could be used as a communications house in Nogales. It would be cumbersome and expensive because somebody would have to be there all the time watching and listening. There would be a lot of foot traffic that might arouse the neighbors' suspicions. Of course, the rent was something they didn't plan on, and didn't know how they would come up with the money for it and utilities. The hardest part, though, was that everybody who would work it lived in Tucson. Travel time and overtime was going to kill them.

"Bad guys don't worry about this shit," he commented, "but, cops do. We were, and I emphasize the word 'were,' going to pay hell to cover our expenses on this job. Now we don't have to worry about it. This new surveillance unit will transmit from Tony's apartment to our receivers right here in this building. We've got communications people on around the clock already, so there's no new expense. Presto! Problem solved," he said proudly as a grin swept across his face, the hurt feelings already gone from his shirtsleeve.

"Even better than that," he proclaimed. "This TV, remember, is two-way communication. Tony won't be able to see us, but we can talk back and forth and see him whenever he's home."

"Your tax dollars at work," remarked Martinez. He got up and slowly walked to the front of the room. "I guess I'm greedy 'cause with all this stuff, isn't there any kind of bug that he can wear in his belt or something like a wristwatch? Something we can use to cover him around the clock wherever he is?"

"Yes sir, there is," replied Allbright. "but the Feds who loaned me this stuff thought it was too high-risk 'cause if he's in their place you never know if they've got debugging equipment going. Lots of big wheels use that stuff now. Wow, they would do him on the spot if they thought he was up to something."

There was an uneasy quiet when they realized this was the culmination of their best ideas. Planning was over. Everything was in place. From here on, Tony was the lead character, win or lose.

"All I can say now, Tony," commented the captain, "if you're going to fart, turn off the microphones and camera."

Everyone laughed, but at the same time felt a pang of worry. It was something that was real. It was physical. Tony felt it in his chest and even a kind of a tingle in his fingertips. Worry is something that can be felt like a cold breeze. They could laugh now, but Tony was going to war. One of those quiet wars the public never knows about. It will be one of those wars that is going on every day. No cannons. No jets streaking in on a napalm run or sending missiles down the smokestack of a factory. No six o'clock newscast showing body bags or flag raisings. Just a quiet, scary war played out according to the Constitution and the Supreme Court. The other side could do whatever they wanted.

*

Two days passed with little to occupy his time. Moore and Allbright used the down-time to fill in the blanks with Tony: don't write notes to yourself; don't forego the obvious, but be aware of the less obvious; look in the shadows; learn the formal power structure, but delve into the informal power structure. That is where the real strength of the organization will be found. Drink when it is socially acceptable, but limit yourself; smile and have fun, but remember this is work; go with your gut feeling — don't rationalize yourself into doing something you're uncomfortable with. Never forget this is playacting; don't get too involved with their game; never, never lose sight of your role; they are your enemy, and you are their enemy. You know it, but if they find out, you're a dead duck. Last, but not least, don't trust anybody! If push comes to shove, the smart thing is to just get in your car and come home. There will always be another day.

It was late Thursday morning when Tony's cool phone rang. He sat at his desk killing time, waiting for the call. Time drug slowly. In one way, he never wanted the call to come, but in another way, he was anxious to get started. On its third ring he grabbed the phone from the receiver. His heart pounded.

"Yo, it's me," he said with a cheerful voice to Sara.

"You sure do sound in good spirits today," she said with a giggle. "I'm doing some grocery shopping for the weekend and everything's a go. I did what I said I would do, lover boy. Now it's up to you."

Tony tensed for a moment. She never said that before — lover boy. Did she have that feeling, too?

"Give me some details," Tony said brusquely. He pulled a folding chair away from the wall and popped it open. On the desk was a yellow legal pad and a box of pencils. He grabbed one and started making notes. He leaned forward, cupping the phone between his chin and shoulder as he scribbled notes that only he could decipher. He spent several minutes writing and listening without asking any question, just making notes. He realized he was perspiring when water dripped off his forehead and onto the legal pad. He stopped writing and leaned back with his feet on the desk. She was covering details as best as she could and now she was doing what he always referred to as the "nervous twit." Just talking to relieve stress.

"I can relate to that," he thought to himself.

When she talked herself out, he leaned back over the desk and started making notes to himself. "Listen to me now," he said. "I need to have some questions answered and I need it now."

"I'll do what I can," she replied softly. "You know that, Tony."

"Missouri," he snapped. "I need to know what the hell is with Aguilar, Guzman and Martin and I need the right answer. No bullshit." He never before told her anything about what they found in their investigation, but they were down to crunch time. Was she holding out or was she telling everything she knew? This was the last time he would have to check her out. Today it was do or die.

"Damn it, Tony, quit bitching. You know I'm straight with you." There was a long pause, and then she started talking again. "I don't know much, and I'm guessing at most of that. Anyway," she said, "Aguilar was going to set up a whole new deal for the Midwest, so I guess it was that thing in Missouri. I know he was supposed to have bought some land, but that's about all I know. Why, Tony, what's this all about?" she asked angrily.

"I just need to know everything you know, that's all," said Tony, quieting his own voice and hoping to calm her down. "Have you told me everything? Absolutely everything?" he asked.

"I guess so," she answered. "You knew they split up, and we

both know Rey gave the word to have him killed," she said quietly. "I can't prove it. It's just something I know."

"What about Martin?" Tony queried.

"She's Reynaldo's bookkeeper, but she does other stuff, too," said Sara. There was a pause.

"Like?"

"She's thorough, to say the least. She's Rey's right hand man, so to speak. She's smart. Rey and she knew Aguilar was up to something so when he was out of town, she called his house. Aguilar's maid always answered the phone. Sometimes the maid would call Mary Elizabeth — you know, Martin. That was part of the deal."

"Whoa, what a minute. What deal?" demanded Tony.

"About their maid, that's the deal," Sara snapped.

"Hang on one damned minute. Why didn't you tell me this before now?" said Tony, working to calm himself down.

"Because you never asked. That's why," responded Sara honestly. Tony paused and leaned back in his folding chair, hoping the legs wouldn't break off as he tilted back. He thought for a moment about his own stupidity. She's right. He'd never asked, and she'd never told. He violated another one of the most basic tenets of developing an informant. The cop is supposed to know what to do and maintain control. He screwed up again. Another strike. How many would he get?

"Okay, give it to me. I didn't know about the maid. A woman named Marta Espinosa. Tell me about her," he barked

"No shit, Tony. I never lied to you. You just never asked so I figured you already knew, or it wasn't important. Anyhow, she's from Mexico and has family there, so it was real easy. Nothing really very much. Just call Mary Elizabeth whenever Mr. Aguilar did something. You know. Kind of like," she paused. "Kind of like when he would take a trip, the maid would tell Mary about it, that's all."

"And?" said Tony.

"What else do you want from me? You're the cop. You're supposed to figure this shit out."

Tony bit his lip and shuffled around in his chair. "We're too late in the game to be farting around like this," he barked. "Everything now!" he demanded.

"Okay, but remember this. I never did want to get that poor lady in trouble. I just know what I heard Rey talk about with some guy down at the ranch a day or two before all this happened. I don't have any idea who was there. I never saw him or anything, but I know somebody was there because Rey stayed up late and I went to get him to go to bed. I heard a little bit before I realized that he was having a meeting with somebody, so I turned around and went back to bed. All Marta was supposed to do was make sure they were home 'til about eight-thirty. I heard that much and knew I wasn't supposed to hear it, that's all. She didn't know anything like this would happen. I promise, Tony, that's all I know and it's the truth."

There was a long quiet, and the telephone connection felt like a wall a mile high, separating them — impenetrable so they couldn't reach out and find one another. Tony heard Sara crying softly, yet there was so little he could do.

"That's all Tony. That's all. I'm so sorry."

"What did they have on her?" asked Tony.

"They would get her legalized and let her bring her husband and kids to the states. It's a mean friggin' world, Tony. Real mean," she said.

"Back to the bookkeeper, tell me about her."

"Pretty simple, really," answered Sara. "She went to Missouri and checked wherever they have deeds and found where he bought a farm. She just verified for Rey that Aguilar was working his own deal. I guess that's what finally got him killed."

"Damn it," said Tony. "You know all sorts of shit. Why haven't you told me any of this before? You know when this is done we'll use you as a witness. You'll have to testify and corroborate all sorts of stuff. There's no hiding from what you know. He paused for a few seconds and gathered his thoughts. "How long have you known all of this?"

"Tony, I live with him. How much do you know about your family? A lot! So much that you don't even think about it. How much do they know about you that they don't even think about? Yeah, I live with him and he screws me. He doesn't make love; he fucks. Do you get the difference? I don't know what he does or who he does it with, but I'm not an idiot. I can put two and two together. Listen to me, Tony," she commanded sternly. "You and I both know what happened, but we can't prove it. I can only take you so far, and then it's up to you."

There was a long quiet time before Tony spoke. "This may be our last time to talk. Don't hold out on me." His voice was tired and he leaned an elbow on the desk to prop up his head.

"That's it. Good-bye, Tony." She hung up before he could respond.

CHAPTER 10

The midday sun glared through the window as Tony got up and adjusted the mini-blinds. He stood silently for a few seconds, watching the noontime lunch bunch sweeping into the street, heading for their favorite haunt. "They were so far removed," he thought. They rush from their offices like rats from a sinking ship, getting as far away as possible from the drudgery of their work modules — telephones, terminals, debits and credits, market shares, the bottom line, unhappy customers — a world a million miles from his own. So close, but not really close at all.

Tony turned and looked at his desk. Clean, nothing out of order, an empty in-basket, no sticky notes hanging on file cabinets, everything filed away or reassigned to someone else. He was done with it all until who knew when. Next month? Next year? Probably somewhere in-between, but a long time before he would be back here. He was ready to go. It actually felt good to be able to stop planning and thinking about what was ahead, and instead, start doing it. He made one last round to see the Captain Martinez and Lieutenant Jacobs for any last minute instructions, and then started down the hall for the elevator. He headed home early, something he seldom did.

"Whoa, hold it up a sec," Ann Deberg shouted. She ran to catch up with him. "You can't get way without a hug," she said, throwing her arms around him. "C'mon, I'll go to the garage with you." She pulled him close to her as they walked to the elevator. "I like you, Tony. You're not like the other cops I've worked with. You're different, and I want you to be careful. Tell Muncie to call me at home if she needs anything."

When the elevator door opened she spun him around and put her lips to his, just a light peck, filled not with passion, but with feeling. "Be careful," she whispered as he stepped into the elevator, "you're every little girl's dream. Don't let anything happen to you."

"Be seeing you," he replied, and the doors closed.

Ann suddenly stuck her hand between the doors, bringing them to a halt. Slowly, they rolled back to the open position. "Remember, Tony, Sara was a bitch, is a bitch, and always will be a bitch. I heard the guys saying it and it's true. Don't you ever forget that."

They stood silently for a moment, looking at each other, then Ann lowered her hand and allowed the doors to shut.

*

Tony and Muncie spent an easy afternoon, much like they might on a Saturday — trimming the lawn, cleaning the pool, and doing the normal things that other couples do around the house. They didn't discuss it, but each put forth the effort to keep things normal without talking about where he was going or what he would be doing. Talking wouldn't make it any easier, and it was going to happen anyway, so put it aside and get on like normal people.

The shadows were long, throwing their deep purple casts across the yard where Tony was pulling the last of the weeds in the flower garden. "I'm getting hungry, babe," he said as Muncie tossed her rake in the wheelbarrow.

"I can take a hint. If you'll finish up here, I'll have something for you in a few minutes. Tuna on toast or do you want something better to remember me by?"

"Oh, I think I can come up with something besides a tuna sandwich to remember you by," he replied. He grabbed her from behind and began kissing her ear — first tender and light kisses, then passionate breathing and licking and tugging on her with his teeth. "Yeah, I'll remember your tuna on toast, too."

Their sandwich and potato chip dinner came and went, and after playing a video game with the kids, it was time to get the boys bathed and in bed. It was after nine before Muncie softly closed Matthew's bedroom door. "Shh," she whispered. "They're finally asleep."

Tony walked with her as she went in the bathroom and turned on the hot water and started filling the tub. He leaned against the counter top as she stood before the mirror and brushed her black hair. There was just enough natural curl that she didn't need to do much before her hair was perfect.

"I don't know why you do that," he said with a grin. "You know I'm just going to mess it up."

"But will you respect me in the morning?" she countered.

She put her hand under the faucet and adjusted the water to

the right temperature, then sat on the toilet seat and took off her sneakers. She leaned back against the toilet tank and stretched her legs out and pointed her toes at Tony. "Kiss me," she said.

He went to his knees and took her bare feet in his hands. He lifted her feet to his lips and delicately kissed her toes, then leaned forward and took her in his arms. His true love. This is real life, simple and pure. Uncomplicated, as Margo would say.

It was Sunday afternoon before Tony drove his Saleen to the garage where Jerry Rice was waiting. Traffic was light when Tony cruised passed the university, then turned north on First Avenue. A mile later he wheeled into the shabby, innocuous looking garage in a rundown light industrial area. It was a perfect setting for a maintenance garage for all of the city's undercover cars. Lube, oil, new transmission, or even pound out a few small dents. The police garage crew was as good as they came. Not only fast and efficient, but knowing they held the keys in their hands to every undercover operation in the region, they treated their work with the highest degree of confidence and respect

"I was about to give up on you." Tony spun as Jerry Rice, the head mechanic, walked from the garage, wiping grease from his hands.

"I've got everything ready for you." Rice nodded toward the pickup truck sitting in the dim light of the garage. They shook hands and Tony gave him the keys to the Saleen.

"Take care of it," said Tony with a smile. They walked together across the parking lot at the rear of the garage.

"She's in good shape," the mechanic said as he nodded toward the truck. "I even gave it a lube job and put a sticker on it from some California outlet. We covered your tail, my friend. Everything's taken care of." He laughed and he pointed to the plastic Jesus on the dashboard. "Told you we got everything taken care of," he said with a grin. "We even took it out last night and drove the shit out of it to get some bugs squished on the windshield and grill. We've got to make you look like you drove in from the coast."

*

Twenty minutes later, Tony was driving on the up-ramp to Interstate 19 going south toward Nogales. He settled back into the seat as he gazed across the expanse of the Sonoran desert at the old mission, San Xavier Del Bac, the White Dove of the Desert . . . so peaceful and serene — so distant, it seemed, from his world. He brought his eyes back to the highway, looking at the plastic Jesus with its head swinging to and fro with the rhythm of the road. "Wrong, little guy," he said as he flicked Jesus' chin, making the spring loaded head go up and down. "That's the way. Shake your head 'yes.' Say 'yes Tony, this thing's going to be all right.' Don't be shaking your head 'no' to me. That isn't good for my psyche," he laughed to himself. "Good little Jesus."

His trip took him past the historic town of Tubac, and a few miles later he saw the gate to the Santa Rita Hereford Ranch. It was on his left, and he slowed to look at it, then glanced quickly to his right at the utility pole with its fake transformer, taking pictures of cars coming and going from the ranch. To the average person, the ranch fit in with the beauty and dignity of the surrounding area. This was the land of the conquistadors, of the Indians and missionaries, and later of the ranchers like Pete Kitchen: people who lived and toiled on the land for food and for souls. Yet, there it was. A curved whitewashed adobe wall at least seven feet high; a wrought iron gate with the initial "G" emblazoned on it. Overhead, arcing over the gate was a hand-carved wooden sign proclaiming the name of the ranch. Just like a damn cancer, he thought. You don't see it for what it is, but it's right there in front of God and everybody.

He was coming closer and closer to Nogales, and could feel a pit growing in his stomach, gnawing at him and giving him a cold chill. His mind floated over all that happened in the last few weeks, finally focusing on the women. There were so many of them, and so different from each other. Muncie: honest and pure and true. Just a wife? Nope, he thought. There's a lot more to it than that, but he couldn't think how he could describe her — maybe just somebody special. Yeah. That's about it. She's somebody special, but not like people might think. She's really special. He laughed a little to himself and thought that after all of these years, he just now figured out what love was all about.

Alice Chambers and Sonya Reynolds. "Now there's a pair to draw to," he thought. Control freaks if there ever were any. He could visualize them in the Command and Control Center of an aircraft carrier, pushing all the buttons, making sure all the planes were launched on time; everything was rigid, military discipline. That's them! Absolute control, no loose ends; it's all about things, not people. Just lean back in their executive chairs and call the shots, but be sure to be critical of every little hiccup. "Yeah, that's them" he thought.

And of course, there was Sara; beautiful Sara, her olive complexion and silky black hair: her gorgeous, voluptuous, perfectly shaped mouth. A glance of her eyes; a smile from her lips. "Oh Lord." He thought, "She's too much to describe. One of the most perfect women in the world" That's how beautiful she was. But what if he took just the slightest taste of her? What would it be like: taste of honey or maybe hemlock? "How the hell," he said aloud, "can one guy get so involved with so many different women? How did I get myself in this mess?"

He reached for the mirror and twisted it around, looked at himself, and laughed. The last few miles went by quickly. Ann gave him directions to a small apartment that she found for him through an ad in the newspaper. He wanted an apartment, but not in a big apartment complex. There would be too many people there to keep track of, and he wanted to know who he could normally expect to see coming and going. A few years ago, they would have called this a duplex, but now it was called a garden apartment. Tony liked it. There were five red brick duplexes circled around a common driveway. Each apartment came with its own carport and a small patch of grass in front. Behind the apartment was a small patio surrounded by an adobe wall at least five feet high.

He called ahead and mailed in a deposit, so the landlady was expecting him when he knocked on her door. They went through the routine apartment contract and he signed the name Frederico Ochoa, the new Frederico Ochoa. A life history he memorized inside and out. Born in El Cajon, dropped out of high school, worked in a few carwashes, a lettuce farm in the Imperial Valley, on the avocado farms near Vista, and more recently, helping out at the grocery store. He always showed signs of ability. He'd start out at the bottom, and work his way up. If only he would stay in one place, he would make it, but not Freddy. Always eager to hop around. He couldn't stay in one place long enough to make it big. A fast track taking him nowhere, but getting him there in a hurry. He was old enough now to recognize he needed to get his life together before it was too late, and his favorite cousin, Sara, was getting him a job where he could amount to something. Yeah, sure, Freddy wasn't dumb, he was just a lazy screw-off, but now he was ready to give it a shot.

"Now or never," Sara said to Rey one day. "This is Freddy's big chance. It's now or never. If he can't get his act together now, he never will."

Tony pulled his truck into the carport and began unloading the boxes and suitcases. In a few minutes, everything was inside and he began placing Allbright's equipment in the right places. In less time than he expected, he was completely unloaded, unpacked, and put everything where he thought it should go. He took a deep breath and plugged in the television.

"Am I alone?" he asked, looking at a blank TV screen.

"Nope, its me," said Ann. "This is neat; we're all here waiting to see if it works."

"I knew it would," bellowed Allbright. "Walk around the house and talk to yourself so we can check you out," he commanded.

Tony walked through the place, saying the alphabet so they could tell if they were any gaps to be corrected. "Well, what do you think?" he said as he sat on the edge of the tub.

"Perfect, absolutely perfect," shouted Allbright. "We're in this ball game to win."

*

The fun of playing with their expensive toys soon passed, and Tony went to work arranging drawers and furniture to suit him. He looked at his watch and saw that it was nearly five o'clock and he needed to buy some groceries. He stuck the last pair of socks in a drawer and walked into the bathroom.

"Screw you guys," he said. "I'm not going to keep flipping this thing off and on, we're just going to have to get used to each other." He unzipped his pants and lifted the seat. "Ahh, the pause that refreshes," he said when he peed for the first time while the whole world listened.

As he pushed the flush handle, the doorbell rang. Tony assumed it was the landlady. He walked casually to the door and pulled it open. "Sara, hi," he said with surprise. Sara and a big man, much bigger than Tony anticipated. Reynaldo Guzman! None other than one of the biggest crooks in the state standing at his front door.

"Hi Freddy," she said, smiling as she nodded toward Reynaldo. "This is Reynaldo. Rey, this is my cousin Freddy."

Rey shook his hand, and then pulled him into a hug. Tony knew what the kids felt like when they said he squeezed them too hard. Reynaldo was a big man and had a grip like a bear. He released Tony, then put his huge hands on Tony's shoulders and pulled him close and kissed him on both cheeks.

"We are family," he said with his baritone voice. "Sara's family is my family. Welcome to Arizona."

"Please come in," said Tony as he stepped back and gestured for them to enter. Rey and Sara walked into the living room, then strolled over to the sliding glass door leading to the patio.

"Good place you got here, Freddy," said Rey. "Hope you like it."

Then came Tony's second big surprise. "Damn small world we got here," said Rey. "You drive all the way from California and drive right up to my cousin's place and rent yourself an apartment. That's all right. That's an omen. That means you're supposed to be here."

Tony was startled, but controlled himself and smiled. "The folks in Tucson must be crapping in their pants by now," he thought.

"How did you know I was going to stay here?" Tony asked, dumbfounded.

Rey laughed a deep, hearty laugh. "You'll find out I know everything that goes on around here." He laughed again as he centered his silver western belt buckle in a straight line with his shirt buttons and the zipper of his fly. "All joking aside, I brought my cousin some oranges last night and she told me she rented her last apartment to some guy from California, so I figured it was you." He laughed again, proud of knowing things before anybody else. "But," he said, turning suddenly serious, "remember, you work for me. I know everything. Nothing escapes me. That's why I do so well."

He spoke in short, clipped sentences so Tony would catch the emphasis of everything. There could be no misunderstanding. Reynaldo was in charge and knew everything. That was clear.

"Mister Guzman. Do I call you that?" inquired Tony.

"Reynaldo. Just Reynaldo. That's fine," he replied.

Sara broke in. "Freddy, we figured you didn't have food in yet, and Rey wants to honor you with a little party tonight. You're family. Our family. Come to the ranch about eight o'clock."

"We're glad to have you here, *amigo*," Reynaldo said. He smiled and nodded approval to Tony. "You will be my guest of honor. We'll show you off to our friends, and you can meet some important people. Very important," he emphasized.

"Thank you very much," Tony replied humbly. "Say, I've got some cold beer I picked up on the ride here; can I get you one?" he said as he walked to the kitchen.

Reynaldo walked with him to the refrigerator while Sara walked to the sofa in the living room. She stopped in front of the darkened TV screen and used it as a mirror. She was wearing Levis and a cowboy shirt and looked like a million dollars. Her hair was pulled back into a long ponytail and was held in place with a silver and turquoise grommet. She swung around and admired herself in the darkened screen.

"Where's my beer?" she called to the kitchen as she sat on the sofa, flipping off her sandals and curling her legs up under herself.

"Coming," hollered Tony as they walked back into the living room. Rey sat next to Sara. They were in direct view of the front of the TV, while Tony sat in a chair by the door. They passed time with idle chitchat and a little discussion about his new job. It wouldn't be much, maybe cleaning up the place, lubing the trucks, running errands. Something like that to get him started. Nothing was hinted about Reynaldo's "other world." It was much too early for that to be discussed. Rey didn't know exactly where Tony would end up in the long run, but would start him out doing a lot of the odd jobs, even some of the dirty jobs. It wouldn't look good to the others if some relative came in and started out with an easy job, so he would pretty much start at the bottom.

Tony realized that while he was doing menial jobs they could check him out; run a little background on him if they wanted to, or they might simply watch him, and then make their judgment. Either way, everything was in place. Allbright and the others did not leave a stone unturned.

"That's okay with me," said Tony. "I just want you to know how grateful I am to get the job. I won't disappoint you."

"I know you won't," bellowed Reynaldo with a roaring laugh. "If you're anything like Sara here," he said as he wrapped his arm around her shoulder, "then you'll do great."

Tony caught himself biting his lip as Reynaldo draped his arm around her and hugged her tightly. If the son-of-a-bitch knew how she felt and what was happening he would kill them both right now.

Tony sized up Reynaldo as they continued sipping the beer. He was a huge man, especially for a Mexican. He must have been six feet, maybe even six-two, and weighed well over two hundred pounds. A big, powerful man and that was exactly how he carried on — big and powerful. He was wearing a white cowboy shirt opened at the neck. The top several buttons were undone, exposing a huge hairy chest. Two gold chains were draped around his neck. One was very delicate and fit tightly around the neck; the other was a heavy chain that dropped a large medal of the Virgin of Guadalupe onto his chest. His trousers were heavily starched and ironed Levis, and he wore a pair of expensive ostrich-skin cowboy boots. He was impeccable. The epitome of a successful rancher and businessman.

They finished their drinks. Sara and Rey made their excuses and left. Tony closed the door behind them and held his breath, listening. When their car left, he exhaled loudly and walked to the TV. "Well?" he said, "What do you think?"

"Can't believe it," commented Martinez who was watching. "We told you to expect the unexpected, but this was a surprise. They come to your place, and your damned landlady is his cousin. I can't believe it. This is one hell of a start. Well anyway, you're off and running. Now just watch your butt and everything will be okay."

*

It was eight o'clock on the nose when Tony turned off of the Interstate access road and drove through the gates. Two rough looking, but sharply dressed cowboys were standing guard. Tony slowed and rolled his window down. The one on the driver's side smiled, nodded and gave a flick of the wrist for Tony to pass through.

Sara stood at the entryway and greeted other visitors as Tony parked in the dirt lot beneath the eucalyptus trees. The smell of barbecue wafted through the trees. He was hungry and ready to eat, but would have to be on guard. He already went through enough surprises for one day.

Sara hugged him as they greeted each other at the entry to the front patio. He gave her a peck on the cheek and moved into the patio, hearing the sounds of *mariachi* music coming from farther back in the house. About a dozen other people were already there, holding drinks and engaging in polite conversation. Tony found the bar near the fountain. He ordered tequila on the rocks, and then moved off to explore the private castle of Reynaldo Guzman.

Huge oak doors led into the living room. Tony walked in, finding a few other couples and three or four unattached men wandering around, taking in the grandeur of the house. The walls and ceiling were white, with heavy, dark, wooden open beams running the length of the rooms. Each room had a fireplace. Some were not much more than small notches in the corner, but the ones in the living room and dining room were huge monstrosities at least eight or nine feet wide. Expensive pieces of art were mounted on the walls with lights directed on them. Antique statues stood in the corners of the living room. Tony wandered on through the house, following the music to the rear patio.

"This must be the place," he thought when he saw the pool and retaining wall. Indeed, Benny did good work. The wall and tile work were beautiful. "This is where it all started," he thought as his mind raced over the events of recent months.

"Freddy," shouted Reynaldo walking onto the patio. "Good, isn't it?" he said as he gestured toward the pool and hot tub. "I'm glad you're here."

Outside the wall, a man and woman were busy tending a fire

and cooking steaks. "Rico," shouted Reynaldo to the man bending over the hot fire.

"*Si, Senor* Guzman," the old man replied as he lifted the steaks onto a platter that the woman held.

"Come with me, Freddy," said Reynaldo as they walked into the dining room. Sara was already organizing the others to be seated. "Here, next to me," ordered Guzman to Tony as they sat at the head of the table.

The dinner passed pleasantly as Tony was introduced to the other visitors. Most of them worked for Greater America Imports, but a few special invited guests were there also. Tony was introduced to Raphael Dominguez, the chairman of Santa Cruz National Bank in Nogales. Next on the list of influential people was Peter Eichman, the regional director of Latinos United, a nonprofit organization that worked to loosen immigration restrictions on Latin-Americans who wanted to enter the United States. Last, but not least, was an attractive red-headed woman. She was dressed in elegant splendor with an ankle length white dress that Tony recognized as an Apache wedding dress. A strand of silver and turquoise was wrapped around her neck, dropping down between her generous, milky white breasts. She wore only the slightest hint of lipstick. As she opened her mouth to speak, her lips appeared as passionate as he ever saw.

"Mary Elizabeth," said Rey. "This is Sara's cousin Freddy."

Mary extended her hand and Tony shook it politely. "Sorry I was so late, Rey, but the books couldn't be closed until that last shipment of shrimp was entered. But, anyhow," she commented. "I'm never too late for the drinks."

Tony was careful not to drink too much, but still enjoyed the night. Tonight's dinner party was no conspiracy, and most of the people here were probably straight, hard working people. But, some of them were the kind of people that Guzman might be able to use later on when he needed a favor or a special contact. These are the people he would call on. All except Mary Elizabeth. Tony would have to take his time, but she was one he would have to get to know, especially if she is the bookkeeper or accountant.

After dinner the group moved outside and sat around the pool, talking and drinking. The *mariachis* strolled among the guests, playing Mexican music and occasionally stopping to chug a beer or tequila. Tony was aware that the group was starting to thin out, so he decided this would be a good time to head back to Nogales and his first night in the apartment. Besides that, it was a day of too many surprises and he was tired and ready to get some sleep.

He walked into the living room and found Reynaldo coming out of a rear hallway, holding the hand of a young, beautiful, dark skinned girl. She couldn't be more than twenty, Tony thought.

"No man should be alone tonight," Rey said with a smile. He held her hand out to Tony. "My gift for you," he said. "But only for tonight. I promised her parents I would have her back tomorrow."

"Oh no, I couldn't impose on you," Tony said quickly.

"Bullshit," barked Rey. "Her parents promise she's a virgin. She's Yaqui Indian," he said as he looked at her. She held her gaze down, avoiding eye contact with the men as they spoke about her. "She screws you good and goes home. It's that simple. If you tell me she was good, I get her a green card. Tell me she's real good," he laughed, "and I'll get her whole scummy village green cards."

Rey grabbed Tony's hand and handed the girl to him. "The last bedroom down the hall. It's yours, but I want you out before daylight 'cause we've got to get her back across the border," he commanded as he walked away.

Tony put his arms around the girl's shoulder and walked to the bedroom door and pushed it open. The room was huge with a king-size bed in the middle. It was another one of those rooms with a small fireplace in the corner. Candles were burning on the mantle, and the bedspread was pulled back. His mind raced, then he realized that if they didn't do anything, nobody but them would know. He could bullshit Rey and get green cards for the whole tribe. "Screw you, Rey," he thought.

She walked across the room toward the bed, unbuttoning her dress as she walked. "No, wait," he said as he grabbed her arm. She spun around and faced him, still unbuttoning her dress.

"Stop, you don't have to do that," commanded Tony.

"I do good," she replied. "Do good and get green card," she continued.

"No, damn it. Listen to me. You don't have to do anything." She pulled away from him and threw her dress down over her hips. She stood there, naked. "My sisters do this with men and go to America. Me too!" she exclaimed.

He looked at her tiny body shining in the candlelight. She couldn't be more than five feet tall and weighed less than one hundred pounds. Her breasts were tiny, but protruded straight out from her little body.

"I can't believe this," he said to her. "What's your name?"

"The man of the house calls me Marie, so you can call me that if you want to," she replied softly. She turned and threw the spread off the bed and crawled up in the middle of the mattress. "Come on. Green card," she said. "You want me?"

Tony racked his brain. He could not depend on her to keep a secret. Her simple little mind, her drive for an immigration card was too strong. He nearly exploded in anger and frustration. He was only undercover for about five hours, and here he was getting in bed with some poor thing that didn't want him anymore than he wanted her. This can't be. This can't happen. Not now. Not the first day. Nothing can go this bad, this fast. This is wrong. What about Muncie? Oh shit, shit, a thousand times, shit! This wasn't supposed to happen.

If this little Yaqui girl didn't have him, she would probably be stupid enough to admit it to Reynaldo and anybody else who asked. "Damn it," he said. Suddenly he saw the even bigger picture. This was how Reynaldo got girls into the United States. He would get jobs for them in the right places. All he demanded of them was to make a phone call from time-to-time. The grip he held on them was their family in Mexico. If the girls didn't produce, their families faced the consequences.

Sara's words raced back to him, "It's a mean world, and these are OUR rules."

Tony spun around with his back to her and began unbuttoning his shirt, watching her in the mirror as she got off the bed and came to him.

"Hold up a second," he said as he turned around and took hold of her bare shoulders, keeping her at arms length. "You're a virgin and don't know how to do all of this stuff, so tonight lets just talk about it. Who knows? Maybe we can get together again and do some love making after you know more about sex. I've gotta be careful," he said as he smiled at her. "Otherwise, I might accidentally hurt you."

"No worry," she shot back at him. "Man gives dollars to my parents so they send me to a place in Nogales to learn how to do things to make you happy. I know how so you no hurt me."

Her little body looked so innocent as she reached out for his hand and led him to the bed. She sat on the edge of the bed and unbuckled his belt, his muscles quivering, his heart pounding, and his mouth as dry as a sun-baked desert. She guided his trousers and shorts over his hips, and they fell around his ankles. Marie slipped off the bed and untied his shoes. In moments, he was lying on the bed. The flicker of the candles glistened on his sweaty body as Marie touched him with her lips. He closed his eyes and felt the warmth as she caressed him. He folded his arms over his eyes and forehead, not wanting to see her or touch her. He bit his tongue and gave a soft whimper. Marie barely moved. He thought she was crying, but he didn't want to talk to her or even console her. We both were raped tonight, he thought. He watched the candles and wished he was somewhere else. Anywhere else. Then he fell asleep.

He was startled awake. It took him a second to realize his surroundings, then he looked at her. She was on her knees, touching him. "Must," she said. "For green card. No more virgin then," she said innocently. He looked at her and closed his eyes as she rolled over on him. He moaned as he felt her little body touch him, taking that which he vowed to keep only for his Muncie. He tried to put his mind somewhere else. What he was doing was wrong and he could never undo it. No government contract or letter of authorization from the chief could ever make this right. Would it be like Sara said about the Nazis? "I didn't know. Or, I couldn't help it."

She was still on him when there was a tap on the door. The door opened before either of them could react. One of the cowboys from the gate stuck his head through and smiled. "Sorry about that, but she's got to go," he said as he stepped across the bedroom. "Getting late and I have to get her back," he said. He grabbed her arm and pulled her off the bed. "C'mon puta, gotta get you back right now."

The cowboy grabbed her dress and carried it as he led her out the door. "You need to go too," he said as he looked over his shoulder at Tony. "The boss doesn't like people here when he gets up." The cowboy slammed the door and they were gone.

The undercover cop slowly put on his clothes, confused and bewildered about what happened. How could he tell Muncie? Hell, he could never breathe a word of it. He would just have to live with it and get on with his life.

Minutes later, he was outside walking toward his truck. His was the only vehicle parked there. He got in and pulled out of the dirt lot and onto the paved road that headed back to the highway. In the distance, he could see the crack of dawn breaking over the mountains.

He pulled up to the gate where the other cowboy was sitting on a stump, smoking a cigar. "Must have been a good piece," the man laughed as he stepped up to the driver's side window. "Wouldn't mind getting a little of that myself," he commented with a grin.

"Here, this is for you," he said as he handed over an envelope.

Tony took the envelope as though he expected it, then drove away from the ranch and toward his bed. When he was safely away from the ranch, he opened the envelope. There were ten fifty dollar bills and a note from Reynaldo welcoming him to his new Arizona family. As if he needed another surprise, Reynaldo was giving him weekly housekeeping. His cousin, Margaret, would clean, do laundry and change linens each week. No charge for family.

CHAPTER 11

It was a little after seven Monday morning when Tony backed the truck from the carport and headed for his new job. The apartment was about a mile from the warehouses that made up Greater America Imports. Five minutes later, he turned off the street and through the gate. It was a large complex of warehouses, offices, a garage, and parking lots. The small red brick building near the gate was the office, so he pulled into a parking slot near the door and went inside. He introduced himself to an old lady at the desk. She smiled, motioning him to a seat while she turned and pulled open a file cabinet. She gathered together a small stack of papers — an application form that asked just about every question he memorized from his Frederico Ochoa briefing sheet, an insurance questionnaire, and a W-2 form, cramming them beneath the clip on an old clipboard. She handed it to him.

"I know you're Mr. Guzman's family, but you still have to fill out an application. Insurance and that stuff," she said as she returned to the jumbled mess on her desk. In preparation for this moment, Tony memorized his new social security number and other particulars, and quickly filled out the forms and returned them to the old lady.

"Here you go, ma'am," he said, sliding the clipboard across her desk. She pushed her other work aside and gave a quick scan to his application.

"Okay, wait here a bit," she mumbled as she pushed back from her desk and got out of her well-worn secretarial chair. She walked to a desk-top microphone on the counter, grabbed it like she was choking a chicken, and bellowed into it, "Rico, come up here."

Tony fidgeted in his chair and was getting comfortable when the old man who cooked the steaks at Guzman's walked into the office.

"Good morning, sir," he said politely to Tony. "Come with me, please," he said as he gestured toward the door.

"Thanks for the help," Tony said to the old lady.

"*De nada*," she responded without looking up.

*

Tony's first day on the job was anything but remarkable. Rico told him that Guzman gave explicit orders for him to learn the business from the bottom up, and that was the way it was going to be. Tony moved his truck to the far end of the complex where there was a spot designated for employee parking. He went to the green-trimmed warehouse where Rico waited for him on the loading dock.

"This is produce only here," Rico told him. "The yellow warehouse is fish only." He pointed to the other warehouse across the parking lot. "Remember, nothing ever goes from one to the other. Fish and produce don't mix."

He led Tony down the loading dock and through a set of double doors into the warehouse, then worked their way past stacks of empty wooden crates to a janitorial closet in the corner. Rico twisted the doorknob, but nothing happened. He adjusted his grip, then tried it a second time before he took it in both hands and jerked it so hard that Tony thought he would pull the door off its hinges. On the second heavy jerk, it opened so fast that he almost fell to the floor.

"Damn thing," he muttered as he regained his balance. "Always sticks. Anyway this is your office. Maybe the first thing you need to do is fix this piece of shit," he mumbled as he kicked the door.

Tony spent the first undercover week sweeping the warehouses, washing out trailer trucks, helping mechanics fix flat tires, and replacing burnt out headlights. It was anything but glamorous. He learned he had muscles where he never knew they existed, and learned a new appreciation for what some people disdainfully call manual labor. It sucked.

The only blessing he found so far was that he was assigned to the day shift, working from eight until five. This was the large crew with about twenty people on the docks, while the evening and midnight crews were considerably smaller, which sometimes meant they were required to do double-duty on the docks.

He arrived at his apartment a few minutes after five and crashed on the sofa. Part of the Task Forces' communication protocol was that he always said "another hard day," when he came into his apartment. If everything was okay from Tucson's point of view, they would answer him. He routinely gave a brief report to the Tucson communications people, who expected little more from him than a few grunts and groans. No one expected much this early in the game, and they weren't disappointed.

He considered coming up with some story to give him an excuse to go to Tucson over the weekend, but Martinez talked him out of it. "Just too much of a risk this soon," he commented.

At the start of his fourth week, Tony's usual Monday morning foray into his "office" was interrupted when Rico shouted at him over the noise of the diesels and the forklifts grinding up for their days chores. "Come with me," the old man said, straining his voice over the commotion around the loading docks. "Let's go up to the office, you've got yourself a new job."

Tony was elated. At last he, that is, Freddy, was promoted to loader's assistant, a pretty decent job after working as the main janitor and gopher. A loader's assistant did the last count of crates of produce that came in from Mexico and headed north into the retail market. It was an easy job. All he did was make sure they received or shipped what they paid for, regardless of which way it was going. The loader really wasn't a loader in the true sense of the word. It was his job to be back in the warehouse, barking orders to the laborers, who loaded crates and cardboard boxes onto pallets for the forklift. Maybe it wasn't an air conditioned office like he enjoyed in Tucson, he thought, "but this ain't half bad compared to that janitor's job."

The week was uneventful, but at least he didn't moan and groan at the end of each shift. He never saw Guzman or Sara anywhere around the complex. He assumed that Sara seldom or never came there, but that when Guzman was there he would be only in the office. Thursday evening he convinced Martinez that other workers from the warehouse usually drove into Tucson regularly for a little night life and some fun, so it wouldn't seem out of place for him to drive up there once in a while on weekends. Martinez agreed, so

Friday after work, Frederico Ochoa headed north on Interstate 19. He left his pickup at the garage with Jerry, got behind the wheel of his Saleen, and was in Antonio Castenada's home by dinner time.

Four weeks down! How many more to go?

*

Tony and Muncie cooked hot dogs on the grill and played Marco Polo with the kids in the pool. The evening hours zoomed by, the kids were tucked away, and they were left in the quiet of the moonlight by the pool.

"What's it like?" Muncie asked. She was lying on the chaise lounge wearing a bikini, her knees bent and her feet flat on the lounge. Tony got up from his deck chair and went in the kitchen and got a pitcher of lemonade. He brought it out with two Tupperware glasses and poured it for them. Plopping down in his chair and stretching out his legs, he gave her a sketch of his menial work, but explained that they thought it would go about like that, so things were on schedule. He finished his lemonade, got up from the chair and sat on the edge of the chaise lounge. He rubbed his hand on her thigh and talked to her about the first day in the apartment and of all of the surprises, but left out the story about Marie.

Muncie listened, then reached out to him, pulling him to her — kissing him. First softly, then with lust and passion. Their breathing became labored as they kissed each others lips, then took turns nibbling each other's ears, hugging and touching all of those special places. He tasted the sweetness of her lips, holding her gently between his teeth as he put his hand behind her and tugged the string loose, letting her bikini top fall to the deck. Muncie carefully pushed him back, got up from the lounge and spread a towel on the cool deck, sliding her bikini over her hips and flinging it into the pool. She lay back, reaching up to him and taking him to her.

As they embraced, Tony's mind raced through the event with Marie. Again, Sara was right. Guzman and people like him corrupt everything they touch. Tony's mouth was dry and he couldn't find the feeling that was there before. There never was anything like this. Never! He couldn't make love to his own wife because of those filthy bastards. Those dirty, rotten bastards.

"I'm sorry, honey," Muncie said, holding him tightly in her arms. "I know this thing has been hard on you. Let's go to bed and sleep until noon."

*

Tony's next week started with another promotion. "The boss says you're too smart to waste out here," Rico said, smiling and patting Tony on the back, telling him what a good worker he was. "Let's go up to the office. Mrs. Martin wants you up there."

Great, he thought. Maybe, just maybe he would get a chance to start seeing the books — he was on a roll. They knew it would take a while to get started, but once they got the wheels rolling, they were on their way.

Mary Elizabeth greeted him with a smile. She was more than just what he would call good looking. A little heavy-set, but at the same time, an attractive middle-age woman. Her auburn hair flowed casually over the top of her ears, then was swept back and held in place with her usual silver clip. Her milky white skin stood out in contrast beneath her bangs, and her lips were colored with only a hint of a natural colored lipstick. Whether with a bit of pride or arrogance, she typically wore a slightly revealing neckline, giving more than just a hint of her well-endowed bosom. She carried herself with a certain degree of intrepidity, not at all timid of her womanhood, and at the same time, more than capable in handling anything that might come up — unhappy employees, a hard-drive crash, a late shipment. It didn't make any difference to her. She dealt with it and got right back to business. She was an absolute professional, but nevertheless, could be downright brutal.

Ten women worked at computer terminals or shuffled packing lists all over the place. No one looked up from their work stations as Mary Elizabeth gave Tony his assignment. She gave him a few quick tips on their newest version of Vista and got him into a spread sheet. His job was simple, but important and boring. He compared packing lists that came in from the trucks with data that was entered by Mary Elizabeth's staff. If there was a minor error, he must correct it. If the error was major, he brought it to her and she took care of it. If he caught anybody with more than three errors on the same shift, he also brought that to her. She did not tolerate sloppy work, and fired people she could not depend on to get it right.

The week flew by before he knew it. The job wasn't hard physically, but the intensity and volume were staggering. He went to the apartment at night and crashed on the sofa for a few minutes before he gave his ho-hum report to Tucson. He was relieved that Margaret came in and cleaned the apartment, because he was too wiped out to do it.

He wanted to go home again for the weekend, but Martinez nixed the idea. It was too risky to be running back and forth every weekend, and there were too many chances of his running into someone. No! He would have to stay put. "Go across the border and see a bullfight or something," Martinez suggested. "Be Freddy."

The next week started the same as any other. Work, pick up some groceries on the way home, give a boring report and fix dinner. Tony settled into a routine. He knew things would take time, and he must be prepared whenever it happened. Tuesday night he made his usual stop at the store and went home. He started talking into the radio as he stuffed the milk and delicatessen potato salad into the refrigerator. He gave the usual passwords that they agreed upon before he left Tucson. "Another hard day," he said. He paused to hear the usual response. Jacobs, Margo, Ann — somebody should say something back to him. Anything!

"Glad to see you, or you look tired." Anything, but there was no response . . . just deathly quiet. Not a sound other than his own breathing. He stopped putting away his groceries and froze in his tracks. Something was wrong. Very wrong.

"Another hard day," he said, wishing to just hear a friendly voice come back at him. Once again, he paused. Was something wrong with the electronics, or was it something else? No answer. He looked at the master power switch. It was still turned on. Slowly, he walked through the apartment, opening closet doors and listening. Nothing!

Allbright planned for contingencies such as this, so Tony went to what they called Plan B. He flicked on the radio, turning the volume up to ear splitting levels, and then went to the closet. He pulled his suitcase from beneath the rack of cloths and took it to his bed. He pulled a pocket knife from his pocket and flipped open the screwdriver blade. With three quick twists of the screw holding down one end of the handle strap, it slipped out of its inset and fell into his hand. He worked his knife blade under the seam and a small spring-loaded wand popped out. The whole thing was no bigger than a pack of cigarettes with a three-inch wand protruding from its side. Tony went back and flipped off the master switch so that there would be no interference from his own listening devices.

He started at the front door and walked slowly toward the patio door. He held the wand level and worked to control the shaking of his fingers. When he approached the patio door, the wand began making a slow arc, pointing to his left in the general direction of a table, lamp, and some miscellaneous junk that he had not put away.

He put the wand back in its original position and then went to the kitchen doorway. He walked slowly toward the front door. Again, he focused to control his labored breathing and shaking hand. The wand made a slow arc, this time to his right and once again pointed to the lamp and table.

He folded the wand into the tiny pack and shoved it into his hip pocket. He took a deep breath and walked back to the kitchen to turn on the master power switch so Tucson could see what was happening.

Tony stepped in front of the TV and smiled. Without muttering a sound, he pointed in the direction where the wand pointed. Very softly, he stepped to the wall and removed the picture. There was nothing stuck to the back of it, so he hung it back in its original position. He held his breath as he lifted the lamp and looked beneath its base. There it was! No bigger than an old hearing aid with a piece of tape holding it in position. Tony carefully put the lamp down and nodded in the affirmative to the blank TV screen. Once again, he turned off the master switch and searched the rest of his apartment with the wand. Nothing was in the kitchen or bathroom, but there, taped to the leg of the bed under the headboard was another bug. Tony recognized the equipment as stuff the police used ten or fifteen years ago, but abandoned for more sophisticated equipment. This was junk that could be bought at any spy store for a few dollars. It was good for a range of only fifty or seventy yards, but was close enough for a receiver in Margaret's apartment to pick up anything.

Tony got a piece of notepaper from near the phone and sat on the sofa, using a coffee table as a desk. He waited three weeks for the telephone company to install a phone, but he knew it could never be used for police business. Even though they never were suspicious of it being bugged from this end, it was a simple task for anyone to tap into a conversation anywhere along the line. The phone was as much for appearance as for anything else.

He carefully printed a note about the bugs and squatted down in front of the television set. He didn't know how close or far he would have to be for the camera to focus on the note, so he took a guess that if he tried three or four distances, one of them would have to be right. He held it up for a few seconds about three feet back from the screen, then scooted back to four, then to five feet. Finally he gave a big grin to the screen and scribbled another note on the back of the first one. "THANKS," he printed in big letters. Now, at least, he knew what the staff in Tucson knew, and it was a good feeling to know that they could communicate and stay one step ahead of Guzman. Their communication was not only important, it was critical. They must always stay at least one step ahead of Guzman. Anything less could be fatal.

Rather than worry about the bugs, he decided that Guzman was checking him out before bringing him any deeper into the company. Tony never trusted Margaret, and assumed that she either placed the bugs, or let someone else in to do it. Either way, he felt relaxed. They didn't find anything and they wouldn't if they looked for a million years. He grabbed a cold beer from the refrigerator and went back to the sofa. He lit a match to the note and dropped it in an ashtray and watched it burn. He made sure every bit of it was unrecognizable, just in case they were checking his trash. When it was cool, he picked it up and put it in the palm of his hand and crumbled it into ash.

When there was nothing left, the Tucson crew watched him leave the sofa and go out of view of their camera. Seconds later, they heard the toilet flush.

*

"Wow that was too close for me." Chipper Gephardt, an entry-level communications operator said. He was in his third week on a new job. The work was more boring than he ever anticipated, watching the monitors as they stared out at Tony's normally quiet and empty apartment. Nevertheless, he watched until his eyes were almost glazed over before calling a relief so he could get up and stretch his bones; let his eyes wonder around the office, then slide back into his chair for another dose of tedium.

"What time did she come in?" queried Jacobs.

"She usually cleans about nine or so, and it was about then. Except this time she was in and out in a minute or two. I couldn't tell exactly what she was doing, but I saw her lifting up the lamp and doing something. Next thing I know, I can hear her doing something in the bedroom. Bim-Bam thank you ma'am and she was gone."

"You did well," said the lieutenant.

Chico, Ann and Jimmy stood behind the lieutenant while he re-ran the tape of Margaret planting the bugs. "I can't believe all this crap," said Jimmy. "Is everybody a crook? Screw'em. We should just go and nuke all of them," he said with disgust.

"Well, we are getting the big picture, and that's what we want. We ain't got no murder case or nothing," Jacobs said more to himself than to anyone else. "We'll get that bunch of bastards. We'll get'em. You watch and see," he said with a grin on his face.

*

The next two weeks passed uneventfully. Tony worked and wrote notes to his TV; Mary Elizabeth drove her workers to the brink with more work, and the summer quickly passed into fall. Tony twice tried to pry a little more into the business, but twice she shut him down. "You'll know what you need to know when you need to know it," she barked. "We have a lot of business and you work for me, so you do what I tell you."

Tony began to double-check himself as a precaution. He drove home on different routes, doubling back to see if he was being followed. He swept his truck with the wand, but there weren't any bugs. Caution was his byword. Be careful, but don't be paranoid. Nevertheless, he was getting lonesome. He stopped at the drug store and used the payphone to call the office. He figured that they didn't have every phone in town bugged, and by damn, he wanted to go home. He didn't intend to surrender his whole life for this. He got the captain on the phone and pleaded his case and finally convinced Martinez to let him make an occasional trip to see his wife. "What the hell," he said in exasperation to the captain. "Every stud down here goes to Tucson to get laid or go to a flick and I'm no different." There was a long pause, both waiting to see who would blink first. "I want to come home."

"Okay, you deserve it, but be careful. Don't set a pattern and don't push it. Better a little from time to time than overdoing it and raising suspicion."

Each time he was home he called Martinez for updates, but there wasn't much. "Only one thing we missed early on," Martinez said over the phone. "The crime lab reviewed the photos of the shoe tracks in the arroyo and found something that they missed on the first analysis. The Vibram-soled shoe or boot was well worn, but under closer scrutiny, they found a V-shaped notch on the front of the heels. 'Prison notches,'" said Martinez. "Every inmate turns in their personal possessions when they are booked into the prison, except for one item — their shoes. A standard part of the booking process is for them to remove their shoes and the cobbler chops a notch in the heel. It just takes a second because he does it with a paper cutter type device. He holds the shoe under the cutter, and 'Whomp,' there is the notch. If they escape, the notch gives the guards something to identify wherever he goes.

"That's not to say it was an escapee," said the captain. "Could be he went in and served a few months and got out. Not a whole lot, but we'll put it with everything else as it all comes together."

*

A couple of days later Tony walked into his apartment just as the phone began ringing. He grabbed it on the second ring. "Hello," he said.

"Freddy, this is Marty. I'm the evening shift boss. I've never used you before, but we are getting stacked up on our loads."

"Sure, what can I do?" responded Tony.

"I know you are not a regular driver, but I've got a load that should be ready for the morning run. I need you in here by five o'clock to take a load up the highway for us."

There was a pause. "I know you just got off work, but you'll get paid for a double shift. Get some sleep and be here dark and early. We've got work to get done," he commanded.

There was a click when Marty hung up. Tony turned on the radio and wrote a note in front of the TV. He didn't know where he was going, and it was up to Martinez to decide whether or not to put a tail on him. Tony grabbed a beer from the refrigerator and sat on the sofa. He looked at the TV, smiled, and gave a thumbs up. Things were starting to happen.

CHAPTER 12

Tony found an empty slot in the employee parking area and pulled in. He looked into the darkness at the distant mountains. The wind blew from the northeast, and a steady rumble of thunder rolled down the mountainside and across the valley. A big rain was on its way. He hurried toward the yellow warehouse as rain drops pelted the ground. Before moving into the office, he worked in what was referred to only as the "green" warehouse. This morning, though, he went to the opposite side of the yard to the "yellow" building to meet the shift boss.

Eighteen-wheelers, one-ton and half-ton trucks were backed up to the loading docks, but only a few people were visible as everyone else scurried out of the weather. Tony climbed the stairs at the end of the dock and walked toward the shipping manager's booth in the center. He was almost there when an older man stepped out of the warehouse door.

"Freddy, hi. I'm Johnny," he said. "I'm the midnight boss. Glad you could make it. C'mon, I'll show you your truck." He took Tony's arm and walked back toward the end of the dock where Tony came up the stairs.

"Here's your shipping order and the address where you need to take it," he said with a smile. "You know those Chinamen, love their fish," he laughed. He went over the bill with Tony since it was his first road trip. He quickly covered the packing list, noting a few of the ordered items and a couple of substituted items. There was a signature line at the bottom to be signed, and an official note requiring payment within thirty days. "We always guarantee fresh frozen fish," he said. "You just need to climb in and get it to them before seven o'clock."

Tony opened the door and slipped in behind the wheel. It was a one-ton stake-bed truck with a large reefer box bolted to the bed. The freezer door was closed with a padlock. Tony checked the key ring and made sure the key was there.

"You think you can find the place?" asked Johnny. "It's some little Chinese store in the El Rio neighborhood in Tucson. Don't get lost, and be damned sure to get there on time," he commanded.

Tony started the engine and eased the truck out of the lot. Minutes later he was on the Interstate with his load of fish and whatever else might be in the truck. Rain fell as he left the Nogales city limits. First it was a light shower, then turned into a heavy monsoon with wind pelting the rain against the windshield and lightening throwing strange shadows in the night darkness. He flipped on the dome light to check the address. Sunshine Market on El Rio Drive, behind the golf course.

He knew the neighborhood well. The teenagers who lived there called it "*El Sabaco*," the armpit. That's what it was. The armpit of society. Dope dealers, little gangsters, car thieves and burglars mixed in with a few old people who didn't have enough money to move out. "Gotta be," he said to himself. "Gotta be carrying a load of dope."

He looked in his side mirrors, but the highway was dark and deserted behind him. Wind, rain and lightning were his only companions. He was curious whether Captain Martinez was able to get anybody in place to set up surveillance on him, but quickly decided that he probably hadn't. For whatever reason. Maybe not enough time, or maybe afraid that they would be spotted on such a lonesome road. Either way, he decided that he must go it alone and it gave him a creepy feeling. He was in the war without a backup — nobody to help him if he needed it and he didn't like the feeling. He felt like a spy behind enemy lines and it wasn't a good feeling.

He kept the truck well under the speed limit as he drove the deserted highway toward Tucson. He felt calm, but his hands were sweaty and his lips were dry. He wanted a cup of coffee and cussed himself out for not planning ahead. He had a small thermos jug and should have brought it along, but here he was in the middle of nowhere and dry as a bone. It was going to be a long drive, but he might catch a Denny's or Dunkin' Donuts for a quick cup. He smiled to himself. It was another lesson learned.

He passed the Guzman ranch and settled into the hum of the road as he guided the truck around a curve on the wet highway. Far ahead he made out flashing yellow and red lights on the highway. He took his foot off the gas pedal and slowed the truck, staring thorough the rain. As he got closer, he saw it was a border patrol checkpoint. He slowed and dimmed his lights as he drove between the traffic cones that funneled traffic into a single lane. A green Border Patrol trailer was parked at the side of the road, and a Department of Public Safety patrol car was straddling the lane markers in the middle of the highway. A green-jacketed Border

Patrol officer ran out of the trailer and came to the driver's side window. The wind and rain buffeted against him and blew his hat from his head. He looked at Tony and waved him through, then raced after his hat as it blew into the ditch. "Your tax dollars at work," grinned Tony as he drove the fish and whatever else he might be carrying away from the check point. "It's like a sieve and they don't have a chance."

The rain slackened as he got closer to Tucson. By the time he exited Interstate 19 and got on I-10, the rain stopped. He considered stopping at a phone booth and calling the on-duty communications officer, but decided it was too risky. There was no way of knowing if anybody, good or bad, was following him. He was early, but still needed ten or fifteen minutes to get to the store. He exited the freeway at Speedway Boulevard and turned left into the barrio. He wasn't sure exactly where the Sunshine Market was, but knew he could find it in a few minutes. A cup of coffee would have to wait.

He found El Rio Drive and turned onto the narrow rough pavement that the city called a street. The rain and wind suddenly slammed against the truck with its full fury. He was startled and took a few seconds to regain his composure. "Damn me," he bellowed. "Calm your ass down."

Down the street on his right one little yellow light burned over the door he was looking for, but there were no other signs of life. The neighborhood was deserted and dark, and the rain suddenly quieted into a steady drizzle. He turned onto the muddy parking lot and felt the wheels spin as they slipped in the mud and water. He pulled to the rear of the store. The back door was open. The storeroom looked small and cluttered when Tony pulled toward the building. He swung the truck around and brought it to a halt, shifting into reverse and carefully started backing up to the door.

Although he still didn't see anyone, he assumed they were inside out of the rain. Two pickup trucks and a car were parked at the rear of the store, but were too far away for him to make them out clearly through the rain and darkness. He watched his mirrors as he slowly backed up, bringing the truck to a halt a few feet from the door. He turned off the engine and reached for the door handle to get out. Suddenly, a large man came out of nowhere and banged on his door.

"Hold it right there," the man growled.

Tony's heart jumped. "What do you mean?"

"Raining like hell," the man said. "No sense in you getting wet, too. Let me have the key and we'll unload everything. New, ain't ya?" he said.

Tony handed over the key ring and clipboard and watched in the mirrors as two other people joined the first man. He couldn't make them out through his rain-spattered mirrors, but knew they were going about their business quickly. He watched the big man carry one or two boxes into the store, but all the other boxes were carried to the pickup trucks and car. In a matter of a few minutes, the big man was back at the driver's window.

"Here's your ticket and keys," he said, handing it to Tony. The man stared for several seconds, then commanded, "You better be getting out of here."

Tony started the engine and shifted into drive. The mud was slippery, so he eased down on the accelerator and slowly pulled away from the building. He watched in the mirrors as the storeroom door was shut and the headlights of the other three vehicles came on. Seconds later he was on the solid ground of El Rio Drive, heading out of the barrio. He never saw which way the others went. Tony drove back to the Interstate and stopped at a Denny's for a large coffee to go.

He couldn't believe how easy it was, and it was going on all over the country every day and every night non-stop. He didn't have any idea what he carried or how much of it there was, but it was easier than he thought it could ever be. He shook his head and realized how badly his side was losing the so called war on drugs. In fact, it was so one-sided that his side probably shouldn't even consider themselves in the battle. Just a few skirmishes, that's all. Just skirmishes.

The rain was reduced to a light drizzle, and dawn was on the horizon as Tony swung the truck back on the highway for the trip back to Nogales.

*

The next couple of weeks went the same. He worked in Mary Elizabeth's sweat shop, and then made a delivery to the Sunshine Market. Each trip was identical. The big man, whom Tony referred to as *"pelon"* for his bald head, always met the truck. He was a least forty years old and weighed well over two hundred pounds. Every bit as big as Guzman, maybe even bigger. The other two appeared to be about thirty. They were small and wiry, but quick and strong with the heavy boxes that they moved. They never took more than five minutes to unload the truck and load their cars and trucks. They were the epitome of efficiency. No talk, no bullshit, no games. Theirs was a serious business and there was no room for screw-ups.

Funny, thought Tony. He never saw a Chinaman. Wonder if we'll ever know whether he is in on it, or if they just use him. Who the hell knows? After his fourth trip, Tony turned in his truck and paperwork and went to his apartment to get some sleep. He unlocked the door and walked in, flipping the door shut behind him. Suddenly, a woman's voice came from the living room. He jumped and reached for his gun. It took him a second to realize that he didn't have one, and that it was his TV talking to him.

"Crap, I'm sorry." It was Ann. "Your landlady came in a couple of hours ago and took the bugs out. Damn, I'm sorry I startled you," she said. "We watched her whip them out in just a couple of minutes, and then she was out of there. I watched a couple of seconds when you came in to make sure you were alone. Sorry for the scare," she said. "Should I sing you a little song if we have to go through this again?" she asked with a touch of humor.

"Tony, it's me," came Martinez's voice through the television. "Looks like they wanted to keep an eye on you for a while to make sure you were clean and not screwing around on them. You did fine. Hang in there and remember, we're never very far away."

Another week passed before Mary Elizabeth called Tony into her private office. She was wearing a green business suit and heels, much out of character for her normal workday. She never was a sloppy dresser, but today she was dressed in her power clothes. She sat behind her desk and leaned back, folding her hands across her chest.

"Have a seat."

Tony pulled up a straight back office chair and sat directly across from her, leaning forward, resting his elbows on her desk. Their eyes met and froze. Neither of them blinked for a few seconds, then she smiled and looked down at her desk.

"I won round one," Tony thought.

Mary got up from her chair and walked to the door, quietly closing it as she turned to look at him. "I've been watching you," she said as she walked back to her desk. She sat on the edge and leaned over and pulled a drawer open. "Cigarette?" she offered, taking a pack from the drawer.

"No, thanks. I don't smoke."

"What vices do you have?" she asked.

"I'm not perfect, but nobody is," he said. "I drink too much sometimes, don't save much money, never held a job where I could see a future, don't have any great plans, so I guess maybe my whole life is a vice. Why do you ask?"

"Because I've noticed that you don't mix business and pleasure, and that's a high mark for a man." She slid gracefully around the desk so that she was directly in front of Tony. She leaned back on the edge of her desk, casually slipping out of her shoes and putting one foot on the edge of his chair. "You don't believe in dipping your pen in the company inkwell, do you?" She lit a cigarette, inhaled deeply and blew the smoke out through her nose.

"You're right," he said. "Sara got me a good job and I'm not going to screw it up." He was staring into her eyes and she stared back. Without a blink, she raised her foot between his legs and slid it up to his crotch. It was a contest of wills. Tony was nearly holding his breath, but he wouldn't blink. She pushed her foot against him harder. "You'd like me, wouldn't you?"

"Any man would," he said with a deadpan expression on his face. They stared at each other for what seemed like eternity to Tony. Neither of them moved or showed any emotion or expression. It was a game of wills, but only she knew where they were heading.

"You just got a promotion," she said with a smile. She turned and went back to her chair behind the desk.

She stubbed her cigarette into an ashtray and leaned across the desk, once again staring into his eyes. "You're the kind of guy I like, and I can use you if you're willing to work," she said seriously. "I do big business and need a few good men. Kind of like the Marines. Just a few good men."

She paused, but never took her eyes off of him. She watched his reactions intensely. "I'm a good boss," she said. "I take care of my people and they take care of me. It's that simple. Are you in or out?"

"So what's the deal?"

"I pay well; you do good work, keep your mouth shut and live happily ever after. Just like in the fairy tales," she replied.

"So you're my fairy godmother?" Tony said with a grin.

"If that's what you want," she said with a shrug of her shoulders. "Or, I can be your worst nightmare. We've come this far and the ball is in your court, so put up or shut up. Do you want the job?" She stared without a glimmer of emotion in her body.

Tony thought that in any second she could lay him or kill him with the same enthusiasm. She was a cold-hearted bitch.

"I'm in! I'm your man. With somebody like me, you won't even need a few good men. You've got me. What else could you want?"

She smiled. "That's what I like in you. You're a confident s.o.b., and I think you'll do great."

Mary Elizabeth stood and reached out to shake his hand. "Done deal," she said just like she was closing a contract. They shook hands politely and she stepped around the desk. "First things first," she said as she walked to a file cabinet. She pulled out a drawer and thumbed through it for a few seconds while Tony watched over her shoulder. "Here it is," she said. She turned and faced Tony, tossing him a large brown envelope. "Go ahead, open it."

Tony ripped it open and pulled out a wad of money.

"Count it if you want. Its two thousand dollars expense money to get you started. I want you to go to Tucson or Phoenix and get some clothes. Business clothes. No more discount shirts or pants, and get rid of those trashy shoes. No more polyester. Dress for success. Half the power of being successful is just looking like you are, and you dress for shit." She flashed a quick, condescending smile. "And, my dear Freddy, I don't mean to step on your cultural heritage, but power people don't drive pickups with fringe around the windows."

"Two thousand will buy me a bunch of clothes," he said. "but not a new car."

"Go to Alto Motors," she directed. "They know me and they will fix you up. But be realistic, use your head and don't blow your first job on your own." She stubbed out her cigarette, reached into her desk drawer and pulled out a pack of Virginia Slims, tapped them lightly into the palm of her hand, and slipped one between her lips. Before she could react, Tony pulled out a lighter and put it to the tip of her cigarette. She inhaled deeply and held the sweet smoke in her lungs as she looked into his eyes. Slowly, ever so slowly, she exhaled, blowing the smoke into his face.

Tony smiled and turned to leave. He stopped at the door and turned slowly to face her. He grinned. "You'd like me, wouldn't you?"

"Any woman would," she responded with a grin.

"I'll get the clothes this weekend," he promised with a smile.

"Good," she said. "Take tomorrow off and get your shopping done."

*

Tony was headed for a three-day weekend. It was something he badly needed. Too much time passed since that fateful day of the Aguilar's murders. He was ready for a break, and besides, he and Muncie would have a ball spending the crooks' money on his clothes.

The long weekend with his family was, as Tony described it, like taking his brain out and scrubbing it. Everything about it felt good all over — sleeping in his own bed; playing in the yard with the kids; sitting in "his" chair in the living room; lying close to Muncie, feeling her softness and warmth as they cuddled up like spoons stacked one against the other, and maybe most relaxing of all, not having to think about somebody always watching or listening to his every move and sound. If ever there was a relaxing weekend, this was it. His whole mind and body were refreshed by the time Sunday night rolled around, and it was time to head south — south toward Freddy, Sara, Reynaldo, and all the other people and places where he played the old television game, "What's My Line" for the week.

He returned refreshed and ready to start his new assignment. Over the weekend he met with Martinez and Chambers for Sunday brunch at the captain's house, and they shared his enthusiasm for the progress he made. Operation Shamash was well underway and going smoothly. Intricate cases don't just fall together with a little luck and some flash, boom, bang like in the movies, but take care and precision to come together with all the pieces in place. All in the right place — all at the right time. For this case, it was only a matter of time. Martinez and Chambers congratulated him for his work, and if anybody ever doubted that he was the right person for the job, those doubts were erased with the clear focus Tony put in moving deeper and deeper into Reynaldo's inner circle. The Task Force would put another feather in its cap — a big feather! Even

Tony felt a degree of cautious enthusiasm in spite of his original trepidation about headline cases. This one was well in hand and under control. They were going the right direction, maybe taking a little longer than they wanted, but so what? It was going well. He didn't like the problem about sleeping with Marie, but nobody else would know and he would get over it. It was business, not something he planned or even wanted. He was making headway, and sooner or later he would get close to Reynaldo and do him. Plain and simple — Reynaldo would take the fall for the Aguilar murders. It was just a matter of time.

While Tony was driving his newly leased Lexus back to Nogales, Captain Martinez, Chambers and Reynolds met with the chief and sheriff in the chief's conference room.

"This looks almost too good to be true," Biggers said with a broad smile sweeping across his face.

"I'm with you," Sheriff Livingston said as he leaned back in his chair and glared at Martinez. "We all know that if it is too good to be true, it probably isn't. You really think you've got your guy into these people and they're going to let him see the whole damn thing?

"Respectfully, sir, Martinez replied. "We're so damned deep into those people, and our cover is so good, they'll never know what hit them until it lands like a bomb on their heads. Then," he said with a grin, "it'll be too damned late!"

"Go on," the sheriff barked. "Let's hear the rest of it."

"We think the office manager, Mary Elizabeth, is the money guru for the whole operation, and our guy is working directly for her every damned day. Granted, he's not into any of the illegal bookkeeping, but he works side-by-side with her on the financial records of the legitimate business, then he does deliveries on nights and a few weekends. She likes him, and we think it is just a matter of time before she moves him into some of the other financial records that they've got to have somewhere around there. And," the captain said as he thumbed through his notebook, "they have him making pretty regular deliveries of what is supposed to be fish to four different businesses here in town. Our guys have done background on all of them, and sure as we're sitting here, every one of them has a track record on drugs. Yeah, Sheriff, we're into them. It'll take some time, but sooner or later we will start putting the pieces together and it'll happen. For sure, we'll have enough drug cases to send a few folks away for forty or fifty years, and with a little luck, we'll twist a few folks and get them started talking about the murders."

"He's right there," interrupted Reynolds. "Right now, we don't have zilch on the Aguilar murders, but the way it looks, we'll get a lot of people on Class One drug violations. When that happens, some of them, and one I would think we can aim for is Mary Elizabeth, will twist off on the murder case."

"Explain yourself, if you would please?" the sheriff asked.

"Sure," Reynolds replied. "Nobody wants to take a fall for first degree murder and get the green needle in the death house. So what we do is we will offer immunity to a couple of people that can tie Guzman to the murders. For their cooperation, we get them a light sentence for the drug case; they spend a few years in the joint, and go free. Actually, it is fairly simple. I think the case is going the right way, and I agree with the captain. It'll just take a little time. And on top of that, we've got the informant. She's dynamite! Pure and simple. She and Tony will tie everything together in a tight little knot, and we will be able to squeeze the crap out of every single one who's involved in the drug or murder cases." She paused and looked at Martinez. "I've got to give your Task Force people credit. They have got their act together, and they're going to pull it off."

"Okay, you sold me," the sheriff said as he looked to the chief.

"Me, too," Biggers responded. "But I've been sold all along." He leaned back in his chair and slowly spun it around, looking out the window of his conference room as the full moon rose brightly over the top of the distant mountain peaks. The room was silent as he got up and walked to the window to enjoy the beauty of the quiet evening. "We did it," he finally said. He turned to others and smiled. "This is the first time I've felt this good in a long time. It's a go!"

*

Tony met with Mary Elizabeth in her office before the others got to work on Monday morning. "You look good," she said with a smile. "Play your cards right with me and you'll go a long way." Once again she was looking deep into his eyes. She sat behind her desk with her cigarette curling smoke up from the ashtray. "Yes sir, my little Frederico, play your cards right and you will go a long way with me." She smiled and leaned forward across her desk and took his hands in hers. "Understand?" she said.

He squeezed her hand lightly. "Very much." He rose slightly from his chair and leaned toward her and put his lips to her ear. "A very long way."

He smiled and she looked pleased and blew him a kiss, not knowing what was going through his mind. You bitch, I'm going to be your worst nightmare and you'll never see it coming. He raised his hand and caught her kiss and brought it to his lips. "Yes, a very long way."

*

The remainder of the day was spent discussing the import and transportation of fresh frozen fish, and of the vicious war that was under way with the Florida citrus growers. "Dirty sons-of-bitches," is how she continually referred to them. They fought every move from the importers of Mexican produce — tomatoes, grapefruit, and oranges. If it came from Mexico, they fought it. "Dirty sons-of-bitches," she would say. "They don't care if America eats or not. They just want money, the greedy bastards."

Lunch was a quiet meal together in the Emerald Room of the Durango Inn. Mary chose it as her favorite place. It was a short, ten-minute drive from Nogales on the Patagonia Highway, and was an exclusive place for the upper crust of society from both sides of the border.

"Let's go in your new car," she said as they walked from the office. Tony opened her door and watched her slide in, raising her skirt high above her knees. She gave him directions to a shortcut through town, and minutes later Tony was giving the keys to the valet.

Durango Inn sat on a ridge high over the highway, facing the east so the afternoon guest could enjoy a cool drink on the shady side of the building when they sat on the patio with its potted geraniums flowing over the white retaining wall. Small, individually shaded tables were placed discreetly around, giving people sufficient space to drink and talk without feeling intruded upon by others.

Tony opened the heavy wooden door and held it as Mary entered into the cool darkness of the restaurant. He followed, pausing for a moment to allow his eyes to adjust from the bright daylight to the dimly lit extravagance where Nogales' finest met to wine and dine. To the right was a quiet bar, empty except for the bartender who was busy stocking the racks with clean glasses. To the left was the dining room. An elegant place of booths and tables, all presented with white tablecloths and fresh flowers. The booths offered fine, burgundy colored leather seating. The chairs were tall, heavy wooden chairs, also covered in burgundy colored leather. A couple, probably about Tony and Muncie's age, sat at a table in the middle of the room. The young man ignored his food as he leaned across the table, taking the girl's hands in his, whispering softly so that only she heard the secrets of his love for her. Another couple, older than the young lovers, sat in a booth to the left of the door. The old man laughed as the woman looked at him and nodded her head, apparently agreeing with whatever bit of humor he shared with her.

The maitre'd knew Mary by name and took them to a booth in the corner. He was followed immediately by a busboy who placed a candle on their table and lit it. The soft light of the flame danced across her face. Tony felt for just a moment how pretty she actually was, older, but nevertheless, a very pretty woman. Mary ordered an appetizer and glass of Chablis as she lit up another cigarette. Tony scanned the wine list and asked for a glass of Cabernet Sauvignon.

They passed the meal with polite chitchat, neither willing to spar with the other before Tony felt comfortable to start talking about the business. She finished a second glass of wine with her meal, and had a Bailey's Irish Cream for dessert. She was far from being drunk, but felt giddy and talkative, rambling on about whatever seemed to be on the tip of her tongue at the moment.

"There's more than just fish and oranges to this thing we're doing. Are you going to fill me in? I've been around here long enough to know two plus two. I can do you a lot of good if you'll let me."

Mary stopped cold in her tracks and looked at him.

He continued, "Trust me. I know you want to, but you've got to give me a chance. I know what I can do for you, and we'll both make a fortune. I'm the guy you've been looking for. I know I am."

"Later," she said as she sipped her drink. "When the time is right and not before then."

Tony finally looked at his watch and smiled. "Hey, we can't do this," he said. "We've been gone nearly two hours and we've got work to do."

"I think you're a bastard," she said with a grin as she reached for his hand. "Or you're plain dumb. You didn't even touch me. I gave you a shot when I got in your car, and you didn't even look. I'm not wearing any panties for you."

"You're the boss," he replied as he cupped her hands in his. "I need to be careful and work this out. Besides, I've always been told that its bad business to dip your pin in the company inkwell"

Mary lifted his hands and kissed them passionately, rolling them over, touching each of his fingers with her tongue.

"Just hope you're not too good," she said as she slowly let him go and scooted out of the booth.

"You're right, we need to get our butts back to the office," she said as she blew him a kiss.

*

The next several days passed with Mary devoting almost all of her time taking Tony through the business administration of Greater America Imports — Accounts Receivable, Accounts

Payable, Depreciation, Inventory, Capital Assets, Investments, and it went on and on. Even Tony was starting to doubt, but not for long, the theory of Greater America Imports being involved in all of the crime and violence that they thought. It wasn't until the eighth week that the first crack became visible in her facade.

It was late in the afternoon after the office workers went home that Mary asked him to come to her office. He pulled up his usual straight-back chair and sat across from her. It was a ritual. He sat. She smoked a cigarette. They watched each other respond to the expressions of the other. He wondered why it was that she always played this weird game.

"Tony," she said. She walked to the window and watched the laborers on the docks. She kept her back to him as she spoke, "Can I trust you?"

"With your life," he said with a voice of authority.

"That's exactly what I'm going to do. You can't back out now, or," she said as she turned and looked at him, "I'll kill you."

Tony did not respond. He only stared as she walked back to her desk and pulled out another cigarette.

"Those things will kill you if you keep it up," he said seriously.

Mary Elizabeth sat at her desk and explained her new business proposition to Tony. One of Greater America's partners died unexpectedly a few months ago. He made some bad business deals before they could stop him and now they needed to recoup their losses. There were hundreds of thousands of dollars out there to be collected, but she and Guzman could not go to conventional means to collect the debts. "It was just a different kind of business," she said.

"I'm not dumb. I didn't fall off the back of the turnip truck this morning," Tony responded.

"I didn't think you did," she said. "There are just certain words we never say. We never know who is listening," she said as she pointed around the room. "Who knows who would betray us and plant a bug in here or somewhere else?" she said with resignation. "We're very careful in our business. Every couple of weeks we bring in some special people from Mexico to sweep my office and Rey's house." She looked around the room with a sad expression on her face. "Sometimes I get tired of all of this, but that's the way things are. It takes them almost all night to get it done, but we can't be too careful. Even Rey's lover, your cousin, doesn't know about our sweeps." She smiled as she was thinking to herself, then continued. "Sometime I want you to watch them do it. It's quite a big deal. I've learned a lot from them. They do a radio frequency check, a wire line check, and what they call an acoustic leakage check. They are thorough to say the least, but Rey pays them a bundle. They even take off all the ventilators and electric plugs and everything else." She looked at him sternly, a sudden switch from the way she was a few moments earlier. "We can't afford mistakes."

She got up from her chair and sat on the edge of her desk in front of him. "You're job is quiet simple. You'll be paid well. Probably better than you expect," she said. She leaned down and put her hands on his shoulders. Tony reached out and put his arms around her and took her into his lap. They slowly touched their lips to each other in a gentle kiss. Mary leaned back slightly, taking his hand and put it to her breasts, gently holding it against her. "I'll be yours," she said softly. "but not tonight." She smiled at him and kissed his cheek before she got up and returned to her desk.

"It's very simple." Once again she was pure business. "I give you a name and address and you go there. You talk to them however you please. You get our money or you don't come back." Tony saw the fury in her face. "That bastard partner of Rey's about did us in, but you're going to bail us out."

Now was the time. He had to ask. He must get her to talk. "How do you know this for sure? Who is the partner?"

Mary Elizabeth was primed and in the mood to talk. For the next thirty minutes she talked about Aguilar; how he and Rey were friends and partners for years; and, how somebody decided that he got too greedy and he had to pay for his sins. The family? Too bad it turned out that way she was sure, but he brought it on himself. How did they know about his cheating? Simple enough. The maid kept Mary informed on some of what was going on, but the real answers came from Aguilar's home computer. They figured out he was screwing them and "somebody" decided to do him. Once it was over, they got their hands on all the floppy disks, thumb drives, and CDs he kept at home. Once again, thanks to the maid. Every transaction was there and it was worse than they ever imagined. They stashed everything in a safe place — a very safe place, and we're going to track down every last dime. She hired some of the people from Mexico to do a little intelligence work to get started, but didn't want them to get too deep in it with her and Reynaldo. That's where Freddy came in.

Mary opened her desk drawer and removed a brown envelope and dumped its contents out on her desk. "Here's your first one," she said. Her anger was nearly boiling over as Tony reached over and scooped up the papers and a picture.

"That asshole is Randall William Koch," she snarled. "He owes us a hundred thousand dollars even. No less and no more. He's a doctor and lives in Arlington, Texas. He lives off of Green Oaks Road and has an office on Collins Street near the hospital." She grabbed the picture from Tony and held it up for both of them to see. "This is his little girl, Patricia. She'll be two in a couple of months, but if that asshole doesn't come across, she'll never make it.

"He's a crappy doctor and couldn't do any better, so our former partner went in cahoots with him. They thought they would make a bundle and probably did at our expense. Come back with our money," she said as she threw the picture at Tony. "Get our money and we'll have a hell of a party at the ranch."

She laughed, and leaned across the desk "I hear you like little virgins. Well, I'll just see if we can't do better the next time."

*

Tony spent the evening talking with his television set. Chipper Gephardt was on duty again, and this was far beyond his authority to handle. It took nearly two hours for him to round up Martinez, Jacobs, Chambers and Reynolds. Tony told his story and heard a jumble of conversation in the background. A couple of times he heard raised voices as they debated how far they would let him go. Jacobs argued that they were on the verge of overstepping their authority, and might even get Tony killed. No one else shared his opinion, but they were still in a quandary about how to handle the legalities of his debt collection. Jacobs insisted it was extortion, but the others couched it in different terms. Tony heard Martinez take on his Marine voice and snap at Jacobs to shut up. "You're overruled, damn it," he commanded.

Chambers finally took control and called for a time out while she made some phone calls. Tony took advantage of their confusion to make a sandwich and pour a cold beer. "What a screwed up mess," he commented. "And I've gained ten pounds since I started this job." He walked to the bathroom to take a leak. He unzipped his pants and began answering the call of nature when a touch of humor crossed his mind. He picked up the razor and peeked carefully at the microphone. He smiled to himself as he put it to his hips and farted.

"You asshole," screamed Chipper.

"Quite right, Chipper boy," answered Tony.

Nearly an hour passed before Chambers called the group to order. She talked to the Texas Rangers in Austin. They were ready, willing and able to lend a hand: it was a go. They talked to an assistant attorney general and got the green light. The Rangers would meet Tony at the Dallas/Fort Worth Airport and set him up with a body bug and surveillance. "Hells fire," said the Ranger. "We'll give your good ol' boy a clean Suburban to drive. Sheeit," he drawled. "we'll fix him up mighty fine."

Twenty-four hours later, Tony checked into the Home Run Inn near the Rangers Ballpark in Arlington. Just like the Texas Rangers said they would do, they got him a nice Suburban to drive. "Justice, my friend," said the Ranger who turned the Suburban over to him. "We just took this mother from a doper last month. Anything else you're fixin' to do, just give a shout, otherwise, see ya fer grits and eggs in the morning."

At ten o'clock the next day, Tony was in Dr. Koch's office. Since he didn't have an appointment, the receptionist made him wait until the doctor finished with his morning patients. Fortunately for Tony, he probably was a bad doctor, because there were only two patients ahead of him.

Two Rangers sat in the parking lot in an old bread truck running the recording equipment while Tony sat in the office. Typical, he thought. Never anything newer than last year's magazines. Cheap son-of-a-bitch.

The receptionist finally invited Tony to have a seat in the doctor's private office. "He'll be with you in a minute," she said as she walked back to the front counter. Tony sat in a heavy leather chair and looked around the office. "No different than any other doctor's office," he thought. An Ego Wall showing all the schools he attended — everything from William Jefferson High School in Port Arthur to his medical degree. Hell, he even had his varsity letter for track and field framed and hanging in a place of honor by his wife's picture.

"Hi, can I help you?"

Tony turned in the chair when the doctor walked in and shut the door behind him. He was about Tony's age, tall, dark and handsome. He looked like a doctor, Tony thought. A very successful doctor.

Koch sat at his chair behind the desk and shuffled some papers to make room for whatever business this man might have. "What can I do for you, sir? I don't believe we've met, have we?" he asked.

Tony leaned back in his chair and said nothing. He stared stoically at Koch. The doctor fidgeted in his chair and shuffled papers around on his desk. "Can I get you something to drink?" he asked.

"Cut the shit," replied Tony. "You know why I'm here and what I want, so don't screw around with me." He never changed his expression, but sat back in the comfortable chair and crossed his legs, feeling a little bit like Al Pacino in The Godfather. "I'm here 'til you pay up," he said.

"Damn it," said Koch. "I told Aguilar that I didn't think I was ready for all this, but he told me I could make a killing. What the hell do you want from me? I don't have the money."

Tony got up and walked slowly around the offices, looking at the diplomas and then looking at Koch. "Look," he said, "we know all about you." Tony moved to the desk and sat on the edge in front of Koch. "You're a stinking waste, that's what you are.

You wanted to play with the wolves, but you can't howl. You got in over your head, and you owe us."

Tony allowed a hint of compassion in his voice. "Listen to me. Your old man is a surgeon in Austin, and your wife's mom is a pediatrician in Shreveport, so don't say you can't get the cash."

Tony returned to his seat and leaned back. "You were in over your head when you went to medical school. Look at that piece of shit you call a diploma. It's from Granada. What is that, the University of Flunkies? Get on the phone, 'cause I'm not leaving without my money."

"You can't do this, please," cried Koch.

"Look, you can call the cops, the IRS, The FBI, DEA, or a priest. You're in way over your stupid head. Give me the money, now!" He pushed the telephone toward the doctor, sat back in the chair, crossed his legs and stared bullets at Koch.

*

It was mid-afternoon when Tony walked into the main branch of Lone Star National Bank and sent a wire transfer of one hundred thousand dollars to the company account in Nogales. He sat at the desk of the assistant manager and called Mary about selling their used refrigeration equipment. "Finally got us a buyer," he said to Mary as he smiled at the bank officer, giving her a wink as she adjusted her skirt, showing her shapely, tanned legs to this handsome guy from Arizona.

"You're serious, aren't you? You really got it just like you said you would."

"Hey, boss," he said with a grin as the banker continued to

adjust her clothes, this time using her compact mirror to align her necklace that hung delicately over her neckline, "when you send me to do a job, you know I'll deliver."

"Freddy, you're a tease, but a hell of a good worker. Get home and let's celebrate."

"See you tomorrow ma'am," he said as he hung up the phone.

*

Mary lied when she said they would have a party. Tony picked her up at her house on the outskirts of the city and drove to the ranch to meet Rey and Sara. Mary took advantage of the ride to tell him more about the financial end of the business, particularly of income tax. "Remember Capone," she said. "One of the biggest racketeers of all time, and they got him on income tax evasion." She shrugged her shoulders and lit a cigarette and then threw it out. "Sorry, won't smoke in our new car," she said with a smile. She went on to explain that the business records would show Tony's transaction as a sale of used refrigeration equipment for a gross of one hundred grand. "Always clean up your money," she said when they pulled through the gate to the ranch.

Reynaldo was an excellent host. Tonight there would be no hired hands cooking or serving drinks. Rey and Sara wanted to treat their new business executive right. Sara made a salad with fresh spinach with sliced hard boiled eggs and slices of fresh tomatoes, straight from Mexico. Rey built a perfect fire on the grill by the pool and cooked four prime steaks. "The best for the best," he boasted to Tony as he lifted a glass of wine.

The evening was pleasant and relaxing. No one talked business. They acted like normal people. The county tax rate was too high; the Arizona Cardinals looked forward to another miserable year; traffic on the Interstate was too dangerous on the weekends with the tourists, and Reynaldo even had the brass to talk about today's young people not having respect for adults. It was a fun evening and a good evening. Rey was getting comfortable with Tony. Still too early to talk business, but they were on the way. They ate dinner in the luxurious dining room, then moved to the patio. Sitting by the pool, they enjoyed the evening breeze and the sounds of a dove cooing somewhere in the distance.

"Listen," said Sara. "Hear that chirp? That's quail. We've got a covey of quail around here," she said as she got up and went to the wall to look for the birds.

Reynaldo followed her, wrapping his arms around her waist and holding her from behind. Mary and Tony sat in the chairs and watched Reynaldo kissing her neck and ear. Sara leaned forward across the retaining wall as Rey lifted her blouse and rubbed her back.

Mary sat up and reached for a pitcher of margaritas on the table. She refilled her glass and topped off Tony's before walking to the pool and sitting on the edge with her feet in the water. Rey was getting more passionate with Sara, kissing and rubbing her back before he spun her around and removed her blouse. She stood there for a moment and looked at Rey, then at Tony. She was not wearing a bra. Her breasts were more beautiful than Tony could ever imagine — a gorgeous silken tan, beautifully curved. Delicate nipples that stood erect, aroused by the man she loathed. Reynaldo touched her and began kissing her lips, then her breasts. He kissed the Spanish Gypsy. Tony's dream-come-true was being violated right in front of him and there was nothing he could do about it.

Sara put her arms around Rey and held him as he put his lips to her breasts, but her eyes were frozen as she looked at Tony. As she said earlier, he doesn't make love, he just takes me.

Mary looked back at Tony and nodded for him to come to her. He got out of his chair slowly, thinking about what he was getting into and the improbability of getting out of it. He stood beside Mary and took off his shoes and socks and pulled his pant legs up before sitting on the cool deck and putting his feet into the water. Mary put her arms around him and began kissing him passionately, slipping her tongue between his lips, caressing his tongue, stroking it. Her lips were delicious. Everything about her was delicious. He knew it and hated it, and knew where they were going. Her kisses were the most profound, enveloping, and arousing he ever tasted.

By the time he and Mary got up from the pool, Rey and Sara were gone. "They went inside," Mary said. "He likes to do that in front of people 'cause it gives him a charge. I've seen him do it before." She took his hand in hers and walked toward the house, through the dining room and down the hall. That same hall from his first night. "You won't get a virgin tonight," she said as she shut the bedroom door. "but, you'll do better."

The sun was shining in the window when Tony woke up and looked around. He was naked, on top of the sheets, perspiring in the morning heat. Mary sat in a chair, smoked a cigarette and watched him.

"Been there long?" he asked.

"Not long enough," she said. "You're beautiful, and I think we have something special between us," she said as she came back to bed.

*

The next two weeks passed much the same. Tony made three trips. One to St. Louis; one to St. Paul, Minnesota; and one to Naperville, Illinois. "Two out of three ain't bad," he said to Mary after he got back from Illinois. He collected ninety thousand dollars in Missouri, and sixty-eight thousand in Minnesota.

"Somebody beat us to the punch on that Naperville prick. He owed too many people," he said as he plopped down in her office. "Somebody blew his whole damn head off a couple days before I got there," he said with a little tone of resignation.

"Freddy," Mary said as she got up and went to the door to close it, "you're the best thing to happen to us in a long time." She turned and walked slowly toward him. "I love you, Freddy. I really do." She stood behind him and put her hands on his shoulders and rubbed his neck. "I'm twenty years older then you, I know that. But I love you and want to marry you."

Tony reached behind him and took her hands in his. His heart raced and his mouth was dry. He hated her and at the same time found she was a passionate lover. "I feel something special, too," he said through his parched lips. "Let's be careful. You know the rule. Don't dip your pin in the company inkwell."

She leaned over and kissed his forehead. "Rules were made to be broken."

CHAPTER 13

Sara stood at the sink slicing a tomato for her salad. Reynaldo was gone on one of his trips for two days and she didn't know when he would return. It was dinner time, so she did as she did a thousand times before — eat alone. It was a beautiful, peaceful evening. She opened the kitchen window and listened as the birds sang their magical songs at the close of another day. In the distance, beyond the pool, toward the river bottom and the mountains in the background, shadows grew long, reaching out and covering the land for its night's sleep. A final burst of sunlight flashed in the sky with the colors of the prism, then faded into the growing darkness. The eucalyptus and mesquite trees waved softly in the cool evening breeze. Sara Hurtado was at peace. The end was in sight.

The front door suddenly slammed shut and Sara heard Reynaldo's footsteps coming through the house.

"Hi honey," she shouted. "I'm in the kitchen."

Reynaldo walked into the kitchen without speaking and leaned against the sink. He wore Levis and his usual crisp, clean cowboy shirt. His white Stetson showed a band of sweat around the hat band. He stared for a moment, looking deep into her eyes. Hate! Pure, unadulterated hate — enough to kill.

"Why?" he asked. "Why, after all I did for you?" he shouted, holding a small piece of paper wadded up in his hand for her to see. "Why?" he asked again.

Sara felt her heart pounding. Her breathing became labored and she felt her hands tremble. It was a feeling she never before experienced. There was a pit in her stomach and she thought she was going to throw up. It was Tony's telephone number — the number he gave to her when they first met! She wrote it down until she could memorize it, and she meant to throw it away. It was just a tiny scrap of paper with seven numbers on it.

"You ungrateful bitch," he bellowed as he leaned forward, screaming into her face. His breath was strong with liquor. He was drunk and mad, either of which was deadly. "You ungrateful bitch," he screamed again. "I was looking for your keys 'cause you blocked me in and I found this in your purse. Now look at me!" he commanded. He grabbed her chin. "You look at me when I'm talking. You cheap bitch. I don't know the fucking number but I know people at the phone company. They work for me; everybody works for me. So they tell me the bill gets paid every mother-fucking month by the attorney general's office." He released her chin and gave her a small back-handed slap across her mouth. "Fucking whore, that's what you are and you go and talk to the cops."

He leaned back against the counter and stared at her. "Bitch! What did you tell them? Who is it? What did you do? You think you're so smart, but you can't stay up with me. I know what you did. There's only one new person anywhere around here and that's your little prick cousin Freddy. They sent him in here didn't they? I'll find out!"

Reynaldo turned and threw open the sliding glass door and walked out onto the patio. Sara could only watch as he stepped into the waning lights of the setting sun. What was so peaceful and serene only moments ago was now filled with anger and hate.

There was a sound, ever so slight behind her. She spun around to see a hand swinging a black sap down toward the side of her head. Everything suddenly went into slow motion as the hand came down. It was as though a bolt of black lightening struck her temple. She felt the explosion of pain as it spread throughout her head. The noise was deafening. She knew she wasn't shot, but the sound of her head absorbing the impact of the sap was beyond imagination. The pain spread from her brain and went into her teeth. They felt like they were becoming ice cold and brittle. For an instant, she knew she was about to die. All so unexpected. All so soon. Everything had appeared as if it was going so well and she would be free from Reynaldo's grasp.

Her eyes were still open, but everything was shaded in a light pink color. She tried to focus on the refrigerator, but it kept moving like she was in a house of mirrors. Sara was aware of her feet moving when she tried to regain her balance, but it was as if she was walking on a cloud. There was nothing to hold her up. Her knees gave away, and she tried to grab something to hold herself up. Her hands floated on their own. The side of her head banged off of the tile drain board as she crashed into the floor like a helpless rag.

She lay there, working to focus on something. Like the iris of a camera lens, black began to close in, leaving only a tiny spot of pink for her to see through. No, I won't, she thought. I won't let them kill me. She struggled against losing consciousness. She gasped for breath, fearing that if she passed out she would never wake up. The pink and black slowly faded, and she began to refocus her eyes. All she could see standing in front of her was a pair of bare feet. Long, bony, callused, dirty feet.

Sara gasped, catching her breath. She started to speak when the man brusquely reached under her skirt and ripped her panties from her. She again tried to form words with her lips, but he shoved her underwear into her mouth. She gagged and tried to breath and thought that she was going to choke to death, yet there was the slightest opening for her to suck in the sweet, life-giving air. She could breath. She would not die yet, but was unable to mutter a sound.

He spun her around flat on her stomach and pulled her hands behind her back. She heard the ripping sound she recognized as tape being torn from a roll. She tried to look back over her shoulder, but he put his dirty foot against the side of her head and shoved her down. He grabbed her hands and pulled them behind her back and quickly taped them together. She thought that her shoulders were going to be pulled from their sockets, but found that if she pushed her shoulders back, the strain was lessened.

Just as quickly, he pulled her ankles and crossed them and taped them together. She felt totally helpless, lying there on her kitchen floor. The skinny man leaned over her and pulled her ankles up to the middle of her back and taped her feet to her hands. She was hogtied and totally defenseless against whatever might happen to her.

Sara tried to turn her head to look up just in time to see the man take a large trash bag and pop it open. He stepped forward and rolled it down over her head, all the way to her waist, and then taped it tightly against her body.

She thought that she would suffocate. She would die right there in her own kitchen — the very place where only moments ago she felt true peace.

The air rapidly grew to an unbearable temperature, sweat poring from her brow and into her eyes, stinging. Her clothing became soaked, but there was nothing she could do. Reynaldo would have his revenge. Sara felt the man grab her taped hands and feet and spin her around on the floor, then start dragging her through the house. She felt the bump when they went through the front door and across the patio, then down the step and into the dirt parking lot. They stopped and she heard the familiar click of a trunk lid being opened. Her mind raced, but there was nothing she could do. She could not scream or run, she could not fight or plead. She was being taken away.

The man lifted her like a bag of flour and threw her into the trunk. Her head crashed off of something hard — maybe the spare tire or jack. She began crying. She was frightened, hurt, and alone, more than she could ever have imagined. The trunk lid closed, throwing her into complete darkness. The heat was stifling. There was no air to breath. Just her own hot breath and the smell of plastic. She choked and tried to spit to clear her throat, but only made it worse. The car door slammed, and seconds later she heard the car engine start. She felt the car turn around in the lot outside the front door, and knew that they were pulling onto the driveway, heading toward the highway. She lost track of time, fading in and out of consciousness in the stifling heat. Nevertheless, she knew that the car was stopping and starting — maybe at traffic lights or stop signs. Who knows? There was the smooth hum of the highway, then the bumping and shattering of her bones against the bottom of the trunk as the car bounced along a dirt road. Sara strained to hear sounds, hoping to find something familiar. The car slowed, then moved forward and stopped. They were in traffic.

They were in civilization. Nogales? Tucson? How long were they driving? "Oh God," she murmured. "Where am I?" There were voices — more than just two or three, but who were they? What were they going to do with me? They were speaking in Spanish, but their voices were muffled. She couldn't understand them, but at least she wasn't alone. Maybe somebody would help her. The car lurched forward, then stopped again. The voices were almost right beside her. Somebody talked to the driver, but who? Suddenly she understood. "No. No." she screamed to herself through her gag.

"*Pasa. Pasa. Adelante!*" Oh God, no, she thought. We're at the border. Oh God, he's taking me into Mexico. Please God, help!

The car continued on with its human cargo securely bundled in the trunk. She could feel it taking a right turn, moving slowly through the jumble of street vendors, traffic lights and pedestrians, before making a left turn. Now she knew where they were. Calle Obregon. She had been there so many times before, working her way through the city to the Methodist orphanage on the south side of town where she delivered meat and vegetables every week. They were in Nogales, Sonora. Whoever he was, he was taking her far away. For the first time in her life, she knew unmitigated helplessness.

The car gradually picked up speed as they left the city, and Sara began to cry. The heat and the hum of the highway hypnotized her, and once again she drifted in and out of consciousness. Her head suddenly bounced hard on the spare tire, shocking her back to reality. They were off the highway, turning and bouncing on a dirt road, its dust quickly choking the life out of her. She gasped as the heat and dust and fumes filled her nostrils. Finally, there was no more air. She was dying. Sara fought the trance that swept over her, then surrendered. She closed her eyes, accepting the hand of the grim reaper who surely would take her to her just punishment.

A cold bath of fresh air washed over her. She was still bound and the trash bag still held her prisoner, but the car stopped and the trunk opened. A single pair of hands reached in and pulled her from the agony of the cramped prison and dropped her on the hard dirt. Once again, the hands grabbed where her hands and feet were taped together and began pulling her through dirt and rocks before her head hit something hard. She was being taken into a shed or barn. There was a dirt floor, but she knew she was inside a building.

The man cut the tape that bound her hands to her feet and lifted her up on a wooden chair. He still did not speak to her. She sat there in silence, feeling his presence, and her body began to tremble in fear.

"Be good, lady," he said in English, but with a strong Spanish accent. "I'm not going to hurt you." She could feel the dull edge of a knife against her stomach as he slashed the bag and pulled it off her. Sara squinted from the glare of a light, then focused her eyes on the gaunt figure before her — unsmiling, dirty, skinny, a pig of a man. He stood in front of her, staring. Her hands and feet were still taped, and her panties were still stuffed in her mouth. She watched him watching her, wondering what he was going to do. Kill her? Probably rape her first. Have his fun, then go about what it was that he was hired to do.

The man suddenly turned and walked out of the building. There was no door, just an opening that he went through to the outside. Sara looked at her surroundings and shuddered. It was the most horrible thing she ever saw. It was an old adobe building with a dirt floor. The one window was without glass, just as the doorway lacked a door. A single dim light hung from a strand of wire directly over her head. In the corner to her left was a small pile of scrap iron — an old hatchet, some hammers and picks, some iron rods, and an old rusted machete with a broken blade. In the opposite corner, near the window, was an ancient butcher's block standing on three legs, with the fourth leg broken and hanging uselessly. The table and walls near it were covered with old dry stains of some liquids that were splashed on it. Blood! It had to be. Sara closed her eyes, bowing her head in a silent prayer.

She started to cry as the man walked back into the room, drinking a can of beer. "No, no. No need to cry," he said. "It's over. You're okay." He sat the beer on the floor as he pulled the panties from her mouth. "It's done," he said. "Tonight you can go home and take a bath. You can sleep in your own bed. *Senor* Guzman wants you back, don't you see? He loves you and wants you home."

The man smiled and wiped a tear from her cheek with his dirty fingers. "You're okay, just tell me about the cops and you go home, pronto. *Comprende?*"

"I don't know anything," Sara pleaded. "It's Mary Elizabeth, she's the one. She always wanted Rey and the money. It's her," Sara pleaded through the tears that ran down her face. "It's Mary, not me. Can't you understand? She wants everything."

The man smiled as he took his beer and sat on the floor, leaning against the wall.

"Listen," Sara commanded. "She always wanted my man and his money. This is her trick, can't you understand that? She's evil and she lied to you and Reynaldo. Please listen to me. I love him, I swear."

"My name is Julian Espino Gatica." He got up and walked back toward her. "Your husband wants you home tonight, and I gave my word that I would bring you back to him. I do not lie. I will take you home, but you must tell me about the cop that you brought to *El Patron* Guzman."

He looked at her and nodded, "Its okay, you can tell. You have been brave and with great honor. Tell me so I can take you from here."

Sara began to cry even harder, "Please believe me, please."

Julian turned and walked outside. It was night and there were no lights other than the one over her head. She heard him doing something, then recognized the sound. He was ripping open a bag of charcoal and dumping it out. The strong smell of lighter fluid drifted through the window.

He's going to fix something for us to eat, she thought. He's going to feed me and take me home. I'm okay. I really am. He believes me, and will take me home. Thank you, God. Thank you.

"Well?" he said when he came back in the room. "What about your cop friends?"

Sara was puzzled. She thought he believed her, but now what? "Please," she cried out. "Please." She pleaded her case, crying, begging, calling God as her witness, but he only smiled and shook his head. He did not believe her, not now or ever. It made no difference how much she begged and cried. She only showed her weakness. He would never believe her.

Julian stepped past her and walked into the dark part of the room. Sara twisted in her chair to watch him. The room was dark, but she saw him standing at two pillars that ran from the floor to the ceiling. At the top and bottom of each was a pulley with ropes running through them. He pulled the ropes through the top pulleys and walked silently to her and cut the tape from her wrist. His hands and fingers were as fast as a rattlesnake as he tossed the tape aside, wrapping the ropes around her wrists. Julian grabbed her shoulders and forced her to face the front as he pulled her arms up and behind her neck. She started to cry as he pulled hard on the ropes, pulling her over the back of the chair and into an upright position between the pillars. Her feet barely touched the ground as he tightened the ropes to hold her in place.

Julian looked at her and smiled as he leaned over and cut the tape from her feet and bound them to the other pulleys. He smiled again as he stepped back to look at her and to admire his work. She stood there in her sweat-soaked blouse and skirt, choking back the tears, spread-eagled between the two posts. Bastard, she thought. You'll never see me cry again.

"*Digame*, tell me!" he commanded. "Tell me and save yourself. Tell me about the first time you went to the cops. Tell me what you told them. What are they paying you?" His questions were rapid fire, one after another before she could have time to think. "Senor Guzman gave you everything you desired, yet you did this to him. Why? How much are they paying you?"

Sara choked back her tears and closed her eyes. "I've told the truth; please believe me," she said.

"Bullshit! Tell me while you can, you lying bitch." He stepped toward her and slapped her face. Once, then twice again until blood dripped from her lips. "Tell me and sleep in your own bed before the night is over, or tell me while I kill you. The choice is yours. Tell me about your stinking cousin. He's no cousin, is he? He's a stinking cop, a *federale* no? You ungrateful whore bitch. Tonight you will reap your reward."

Julian turned and walked outside. She heard him scraping something and thought he might be fixing his dinner on the grill. He can't be eating, she thought. Not now. Sara looked up over her shoulders at her hands. It was useless. They were tied to the pulley. She lowered her eyes and looked at her feet. Somewhere she lost her shoes, or did she ever have them on? She wondered.

"What's that?" she said to herself as she twisted around to see more clearly between her feet. There was a small pit about a foot deep between her ankles. It was filled with ashes!

Julian walked silently back into the room and stood directly in front of her. His nose was nearly touching hers. "Well?" he asked.

"You know the truth," she replied.

Julian stepped behind her and began rubbing her neck and shoulders with his bony fingers. Sara held her breath, waiting for the rape that was about to happen. Suddenly, he grabbed her collar and yanked hard, pulling her blouse off and leaving her standing there spread-eagled and helpless. Arrogantly, he stepped in front of her and smiled as he flipped open his switchblade knife. The dim light glistened off the blade as he played it back and forth in front of her lips. "The truth," he said.

"It is the truth," she said. Her lips quivered, but she continued, "It is the truth."

He slipped the sharp blade between her breasts, and with a sickening grin, slowly cut away her bra and let it fall to the ground. Julian lowered the knife to her waist, and with a quick flip of his hand, cut the buttons from her skirt. He caught it with the blade as it fell from her hips. In one smooth motion, he threw is aside and looked at her standing there, naked.

But there was no shame for Sara. She was long past the point of pride or embarrassment. She only wanted to live. To tell the truth now would most assuredly be the kiss of death. She must convince Julian of Mary's evil plan. She must.

Julian looked at her nakedness, then turned and went outside. She heard something scraping, but couldn't decide what he was doing. Her question was answered as Julian returned with a shovel full of hot ashes that he dumped in the pit between her feet.

"What are you doing?" she cried out.

He turned and walked back to his place on the floor and began drinking another beer. Sara looked down and saw the red glow of the ashes. It wasn't hot, but the smoke rose up and stung her eyes and nose. "Please don't," she said. "Please. I'm telling you everything I know."

Julian watched her twist and try to get out of the smoke, but there was no escape. The heat gradually increased, and she looked down at the glowing red embers. It was getting hotter, and her ankles were starting to turn red. "Stop, stop," she begged.

Julian tossed the empty can aside. He got up like an old man and went back outside, returning in a few seconds with another shovel full of hot coals which he dumped between her feet. The heat and smoke rose up immediately, scorching her ankles and legs, the smoke stinging her red eyes and choking her. She twisted to the left, then to the right, trying to find a place away from the heat and smoke, but there was nowhere to go. She looked down again and saw blisters starting to form on her legs. She twisted and pulled, but there was no escape. She was totally helpless, and lost control of her bladder. The sizzling steam and stench rose up and began burning her — first her feet, then her ankles, and quickly up to her thighs. She looked down as the hair of what was Reynaldo's pleasure began to singe, then to fall away and into the pit of ashes. She began to cough and choke, and then she began to bawl. "Take me down," she cried. "I'll tell the truth, I promise."

Her legs felt like they were on fire, and the burning pain began to spread to her lips and stomach and hips. She was being roasted in her own waste. "Please," she cried.

"You tell me, then I take you down and take you home," Julian said with a snicker. He went outside and returned with another shovel full of coals. He was about to throw them between her feet when she screamed out the story of Detective Antonio Castenada. Not her cousin Freddy. The police. It was the murders of the children. They were innocent and didn't deserve to die. If only they hadn't killed the children, then this would never have happened. This was the only way she could ever look at herself in the mirror. It was wrong to take those innocent lives, and as much as she loved him, Reynaldo would have to pay for his sin.

"There is no more," she cried. "No more. That is the truth."

*

True to his word, Julian untied her. She pitched forward and lay in the dust, tears pouring from her eyes. Her wet, burning, naked body scratching in the dirt trying to find comfort.

Julian went away and came right back with another beer. He offered her a drink, and held her head while she sipped the cool, refreshing drink. "Thank you," she muttered. "Thank you."

"See?" he said with a smile as he helped her up. "Here, take your clothes and cover yourself. Let me take you home."

He helped Sara to the doorway while she tried to cover her body with the scraps of her clothes. "Thank you, thank you," she said. She was going home. Reynaldo loved her and would forgive her.

Julian allowed her to step through the doorway into the cool night darkness. She never saw the little pistol come up to the back of her neck. He held the barrel a few inches from her skull and fired it up at a forty-five degree angle, through her brain stem, the cerebellum, and into the cerebrum. She catapulted forward into the dirt.

Matagente stood over her, watching her fingers and toes twitch in the dirt. It was there that she died in the dirt of an old miners shack somewhere in Mexico.

CHAPTER 14

Tony was boarding the commuter flight from St. Louis to Joplin, Missouri as Sara was slicing the tomato for her salad. He would be in and out tomorrow, and be back in Nogales by Friday evening. Saturday and Sunday would be his time with Muncie and the kids. They already planned it. Take a hike to Seven Falls, come home and swim and play Marco Polo, cook hot-dogs on the grill, and just lie back and relax. Maybe even have a few Dos Equis.

Joplin would be a snap. An over-the-hill accountant, Mildred Hamilton, tried to jump-start her career with a bunch of Irish Mafioso from Kansas City and lost it all. She was in for a little more than fifty thousand dollars that she would never recover. She could never be able to come up with the money, but she would twist and spin and be miserable for a while. In the end, she would trade her peace of mind and a shot of staying out of prison for the chance to testify for the good guys. Things were coming together. Chambers thought that if they got three or four more people who sold dope for Aguilar or Guzman, they could serve them with federal Grand Jury subpoenas. Tony's testimony would be critical, but the government would work a deal with the dope dealing doctors, lawyers and accountants to get their testimony. These are people who don't want to do hard time. They don't know how, and they would end up getting themselves killed. Or worse yet, maybe they become somebody's wife in prison. Without a doubt, with Tony hanging over them, they saw the light and wanted to do the Lord's work. They testified against their mothers to save their own skins.

"They'll testify because they'll be scared shitless," commented Reynolds.

"No doubt," Chambers said. "We've got'em by the balls, so their hearts and minds will follow. But we still have a long way to go before we can get Guzman for murder."

The only point of significant conflict between the two prosecutors was Mary Elizabeth, the accountant at Greater America Imports. Surely, she was the one single person who could bring together everything about the money. What went where? Who paid for what? Which were legitimate transactions and which were not? Who were the players? Who called the shots? Who oversaw the payoffs? And, most important of all were the questions about the murders. Who paid whom? How much? When was it paid? What was the catalyst that set everything in motion? Where was the killer now? How could he or they be found?

Mary Elizabeth was the most important potential witness they would have —maybe even more important than Sara or Tony. She and she alone should be able to tie it all together in one neat little package. Well, maybe not so little or so neat, but she was the one key person inside the organization who should have the answers. Follow the money and you'll get your answers. That was the simple theory in any conspiracy investigation and for damned sure, this was a conspiracy and there were more money tracks to follow than most people could ever understand. And that alone — the complexity of the money trails is what was so easy to confuse a jury. Confuse them enough, and sure as hell, you'll come out with a hung jury. Or worse yet, not guilty! Not guilty for the simple reason that the jury got lost and couldn't understand it, so they let everybody go free.

Chambers and Reynolds had vicious arguments about Mary Elizabeth. On the one hand, she should be able to give them what they needed; but on the other hand, she was so deep in it that she should have to take a hard fall, maybe even for murder. What if she made the payoff for the murder? How could they explain to the public how they let her go free? But they always came back to the simple point that she and she alone should be able to put the finger on Reynaldo Guzman, and he was the target of this whole investigation. You could argue this thing forever and never come up with the one "right" answer, but you could come up with several choices of "wrong" answers, and that's what they had to do. Choose the least of the wrong answers and go forward and don't look back and don't second guess yourself.

Eventually, Chambers won out. They would offer immunity to Mary for her testimony on the murders.

"We'll beat the crap out of her with a million charges," Chambers argued. "By the time we're done with her, she'll sell her mother to a whorehouse. We'll get her, but Tony is the link. He'll cut her to ribbons from the stand if she gives us any shit."

*

It was well after dinner time when Tony landed at the Joplin Regional Airport. He was expecting a small town, but was still surprised at the minuscule airport. He could not miss the cops who were meeting him since there was only one gate from the terminal to the tarmac. Two young, clean-cut detectives stood with their badges and pistols on their belts. Not exactly what he wanted to see since he was working undercover, but, what the hell. They walked quickly in the growing mist to their standard detective car, a new white Ford Crown Victoria with dual spotlights. Once again, not something he hoped for with his delicate role, but there was nothing he could do about it. There wasn't a lot to see, but it was their hometown and they wanted to show it off a little bit. They cruised down Route Forty-three through what was left of a once prosperous downtown, being sure to point out the badly aging Southwest Missouri State Bank building, a decrepit red brick building that was nearly empty except for a couple of tenants. This is where they would take him in the morning to see old Millie, as they referred to her. Every cop in the area who worked gambling or drugs knew her. She seemed to be the bookkeeper for every two-bit crook in the Ozarks, but no one ever had any information that she actually started doing some of her own deals.

They parked in front of the lobby of the Royal Ozark Inn on Interstate 44 not far from downtown. It wasn't much, but it was a roof over his head and it started to rain. He checked in at the desk and ran through what was now a downpour to his room. Tony dumped his suitcase on the bed and dug through a couple of drawers until he found the phone book in the drawer with the Gideon's Bible.

It wasn't exactly his idea of a big night on the town, but it was a typical Missouri rain and might last forever, so he called in a pizza order. He spent the evening chewing a doughy, cold pizza, watching television reruns of M.A.S.H. and thumbing through the Gideon Bible. He was far from a biblical scholar, but there was nothing else to read so he decided to kill some time looking at it, much as a person might scan old magazines in a doctor's office.

He stretched out on the bed and fluffed the pillows up against the headboard as he opened a page at random. By chance, or as he wondered later, was it divine intervention that he flipped it open to the Fifty-ninth Psalm?

"O my God, save me from my enemies.

Protect me from these who have come to destroy me."

"Oh no," he said to himself as he tossed the bible back into the drawer. "Don't need that. No sir, don't need that at all."

*

It was ten o'clock in Tucson when Muncie finally got Matthew and Mark into bed. She was worn out. It was not a good day. The kids were full of energy and mischief and ran her into the ground. She was too tired to hang up her clothes, so she just threw them on the bathroom floor, brushed her teeth and was sound asleep by ten-fifteen.

Muncie's alarm clock went off at six o'clock. She reached out and slapped the button with the palm of her hand, sending the clock crashing onto the floor.

"You deserve it, you little prick," she said to the clock.

She rolled out of bed and walked to the bathroom, picked up yesterday's clothes and threw them into the hamper. It was Friday. Tony would get in late tonight or tomorrow and they would have a normal family for a couple of days. She was grateful because the boys were getting too wild and needed their dad to get their attention.

She stepped into the hot shower and soothed herself as the hot water poured down over her head. She lingered, rubbing the soapy wash cloth over her shoulders and let the suds slowly run down her body. It felt good. She stood on her toes and reached her face up into the shower where she took the full force of the water and hummed her favorite song, "Leave Virginia Alone." That song always put her in the mood to make love. Not a quickie, but long, slow, tender love.

It was nearly six-thirty by the time she wrapped a robe around herself and walked into Matthew's room. She always started with him because from the time he was a baby, he was the easiest to wake up. He started each day with a smile and a hug.

"Hi, Mommy," he said. He reached out and pulled her down onto his bed and curled up with her. He loved to cuddle up and stay close.

"You'll make a great husband," she told him. "Girls love to cuddle."

They lay together for a few minutes before she got them up. "C'mon, we need to get on the stick. You get the morning paper while I get your cereal poured." She headed toward the kitchen. She set out their bowls when Matthew opened the front door to go outside. His scream pierced her heart. She dropped the dishes and ran toward the door as he raced back into the house, slamming the door behind him. She dropped to her knees as he ran to her, but he bowled her over as he buried himself in the safety of her arms. They rolled over on the cool hard floor while she wrapped her arms around him and spoke softly to quiet his fear. Matthew tried to speak, but his lips only quivered as tears poured from his eyes, and his nose dripped down over his lips.

Muncie heard the patter of little feet running down the hall and looked up in time to see Mark just before he piled into her and Matthew. He didn't know what happened, but seeing and hearing his older brother was enough to frighten him. He crawled in between Muncie and Matthew and began crying even harder than his brother.

"What is it, baby?" Muncie asked as she tried to get Matthew's attention.

"Mommy, mommy, it's something bad on the door," he said through his tears.

Muncie scooted the boys off of her lap and curled them up close together on the floor of the kitchen.

"Mommy will be right back," she said as she pulled herself up and walked toward the front door. She eased herself quietly to the door and looked through the peep hole but couldn't see anything unusual. She stepped to the side of the door and began softly to twist the doorknob. The door opened, and she saw it. She gave a slight scream, but caught herself. She had to be in control or she would scare her children even more. She opened the door further until she had a complete view of the door and porch. Someone hung a chicken by its neck on a nail that was above the door. They ripped the chicken's intestines out and dropped them on the front porch. The blood oozed out and ran down the step. There, covered in blood on the porch, was a picture from their family album. A picture of Tony sitting in a chair holding the boys on his knees while Muncie stood beside him. Muncie recognized it as one they took last Christmas. Somebody must have been in the house and took it from the album in the living room.

Tears welled up in Muncie's eyes. She closed the door and ran to the telephone. Captain Martinez lived only a mile away, and he was in her living room in ten minutes.

Within a half hour, uniformed officers and detectives strung up crime scene tape and combed the neighborhood for witnesses. Chico, Allbright, Moore, Ann and Jimmy knocked on every door, looked in every trash can, and took pictures of anything that looked like it might be a footprint. It looked like an armed camp, but to no avail. There were no witnesses or anything that could come close to being called evidence. Whoever did it slipped stealthily in and out. They were never seen. It was as if they were never there. Muncie had no idea when she had last seen the photo in the album, but she was terrified. Was someone in the house last night? Were they in sometime while she was gone and stolen the picture? And most of all, why? Who would want to do this "But we're scared and need Tony right now," she thought.

After all of the photos were taken and the blood was cleaned from the porch, one of the uniform officers found the first piece of evidence. He was sticking the dead chicken into an evidence bag when he noticed a small piece of paper sticking out of its beak. The paper was so small and waded up that he almost missed it. He got a grip on it with his fingernails and gently pulled it out.

"Captain, you better take a look at this," he shouted to Martinez. The captain took the paper and slowly unfolded it. It was no bigger than one inch square, and a note was scribbled on it, "How's the family, Freddy?"

*

It was midmorning when Tony heard the car pull up in front of his room. It was another typical detective car, four doors, gray, and an antenna on the rear fender. The only thing that set it apart from the others was that it didn't have spotlights. He recognized the driver as being one of the detectives who picked him up at the airport, but didn't know the other one. Tony walked out of his room as the two men got out of the car. The passenger spoke before Tony was all the way out of the room.

"Good morning detective. I'm Chief Charboneau," he said as he reached out to shake hands. "I need to let you know that everything at home is okay, but there've been some problems."

Tony's heart pounded when he heard those few words. He looked at them with fear and concern written on his face. This wasn't in the game plan. "Home?" he wondered. What the hell could be wrong at home? Somebody sick or get in an accident? Shit, I'm so far away. Damn! His mind raced through a dozen horrible scenarios as the three men went back into the motel room. Tony tossed the spread over his unmade bed and invited the others to have a seat. The driver excused himself to go for coffee for the three of them. Charboneau sat on the edge of a chair and leaned his elbows on the table. The chief went over the information from Tucson in a couple of minutes. He didn't have all of the details, but he knew enough to give Tony at least a little briefing, and definitely enough to know that their Operation Shamash suffered a major hiccup, as he described it. Maybe not fatal, but sure as hell, it was going to have a setback. He assured Tony that his family was being taken care of by the department and by their neighbors. "No need to worry," he said, knowing that there was plenty to worry about, but what else could he say?

"Why don't you go give your wife a call?" the chief said as he got up and stepped to the door. "I'll be right outside if y'all need anything."

Tony sat on the edge of his bed and started to dial, but his fingers shook so badly that he stopped. He put the phone down in the cradle and walked slowly to the bathroom, flicked on the light, and looked at his reflection in the mirror. Just minutes ago he was confident, capable, self-assured, and maybe even a little cocky. But in the period of two or three minutes, all of that came to a screeching halt like he hit a brick wall. Here he was on a drizzly, shitty Missouri morning a thousand miles from home, and some rotten bastard was out there terrorizing his wife and kids. What made things even worse was the horrible memory of what Guzman and his people did to Aguilar's family, kids and all. They were blown to bits. He actually murdered the kids!

"Bastards!" Tony screamed as he slammed his fist into the wall, sending chips of plaster bouncing off the shower door. "You dirty bastards," he screamed as he looked at himself in the mirror. Guilt swept over him as he looked at his mirror image — the Yaqui girl, Mary Elizabeth! He was a bastard himself and he knew it. Why the hell did he let them drag him down to their level? "Because I thought I was so damned good that they couldn't get away from me," he said as he scolded himself in the mirror. "Oh God, I screwed up. I really screwed up, and it's all come to rest on my family. Oh shit, if it would have just been me. Not them. I'm sorry, so sorry," he blurted through his tears as he leaned on the wash basin. "I'm sorry."

He splashed cold water on his face and grabbed a clean, white towel and held it over his face as he caught his breath. Minutes passed before he dropped it on the floor and looked at himself in the mirror. What was behind was behind and couldn't be called back, he thought. But now I've got to get on doing the right thing, and that's my wife and kids. He walked to the bed and sat down. His hands were steady as he dialed, and on the first ring he heard that sweet and beautiful voice of the woman he loved so much. She sounded calm, but he knew it was just a matter of time before things caught up with her. She needed help, and needed it now.

"Tony," she said, "I can't believe they would do this to the kids. Not the kids. They could have killed us Tony. They were in the house."

Her voice was strong, but he read little nuances that told him that she had gone to the edge. She couldn't go much further. They talked for an hour while Charboneau made flight arrangements for Tony to get home. The chief slipped a note in front of him while he talked with Muncie. Tony read it and looked up and nodded approval.

"Baby," he said, "I'll be home at four o'clock. They've got my tickets all set up, and I'm out of here in a few minutes. Tell Martinez to have somebody pick me up at the airport." There was a pause, neither of them wanted to speak, but both of them afraid to break the connection. "I love you, babe."

"Me, too. Hurry home. We'll be waiting," she said as her voice broke.

Thirty minutes later, Tony was on the commuter plane as it raced down the runway. He allowed himself a little smile as he thought about how it all started in San Diego and how he looked at the beauty of the bay, the submarines, and the white crosses on the graves at Point Loma. It was all so far away: so long ago. It was almost nine months to the day since he first met with her. Look where he was now. A ten passenger plane trying to get up enough speed and altitude to make it over the tree tops and the hills of the Ozarks. What a turnaround. Where would it all go from here? His heart suddenly pounded like a sledge hammer trying to get out. Sara! Where was she? What happened? It could only be her. He knew her well enough to know that she hadn't turned on him. She couldn't do that even if she changed her mind and wanted to stay with Guzman. He'd kill her for even thinking about snitching on him. Something must have happened to her, but Charboneau didn't say anything. Maybe they knew, but didn't want to tell him anything. They would figure that he couldn't do anything about it from Joplin, and besides, he had a wife and kids to worry about. Then again, he wondered, maybe nothing happened to her. She just got scared and ran. Yeah, that was probably what happened. She got scared and ran, and who could blame her. She did more than most people would do in her position.

*

Martinez looked at his watch and began giving directions to detectives and uniformed officers to clear up the crime scene. He would leave two uniformed officers in front and back for however much time it would take. He had to take care of his people. Things like this are not supposed to occur and he had to be damned sure that he did it right. None of them had any idea how this happened — how Tony's cover got blown. All this work to end up like this.

"Captain Martinez, telephone." Muncie came toward him with her portable phone. "I think it is your office," she said.

She stepped away so he could have some privacy for his conversation, but from his expression, she knew things were not going well. His voice was hushed and he turned his back to her as he spoke. The call lasted two or three minutes before he turned and handed the phone back to her. "Thanks," he said. "Just more work." He explained that he would have two officers assigned to the front and back of the house around the clock until things were cleared up. "We'll take care of you, I promise," he said as he walked to his car.

Muncie stood in the driveway with Matthew and Mark as the police officers gradually finished up their jobs and left. By mid-morning only the two for guard duty were left. She offered them soft drinks, and then went inside with her children. The three of them went to her bed and curled up. They were asleep in minutes.

*

"Chief, I cannot believe this crap." Martinez leaned back in a chair. He put his fingers to his temples and rubbed vigorously. His headache felt like it was going to take his head off.

"Well, none of us like it, but whether we like it or not, it's a done deal," commented the chief as he got up from his chair in the conference room. The entire team of lawyers and cops sat there in deafening quiet. It was too bizarre for any of them to believe, but it probably was true.

Chief Biggers looked out the window and reflected on his early morning phone call from Commandante Jaspar Rendon of the Judicial Police in Nogales, Sonora. Mexican cops were infamous for not working with American cops, but here was Rendon, the highest ranking cop in Nogales, clearing up the murders of the Aguilar family. "Happy to be of service to my American colleagues," he said.

"Lying bastard" thought the chief. Dirty, lying bastard, but we have to go with him until we get something better.

No sooner had Biggers gotten to his office earlier in the morning than his secretary put a call through from Commandante Rendon. "Sounds really important," she said when she passed the call through. "Says he's going to make your day."

Rendon's story defied imagination. A confidential informant called him to report the murder of a young woman at an abandoned mine about forty miles south of Nogales, near the town of Los Mochis. The informant said the dead woman was involved with the murders of the Aguilar family in Tucson several months ago. Rendon and a squad of armed troops loaded up in trucks and headed out the highway. They were nearly to Los Mochis when they turned off on an old, little used dirt road. The informant said they would see a place where an old store burned down years ago, and that was the place where they would turn to their left.

The narrow road started up the canyon wall, winding around boulders and cactus before reaching the crest more than a kilometer from the highway. From the top, Rendon saw the remains of the mine slag heap and buildings in the distance. It was only about two kilometers further, he said, but the road was rough and took them nearly an hour to get there.

They drove up to a small adobe hut that was at the mouth of the abandoned mine and found her body right away. She was sprawled, nearly nude, by the door of the hut. She was shot once in the head, and it looked as though she was burned on her lower body. "Looks like she got tortured pretty good," the Commandante said. Her purse was found nearby, and it had her driver's license and a little cash in it. "Only two American dollars," Rendon said. The driver's license picture matched the dead woman. It was Sara Hurtado. "Probably somebody you wanted to talk to, right?" said the Commandante.

Rendon described the buildings and terrain around the mine. There was a small hut about one hundred meters down the hill from the hut where they found her body. There were a couple of cots and ice chests in it and looked like somebody was living there. "We found what was left of two more murder victims in the arroyo at the bottom of the hill. Shot in the head," he said seriously. "Just like the woman. Only difference," said the Commandante, "is that one of them was taped up by his hands and feet, hogtied, you know."

"We don't know the details of your murders up there," he said, "but my informant tells me that the shoes these men are wearing are important to you so I saved them if you want them. Don't know why you would want the shoes, but you can have them. Just a pair of Nikes and a Vibram-soled boot."

There was a short pause before the Commandante continued. "Strange thing about the boot, though. It has a big notch cut in the heel. Does that mean anything to you?"

*

Chico, Allbright, and Moore checked their guns with the duty sergeant at the Nogales, Arizona police station and walked the final two blocks to the international border.

"Shit hole, that's what this place is," growled Allbright as they passed under the arch into Mexico. "And these assholes are a bunch of shit holes, too."

They quickly covered the three blocks to the Judicial Police office. It was a decrepit two-story building, one block off Calle Obregon, the main street through Nogales.

"Told you guys it was a shit hole didn't I?" laughed Allbright as they walked up to the desk sergeant. They showed him their identity cards and asked to speak to Commandante Rendon.

"Be seated, please, if you aren't afraid of the shit hole," said the sergeant as he smiled to them. "We're not all assholes," he said as they sat down on a bench next to the wall.

Chico looked at his friends and smiled. "We screwed up, big time," he said. "Really big time."

It was nearly an hour before the sergeant came back for them and showed them to the office of Commandante Rendon. They exchanged stiff pleasantries for a minute before Rendon offered them a seat. His office was modest by American standards, but nevertheless, surprisingly modern for this old building.

"I understand your interest in the shoes the men were wearing," Rendon said as he opened his desk drawer. He pulled out a large grocery bag and dumped the shoes on the desk. "You can have them," he said with a grin. "I understand this will solve your murder case. We are honored to have helped you, now if you will excuse me, I have important business to take care of." Rendon pushed back from the desk and stood up as he extended his hand to the three men.

"We would like to see the bodies, if you don't mind," said Chico.

"That was a little problem," smirked the Commandante. "We do not have all the good refrigeration you have in the United States, so we have to make do the best that we can." Rendon walked to the door to show them out. "We cremated them. Probably did it while you were sitting in the office waiting. We didn't know of any family to claim them, and we can't keep three dead people around in this heat. Sorry. I'll send you the pictures when we get them from our poor lab. Nevertheless," he continued. "we have brought in our best man from Hermosillo to take charge of the investigation. Agent Gatica! An excellent man."

The three American cops glanced at each other, each reading the others mind. This whole damn thing was rigged all the way to the capital. The investigation of Sara's murder was finished.

Somebody paid somebody and it was over. "*La morbida,*" the fucking *morbida*. That's how things get done and there wasn't much anybody could do about it.

They were about to leave his office when he said, "Oh wait, I do have something for you." Rendon walked back to his desk and pulled out Sara's purse. "Look inside," he insisted. "It still has her two dollars and drivers license. Take all of it with you. We don't need it," he said with a smile. "We made positive ID on her, and you might find some family. Maybe they'll want it," he said with a grin.

Chico tucked the purse under his arm and led the way toward the door. Allbright straggled behind, trying to get his old cigarette lighter to work. "Damn thing," he muttered as he stopped at the foot of the dark stairway that led to the second floor. He was blocking the way and stepped aside as someone came down. Anthony Allbright glanced up in time to exchange glances with the policeman when he stepped off the last step. They paused for a moment, then went their separate ways.

"Hmm, I know that guy," Allbright said as he caught up with Chico and Moore. "Did you guys see him?" he asked.

"Yeah, I did," said Chico. "You mean the real tall skinny guy? He was as ugly as shit, but I don't know him."

"I'll remember," Anthony said more to himself than to the others as they headed toward the border.

*

The next few days saw everybody working pretty much around the clock. Mary Elizabeth was nowhere to be found. They held a grand jury subpoena for her but she disappeared without a trace. She wasn't home or at work and nobody claimed to have any idea where she was. Margo tapped into the credit card files to try to find any new travel records but came up with a blank. The Chief Financial Officer of Greater America Imports disappeared off the face of the earth.

"She was a smart and capable woman and went underground" Martinez thought. She had access to unlimited cash and lived a few minutes from the international border. Pure and simple. She was gone.

"Gone, but not forgotten," Martinez said as he sat across from the chief. Biggers sat at his desk, a huge walnut desk, barren except for a picture of his wife and their German Shepherd. As many times as he was in there, Martinez never saw the chief's desk cluttered with any more than one or two pages of neatly stacked business papers. He had a reputation as a neat freak — always organized, on top of everything, in control, no loose ends. And now this! How could this have happened? And now they can't find the money guru who should be able to tie everything together. They were going to twist the shit out of her and charge her with every type of crime imaginable. She'd talk, or she would spend the rest of her life in an eight by six cell remembering the good old days and her hot shot boss, Reynaldo Guzman.

"She's no idiot," Martinez said as Biggers leaned forward, taking his pipe and twisting it until the stem broke. "She knew too much, and she was our guy's direct link to their organization. She knew as soon, and maybe even before Guzman, about Tony and Sara. She hit the road, but we'll find her if we have to chase her all the way to hell."

"Captain," the chief said. "I appreciate your efforts, but I think that lady is long gone and we'll never see her again. Think about it now. That Guzman guy is a heartless bastard. Look at how he killed the Aguilars. The kids didn't slow him down a bit, and he is no fool either. He knows Mary Elizabeth can tie all the crap together, so what do we figure him for? Is he a loving, caring boss or a mean s.o.b.?" The chief smiled as he leaned back in his chair and looked at Martinez. "I'm not a betting man, but I'd lay odds that she is dead as a doornail as we sit here talking about her."

Biggers shook his head. "Nope, Captain, you are never going to see her again. And even if I'm wrong about her being dead, these folks have got tons of money and they could hide her anywhere in the world. Who knows? Maybe right now she's sitting on the porch of her chalet in Switzerland and having a toddy while she laughs at us."

"With all respect, Chief. You're wrong. Watch and see. We're going to nail her ass to the tree."

"Hope you're right," the chief said. He got up and showed Martinez to the door.

*

Martinez, Tony and the different investigators met with the two attorneys trying to calculate strategies for taking their case to a grand jury. They still had the people Tony collected money from and would serve them with subpoenas, but without Mary, their case was dead. Tony never got close to Reynaldo and they couldn't tie him to anything. Everything led to Mary Elizabeth, and definitely to Aguilar, but Reynaldo insulated himself. Without her, Reynaldo was untouchable. A classic case of organized crime. There was no doubt about it; they had to get their hands on Mary.

The crime lab positively concluded that the shoes that were brought back from Mexico were the same shoes that made the footprints at the crime scene.

"Technically," said Chambers as the week grew to an end, "this murder case might be cleared and closed. We know there were two suspects and are only guessing that there might be a third. Both of the suspects are dead, and the fact that they were murdered in Mexico takes their murders out of our jurisdiction."

"She's right," joined in Reynolds, "but, we still have the dope cases and we can still try to twist Mary Elizabeth for conspiracy to get to Guzman for the murders. Damn it people, she is here somewhere, we just gotta find her."

"We ain't done yet, are we?" inquired Jacobs.

"No, not yet," said Chambers. "So long as we have Tony's testimony, we can twist the crap out of everybody and get to Guzman for dope. With a little luck, we'll even get that horse's ass for murder. We just need to find that red headed bitch."

She chuckled a deep, cold laugh as she sat back in her chair and grabbed her pack of Marlboros. She pulled a cigarette out and fumbled for her lighter, but couldn't find it.

"Here," said Allbright as he pulled out his old Zippo. It lit on the first try and he held it out for her. A cold chill ran up his back as she leaned forward to put the tip of her cigarette in the flame. The small yellow flame danced across the tip of her cigarette, and he remembered. The skinny cop! He remembered him from a long time ago. They were working with the army in what nobody officially sanctioned, but was a covert, black operation getting rid of a few revolutionaries in Nicaragua. Allbright himself hired him for a job. A clean hit. In and out. Julian Espino Gatica! *Matagente*!

He sat back in silence. It would wait for a better time.

The days dragged on. Martinez came out of meetings with the chief and the lawyers with a new list of things to get done. They stopped too early for Chambers to be anywhere close to being satisfied, and she wanted verification on everything that occurred. They were going to drag doctors and accountants in to the grand jury, but were afraid that nothing would tie Guzman to anything. They were coming up too short. They could undoubtedly file civil charges against the business and end up owning a bunch of fish and produce and a couple of warehouses, but Reynaldo was going to walk if they didn't find Mary.

Reynolds was relentless in the work she gave to the detectives. When they thought they were done, she demanded more. People decided that they didn't really know her, even after all of these months. She wasn't going to go to the grand jury until everything was wrapped up tight. "No surprises," she said. "I don't want to be in the grand jury room and have somebody throw me a curve. You people better have everything nailed down before you bring it to me."

She was a meticulous and vicious prosecutor. They knew that when she was ready for trial, she would kick ass. Everybody learned hard lessons from the now infamous O. J. Simpson trial. When she went to court she would be ready and nobody would catch her short. Smooth-tongued defense lawyers would be no match for her. "Castrate the bastards," she said. "They're a bunch of blood sucking leeches, and I get my jollies cutting their balls off in front of the jury."

She demanded more from them than they would do for most attorneys, but they would whine quietly, then get it done.

*

Life made drastic changes for the Castenedafamily. Tony, Martinez, and the chief held a long discussion and Tony felt comfortable that he and his family were safe. "Why not?" he said. "They know damned well that we are up a creek without a paddle. I can't hurt them, and they know it. We aren't doing anything covert with them. Shit, they know where I am, and if they wanted to put a hand on me, they could have done it a thousand times by now." He looked at the chief. "Sir, I appreciate what you are trying to do, but believe me. My wife, my kids and I are safe. There isn't a reason in the world for them to want to touch any of us. Hell, if they wanted to, they could have done something a lot worse than hang that friggin' chicken on the door."

"I hear you, Tony, but I've got bigger responsibilities than just making sure you feel good about this thing. I'd never forgive myself, and you wouldn't forgive me either if something happened to those kids of yours." He smiled and shook his head slowly side-to-side. "You're going to have to put up with some pretty close uniform surveillance on all of you around-the-clock until we have a better feel about it. Who knows how long that will be? I sure as hell don't, but I'd rather be safe than sorry."

He looked at Martinez. "I want two uniformed officers around that house twenty-four hours a day. Sorry, Tony," he said as he looked him in the eyes, "but our people are going to be with your wife and kids around the clock, and that can't be helped. I'm sorry. I know this is awkward as hell for you and your family, but we can't take any chances. We have to let this thing cool down. We've got to make sure we have got everything under control. You understand, don't you? I won't get carried away with this thing too much, I guess, so you can travel back and forth to work alone. But," he emphasized, "once you get to the office, you stay until you go home. Understand?"

"Yes sir, I do. And I really appreciate what you're doing for us. I know it is going to be awkward, but thanks anyway."

*

Tony and his family spent quiet evenings around the house simply because it was too embarrassing to go anywhere with the guards following at a discreet distance. They became prisoners, watching television and puttering around the yard. Aimless and without focus. The atmosphere became different from any they ever knew. They didn't laugh and tease like they used to. They didn't swim or cook on the barbecue. Tony felt like they were in a movie — 2001, with Hal monitoring their most intimate thoughts, or even like the Truman Story or 1984, with every word and motion being recorded by Big Brother. Everything they did, everywhere they went, and the guards were close-by. Not so close as to intrude on their private conversation, but still, always there. Always ready for what might happen. For the first time in his life, Tony felt sympathy for the President. What must this be like to live day in and day out, year after year, with someone watching your every move? Even the kids asked how long the policemen were going to stay at their house. To Tony and Muncie, it became the most awkward time of their lives. They watched TV and went to bed. He got up and went to work, then came home, and they repeated yesterday. Their lives became a never-ending circle, and the circle became the sum total of their lives.

After the kids went to sleep was the only time that they could talk. They would lie in bed by the hour, each in their own thoughts. Conversation was polite, but the warmth and spontaneity was gone. It was like they were amateurs in a play and never did a very good job memorizing their lines. Whatever there was between them somehow had slipped away. Things were different. They slept and went through their routines, but their lives were changed. In his mind, Tony heard Sara telling him how Guzman corrupted everything he touched, and he didn't have to look far to see how right she was. First it was the Indian girl, then Mary Elizabeth. He went much too far. And Sara, poor Sara. What a horrible death. Alone. Tortured. And finally, the bullet! Did she see it coming? Did she try to run? How long did she suffer? When did Reynaldo find her out? How did he find out? All of these questions would stay with him until the day he died.

Muncie put her head on his shoulder and draped her arm and leg over him. It was the same scents and body that she knew so well. She listened to his heart beat and heard him breathing, but she was afraid that she was losing him. She took her husband's soft body into her hand and held him, unable to light the flame that so often was there. But these days were different, and in her own thoughts, she knew something bad, something evil had happened. Exactly what, or with whom or how didn't matter. It happened, and she didn't need or want to know more. She knew he was sorry. More sorry than she would ever be able to comprehend, but "it," whatever "it" might be, came between them, and things would never be the same again. Yes, they would have the boys. Yes, the day would come when they would again make love. But, never again would that unspoken feeling be there. It was gone forever.

"I know, Tony," she said. "You don't have to say anything." She cuddled closer and whispered into his ear. "Just be mine again and don't think about it. Don't say a word, just love me." She scooted even closer to him and held him in her arms. "Grandma used to tell me that love is a river from heaven. It never floods; it never runs dry. It's always there, fresh and clean for us to drink and bathe in. Love can't hurt anyone because it comes from heaven, and I love you."

Tony put his arms around her and held her tightly as they drifted off to sleep together.

*

The alarm clock sounded its ugly bleep at six o'clock. Tony rolled over to pick it up and turn it off. "What happened to the clock?" he asked as he looked at the crack in the glass. He had been home for more than a week, but today was the first time he noticed the clock. Muncie explained how she smashed it to shut it up and it fell on the floor. "And I even called it a prick," she laughed. Tony pulled her into his arms and held her. They didn't move or speak, but Tony could feel her tears dripping onto his shoulder. She lifted her head and put her lips to his and they kissed. Her tongue slipped between his lips and caressed him deeply as his hands ran over her breasts.

"Tonight," Tony said as he rolled away from her. "Ann and Jimmy said they would baby-sit if we wanted to get out. Let's do it."

He grabbed her hand and led her into the shower. She adjusted the water and let it pour over them. They rubbed soft wash clothes and soap over each others bodies, taking time to nibble and touch those special places.

"I always wanted to do this," said Tony, spinning her around and putting her head under the shower. The steamy water poured down over her hair and face as he kissed her. "It's the little river from heaven," he whispered.

*

It was mid-afternoon when Tony answered the phone. "Detective Castenedaspeaking."

"Hi, detective. I'd like to report a hungry person, and would be interested in knowing if you would buy her a steak dinner tonight?"

"Excuse me ma'am while I check my schedule," Tony said as he picked up a tablet and rustled the pages. "Yes, it appears that I might be able to arrange that. Anywhere special you would like to go?"

"River Road Steak House sounds yummy to me if you think you can swing the check."

"Yes ma'am, reckon I can," he said with a phony southern accent. "Least ways 'til they figure out my credit card ain't worth a confederate dollar, but by that time we should be high tailing it out of their fine establishment anyway."

"Seriously, Tony. Dinner tonight?"

"Absolutely, sugar. Things here are coming together pretty good for me. We're not doing worth a hoot finding any witnesses that can come across for us, but at least I am in pretty good shape. The uniform cops will stay with us tonight, but they'll keep their distance. They appreciate this mess, and have been real good about how they have handled things."

"Tell me what you are doing now. Just talk to me. I want to hear your voice."

"I have about organized all my notes," he said. "And I finally finished reviewing all those video and audio tapes. By the time I finish tonight, I will have everything ready. Tomorrow I can do my final report and have this sucker behind me. I'll be done for my part anyway."

There was a pause before Muncie spoke. "Tony," she said, "I love you."

"And I love you too, babe. Everything is good." He laughed in a way that he had not done in a long time. "See you about eight."

*

The office was nearly deserted by the time Tony finished his notes. He slipped them neatly into folders and locked them in the file cabinet. He walked out of the main office and passed by the communications room. Through the big window he saw Chipper, tilted back in a chair with his feet on the console, casually watching the monitors that covered the entries and exits.

Chipper saw Tony as he headed toward the hallway and flipped him the finger. "I still think you're an asshole," he shouted through the window. Tony laughed and flipped him back.

"But you're okay," Chipper said with a smile.

Tony walked down the hall toward the elevator as Chipper watched him on the monitor.

The elevator door opened and Tony left the office. Chipper watched the monitors and saw Tony leaving the elevator on the third floor of the parking garage. "Whoa, who is that?" Chipper asked himself. The camera got a quick glimpse of a woman in the shadows outside the elevator door. "Must be his wife," Chipper thought. After all they've been through, they deserve some privacy. He swung around in his chair and flipped off the camera.

*

Tony heard the woman's voice when he reached the door of his bright red Saleen. "You bastard!" He spun around and saw Mary Elizabeth standing in the dim light. She stepped out of the darkness and moved toward him, holding her .357 magnum. She brought it up and pointed it directly at his face. "I want the personal satisfaction of doing this myself."

Tony saw a minuscule spit of fire, not much more than a spark. "What's she doing?" he thought. Suddenly, he felt a bee sting and tried to swat it. He couldn't figure out where the bee came from.

He lay on the pavement of the parking garage, feeling more relaxed than he ever felt. It was soothing. A warm sensation washed over him, like a nice shower after a hard workout. It was the most pleasant sensation he ever felt.

He saw something in the distance, moving toward him. It was Muncie, propped up in bed with a pillow behind her back. She was wearing a long white gown and was nursing Mark. He was only a little baby. Matthew was curled up at the foot of the bed, holding on to her toes. Muncie looked at Tony and smiled, then she began to fade away.

There was something else coming. He turned his head and saw his grandmother walking toward him. She was wearing an old dress and an apron. She loved to cook, and used to tell everyone that they could just send their kids to her. She loved to feed them. "More kids around the table," she would say. "Give me the kids;

we always have room for one more."

She reached out her hand to him and smiled. "*Venga conmigo,*" she said as though she was telling one of the children that it was time to come in. "*No tienes miedo. Dame su mano.*"

"Come with me. Don't be afraid. Give me your hand."

A tiny speck of light was in the distance — it was so tiny, no larger than a pinhead, but it came toward him — slowly, then faster and faster, getting bigger and brighter every moment. It was the brightest light he ever saw. It blinded him, but wasn't painful and it wasn't anything he feared. Only bright, warm and pleasant. As soothing and warm as the hand of God.

He looked again for Muncie, but she was gone.

EPILOGUE

The hours turned into days, the days into weeks and still there were no indictments. Twelve months and eighteen days since the Aguilar murders and the Task Force was no closer than they were then about closing the case. They were devastated. It should have been impossible that somebody could have come to their own building and killed Tony. Biggers especially. It was his call that Tony could travel back and forth to work unescorted. "We don't want to embarrass you," he said. They got hit where he least expected it; in fact, he really didn't expect it at all. Nobody in their right mind kills a cop and expects to get away with it. But maybe that was the point. Whoever did it didn't expect to get away with it, but didn't give a damn one way or the other.

They looked at the snippet of the video dozens of times, but there wasn't enough there. Chipper turned it off too quickly. All they could make out was a shadow of a person who looked more like a female than a male — nothing more. Nobody said anything to him, but Chipper couldn't take the guilt of his mistake and so he resigned. Maybe he would become a missionary or a teacher, but he was done in this line of work. In their own minds, they knew it was Mary but they would never prove it. And there was not a sign of her anywhere. In a desperate move, they served Reynaldo with a subpoena and he showed up with his attorney and took the Fifth Amendment to every question, including his own name. Tony was gone and his written records were worthless without his testimony. It was the same with the Missouri accountant and the Texas doctor. They stood behind their constitutional rights and refused to testify.

They even lost Marta, the maid. Chico took a statement from her the day after the explosion, but went to get her after Tony told them about her role with Mary and Reynaldo, but she was gone. They turned every stone, but she was not to be found. Some thought she went back to Mexico to be with her family; others thought that she paid the price for knowing too much. Either way, she was gone.

"We were close, that's all I can say. Look at it. Marta, Sara, Mary Elizabeth, even Tony. All gone. We've run out of witnesses." Reynolds said. She bowed her head, emotionally and physically exhausted. Slowly, she looked up, tears welling in her eyes. "It's over. I'm sorry."

Biggers, Martinez and all of the others sat around the conference table looking on in disbelief. Biggers stood up and slowly looked around the table at each of them before he spoke. "We're all sorry," he said. His voice broke. "We did our best. Let's go home." He turned and walked to the door as the others got up from the table.

It was over. No glory. No accolades. Nothing! Operation Shamash was finished. They should have never taken that name in the first place. They should have thought about it before they took that stupid name. After all, it was a false god.

Anthony Allbright sat in the back of the room, disappointed at them. Every single one of them. With the slightest nod, he shook his head in disbelief. Quitters! A bunch of chicken shits. "Never call it quits until the fat lady sings" he thought, and she hadn't even started to hum. Nope. The fat lady hadn't even started to warm up. He wasn't done and he didn't need the rest of them. To hell with them. He made a living doing this and knew all the right people. It might take him a while to put it all together but, what the hell, time is free and he was going to have to raise a little cash. His kind of work didn't come cheap, but take your time and do it right. Don't get in a hurry. Besides, let a little water flow under the bridge — let people have a little time to forget. Let them have a little time to put their guard down. There's no hurry, and when they least expect it, hit! Hit hard and fast and get out. Hell, they only needed to look at what happened to Tony and see how it works. Everybody relaxes sooner or later. And then — boom! It's over.

He and others like him did it before, and it was fairly easy. That's the trouble with these kind of people; they didn't even know how to fight a war. They thought they did, but they were mere amateurs. He knew how to get things done, and still come out on the winning side. He would show them how to fight, but they would never know it was him. He was too good for that. Nobody would ever know. That's why it was important to keep up with old contacts — people like *Matagente*. You never knew when you could help each other.

*

Mary Elizabeth sat in her lawyer's office in Rio de Janeiro. She was living well with an apartment on the beach, but missed her real life — life in the United States. Rey sent her plenty of money, but she had no friends or work to keep her going. She wanted to go home. Luxury without someone to share it with turned out to be miserable. She couldn't take it much longer. They had to work a deal that would free her to return and put this chapter behind her and she had just the idea. They had nothing on her and they knew it or they would have already issued a warrant for her arrest. She was going on the offense.

It took only a week for her new battery of attorneys to set up a meeting with Chambers and Reynolds. It was an unusually cold and damp morning for Tucson as they gathered in Chambers' law office. The gloomy weather outside was a preface to what was taking place in her tastefully appointed office: her beautiful cherry wood desk, her diplomas framed, hanging on the wall like they were her license to be in charge of half of the world, pictures of Abraham Lincoln and John Kennedy gazing down — definitely down on whomever gathered in her office, soothing Bose music flowing from the speakers in the bookcase. Everything was perfect — maybe too perfect for the real world she was about to meet.

Mary Elizabeth was represented by Samuel Lazzarato, a prominent attorney who had successfully represented some of the nation's biggest organized crime figures. It was said that his opening consultation with a client started at $50,000 and his hourly rates ran at about $500.00 plus expenses. He was dressed in a charcoal gray Italian suit that reflected his dark but graying hair. His crisp white shirt and navy blue tie complemented his impeccable style. Even Chambers had to admit to herself that his appearance was impressive, if not intimidating. He was assisted by two younger attorneys, both relatively new to his firm. Their purposes were twofold: to serve him in any research projects he needed for the case, but even more important, to watch and learn from the master for the day when they became partners. Clearly, Lazzarato was the best that money could buy.

"Let us come directly to the point," he said after they had exchanged polite introductions. "Do you have a warrant for my client's arrest?"

"Not yet," replied Reynolds. "But we're working on it."

"I doubt that you will ever get there," Lazzarato said with a sugary sweet grin on his face. "If you had a case, you would have a warrant. You know that and so do we, so let's quit playing with each other. After all, time is money and my client needs to complete this in a timely fashion. Tell me what you can do for her."

Chambers leaned forward, her elbows on the table. "We give her immunity and she testifies against Reynaldo Guzman for murder. Short, sweet and to the point. Isn't that what you wanted Mr. Lazzarato?"

"I'm afraid you don't understand this at all Miss Chambers," he shot back. "My client will come here and take the Fifth Amendment to every question even if you give her the moon. Go ahead, lock her up for contempt, but I must point out that she is a very assertive lady and knows the law well."

Lazzarato nodded to one of his assistants who immediately opened a leather briefcase and removed a stack of legal documents. "What we have here, Miss Chambers," Lazzarato said snippily, "is a civil suit which my client wishes to file if she is made to appear in front of the Grand Jury, and I believe that the city and state and whomever else is involved in this cluster fuck you called an investigation would be very embarrassed. Not to say anything about being much poorer by the time we finish with you." Lazzarato nodded to the assistant.

"Summarize it, Leonard!" he commanded.

Leonard, in his dark navy suit and pinstripe tie, sat forward and laid the papers out before him as he adjusted his tiny, wire framed glasses. "What our client alleges in her civil suit that she may file is that your agent, Detective Antonio Castenada, in his guise of Frederico Ochoa, forced her to have sex with him two times. Essentially, he raped her with the threat that if she did not comply with his desire for deviant sex, he would use his cousin, Sara Hurtado, to have our client fired from her position as the Chief Financial Officer of Greater America Imports. He would ruin a career that she built up over many years as a faithful employee of that company."

Reynolds sat forward to speak, but Leonard held up his hand. "Please," he said politely. "I'm not finished yet. Our client further alleges that your detective raped a little fourteen-year-old Indian girl, a house servant. We can bring her to trial to testify, and we have a ranch hand witness who saw them having intercourse and who rescued that young girl from further attack by the detective."

Leonard wet his lips and continued, "We understand your delicate position, but you must understand the grief our client has gone through, so she must defend herself." He smiled as he looked at Reynolds, then to Chambers. "Therefore, our client is willing to go forward with a civil action against all of the police agencies involved and," he cleared his throat to emphasize his next point, "we also will file against the estate of the dead detective. It was he who was the loose cannon, but you were responsible for him. We regret the horror this will cause his widow, but our client is deeply offended. I'm sure you understand."

Chambers sat still, her whole body rigid with anger and hate. The snakes were worse than she ever imagined them to be, and without Tony, there was little she could do to refute their vile statements. Screaming and yelling might have felt good, but would accomplish nothing but to play further into their hands. The filthy bastards would sacrifice anybody for their client, so long as the price was right.

Lazzarato turned to his other assistant and nodded. "We also have prepared to file an order for disclosure to obtain all reports, notes, photos and recordings that relate to this investigation. We want to see everything you have and we are prepared to do everything tomorrow. File suit, go for the disclosure, and maybe the most embarrassing for you people and to the pathetic widow, we will call a press conference. Clearly, the public has a right to know when their government has lost control and has destroyed people. And," he started to say, but was cut off by Lazzarato.

"We are all professional people," Lazzarato said. "I know how difficult this has been for you, and it's not something that we do lightly, but we have to help our client. I feel very bad for the young girl who was raped, and for the widow," he emphasized, "but all of us would like to bring this to closure with dignity." He nodded to his young helpers who quickly packed away their papers. Lazzarato extended his hand to the two ladies as he got up. "Think about it, and I will get back with you tomorrow."

*

Nearly a year went by as Guzman and Mary Elizabeth solidified their relationship. They went through hell, but came out unscathed. Mary semi-retired from the company and stayed at the ranch. She knew his moods; his likes and dislikes; she arranged his travels; hosted his business friends, and provided all the intimate services he could take. She was the perfect companion.

The months continued to slip away, and Guzman was making more money than ever. Tony actually helped him re-establish his business. He was on top of the world. Mary Elizabeth replaced Sara, and, as far as he was concerned, was better than Sara. Not only could Mary make love, but she could still handle the business. The ordeal with Sara and Tony was trying, but they weathered the storm.

"The sign of a real man is how you handle yourself when the shit hits the fan," he said. "I was perfect. Nobody screws with me and gets away with it. Nobody!"

*

No one paid any special attention to Anthony Allbright as he went about closing down his work station. He was brought in solely for the purpose of this investigation, and when it was done, so was he. The two weeks following closure of the case were hectic for everyone. Files to be closed out; evidence to be marked and inventoried before being filed away in the evidence room; workload from other old cases and new ones that were coming in to be allocated, reallocated, or in a few cases, filed away for another day. It wasn't pandemonium, but it was about as close to it as you could get to it without creating a riot. It had never been like this before, but of course, nothing like this had ever happened to them before.

Allbright went through his file cabinets, his desk, even his car as he inventoried everything. Reports were finalized. Logs were closed out, and finally, on Friday night, Allbright turned in his identification card and keys. He was done.

They thought.

COLOR OF THE PRISM

*

On each of his last five nights with the Task Force, Allbright walked out of the office with a fresh high-density, formatted floppy disc and a couple thumb drives. Case log after case log, computer access codes, names, addresses, phone numbers, bank account numbers, credit card numbers — good guys and bad — victims, witnesses, suspects, he downloaded them all and would sort it out later.

He parked his private car, an innocuous old Chevy with over a hundred thousand miles on it, in the carport and went upstairs to his apartment. He didn't believe in driving a good car to get dinged and nicked in the parking lots, but when it came to the place where he would put his head down on the pillow, he splurged to his heart's content. He was married twice. Wife number one was when he was in college at Tulane. He was horny and she was desperate for a husband, so they seemed like a perfect match. Perfect, that is, for eight months, when she filed for divorce. She decided that she wasn't that desperate, and he was still horny for anything in a skirt. It took him all of about two weeks to figure out that he didn't love her, but she was slow. It took her the better part of six months to come to the same conclusion. He didn't contest it, mainly because there wasn't anything to contest, and they called it quits.

Wife number two was a different story. He had a job in Washington D. C. as an aide to Senator Hubert Winslow, the youngest member of the Louisiana contingent of congressmen. Allbright worked for the senator for two months when he met Missie Mulleneaux, the daughter of Doctor Fulton Mulleneaux of New Orleans. There weren't many women who could drink him under the table, but the good doctor's dainty little flower could put him there in a heartbeat. And drink they did, interrupted by a good fling between the sheets until he passed out drunk or was screwed to exhaustion. It had to be love, or so they thought, so they took the red-eye to Las Vegas and legalized their passion at the Lover's Nest Wedding Chapel. And it nearly was love, but by the end of the second year, Missie was going into her second treatment program at the Betty Ford Clinic, and Anthony grew tired of the eight-to-five routine and the honey-do lists, so they called it quits. He had a handful of good political contacts, and in no time was stationed at the American Embassy in Mexico City. His official position was simply listed as "aide" to the Ambassador. In fact, he was on his first assignment with the C.I.A. From there, he bounced around the world for twenty-five years — jungles, cities, deserts, gambling meccas, you name it. All in the name of the United States government and all in the pursuit of truth, justice, and the American way.

*

It was a large apartment, especially for a bachelor. Three bedrooms, two baths, a formal dining room, wet bar, a private balcony overlooking the palm trees and swimming pool, and an unblemished view of the mountains at sunset. Not bad. Not bad at all.

He had a king-size bed, but every year as he got just a little bit older, it got less and less use from the diminishing crop of young damsels. He kept the second bedroom furnished for occasional company from the old days who dropped in, especially during the cold winter months when they tired of the misery of Washington, New York, and other scattered places, so they would look for a freebie in the warm desert to thaw their aging bones.

The third bedroom, though, wasn't a bedroom at all. It was his private room. Always under lock and key with a double dead bolt and its own alarm system. This was his office away from the office.

*

Anthony punched in the code numbers, disabled the alarm, and unlocked the deadbolts. He hadn't used this room for a long time, but knew it was always there when he needed it. He slipped the last two floppy discs out of the inner pocket of his suit coat and placed them in the diskette tray with the others that he took from the Task Force. He didn't waste any time getting down to business. He flicked on the computer. As it booted up, he went to the wet-bar and poured a glass of Chivas Regal, wrapping it slowly around two crystal clear ice cubes in the bottom of the glass.

A retired man has time, and, as they say, idle time is the devil's workshop. Clearly, Anthony Allbright was not idle. Morning, noon, and night he sat at the terminal, hardly taking time to feed his appetite for women or food. He always considered shaving as a waste of time, so he gave that up along with one of his favorite pastimes — sitting on the balcony and watching the most recent covey of young professional women gather at the pool to sunbathe.

When he focused on a job, he gave it his entire being, not letting himself be sidetracked by his erstwhile hedonistic pursuit of pleasures. He loved nothing better than the hunt. Unless, that is, what comes after the hunt — the kill!

His eyes nearly glazed over from the glare of the screen as he searched, aligned, realigned, backtracked, downloaded, dumped, deleted, filed, sorted, and re-sorted, until finally he had a simple list of "donors" as he referred to them. Four likely donors, people weak enough to tap. People who stumbled in their professional careers and looked to line their pockets with the profits of marijuana, heroin, cocaine, amphetamine, and in a few cases, guns. People who were scared of their own shadow, but if pressed, could come up with a fair donation to cover the cost of Allbright's continuing pursuit of truth and justice. But, not necessarily the American way.

Number one on his list was Mildred Hamilton, Joplin's Chief Financial Officer for a dozen or more scumbags running dope in the area from Kansas City to Springfield, and farther south to Little Rock. It seemed only fitting that she should be allowed to make the first contribution since that was where Tony was when his family was being terrorized. Besides, she would be a pushover. She was too old, too weak, and most important of all, to afraid to fight back.

He was right! He scared her half to death with threats that he knew everything about her — which he did. He would make sure every Mafiosi in Missouri knew what he knew, and that it would only be a matter of days before he shared their cooked accounts with the IRS and the state police. She would be "dead meat," he emphasized. It might be slow and painful, or it might be a bullet to the head that she would never see coming, Either way, in a week she would be dead — or so he led her to believe.

She did.

He decided to play games with her to be sure she understood that he was in control of her life. Let her swing awhile. He gave her a week to come up with the money. He wanted fifty-thousand dollars, but she convinced him that she could only refinance her house for thirty-five thousand, so he showed his kind heart to her and accepted her money. But not without enjoying his game and letting her stay terrified a little. Bounce her around, let her keep looking over her shoulder. Keep her honest (to paraphrase the word). He sent her to St. Louis on the commuter plane. When she got there, she was paged to the TWA desk to find a message waiting for her.

"Catch the 4:15 to Kansas City," was all the note in the sealed envelope said. And here she was — all that cash in her brief case, not knowing who was watching her, not knowing what lay ahead of her. Would they take the money and then kill her? She nearly cried as she settled down in the seat for the short hop to K.C.

She walked off the plane, half expecting and at least half hoping that her nemesis would meet her there, take the damn money and get out of her life. But that was not the case.

"TWA passenger Hamilton, please come to the TWA ticket counter for a message," came the voice over the public address system. Mildred hurried, being careful to tuck the brief case under her arm. "I'm Miss Hamilton," she said as she approached the ticket counter.

"Yes ma'am," the ticket agent said with a genuine smile. "Your son said he was paged to get back to the hospital, so he left this note for you." The agent handed the sealed envelope to Mildred. "You must be so proud, your son — a doctor." She said as Mildred took the envelope and turned away.

"Take a cab to the phone booth — the main entrance — Fairyland Park." Short and to the point. Fairyland Park! She couldn't help but find the humor in that — Fairyland! The whole mess was like a tale of witches and goblins, except it was true. Mildred walked through the six o'clock crowds and found an empty cab, no small feat in itself. Another Missouri mist kept everything just wet enough to make her feel miserable, as if things weren't bad enough as it was. The cabby was a decent sort, offering just enough conversation to keep a bit of life in their ride across town. The mist turned to rain, and the wipers scraped and shrieked across the windshield. The interior of the cab, already smelling from cigarettes and body odor, became unbearable with the closed windows and the one hundred percent humidity. Omar, the cab driver, looked over his shoulder as he pulled into the nearly deserted parking lot at Fairyland. By this time, the rain became a steady downpour, water running curb to curb. "You sure you want to go here, lady?" he asked.

"Yes, thank you. Just pull over by those phone booths and I'll be fine," she said with a pleasant smile. Mildred paid her bill, gave him a five dollar tip, and slid out the back door with her briefcase safely tucked under her arm. She was soaked by the time she ran the twenty or so steps to the bank of phone booths. She quickly opened the door of the first one, dashed inside, slamming it behind her as she tried to get out of the rain. "Now what?" she thought. She waited. Twenty minutes, then thirty. She looked at her watch. Maybe something was wrong. She would give him an hour, no more. She kept checking her watch, curious. What happened? Why go to all of this trouble, then nothing?

Fifty minutes later a dark blue Nissan pulled up at the curb, its wipers going full speed to keep up with the downpour. The driver was swathed in his rain hat, raincoat, sunglasses and umbrella, but there was no doubt as to who it was. He never gave her a name, and she was smart enough not to ask. He didn't waste a step as he walked to the booth.

Mildred slid the door open and stepped into the rain. "Back inside," he commanded as he pointed to the phone booth. "You open it. Not that I don't trust you, but with the company you keep, somebody may have booby-trapped a briefcase full of toilet paper, figuring you would blow me all to hell. Get back in there."

The urgency of his voice frightened Mildred, and she backtracked into the booth. "I didn't do anything except what you told me to do," she said. Her voice began to break. "Here! Look!" she said as she stood in the cramped phone booth and opened the briefcase.

Allbright wasn't about to stand there and count the money. It would be right, he was sure. He snatched the case from her hands, slamming it shut as he walked to the Nissan and was gone.

In and out. That's how it is supposed to be, and that's how it was. Thirty-five thousand dollars in the kitty.

The next donor was easier than the first. Dr. Koch, the worthless son of a millionaire doctor, the husband of a wealthy socialite — a pretty little thing from his home state of Louisiana, and whose mommy and daddy had more money than Fort Knox. The good doctor was a snap. "Pay up fifty-thousand dollars or my people cut your balls off and mail them to your wife." Those were Allbright's exact words, and three days later he had the money — worn bills, nothing larger than a fifty, neatly wrapped in a brown paper sack.

"Eighty-five thousand dollars," he thought. That should be enough for starters. I'll hold the other two donors back, and if I need them, okay. Otherwise, well, you never know. They might come in handy some other time.

Five weeks sped by, and Allbright was getting tired. The computer. The traveling. Planning. Always looking back over his shoulder. It took its toll, but the end was in sight. One more meeting before and if all goes well, one after. And that's it. No more.

Former C.I.A Agent Anthony Allbright and the infamous mercenary, Julian Espino Gatica, sat in the bar of the Hotel Splendid in Guymas, Mexico, sipping their drinks and chatting. A little bit about the old days, who was where, who was dead, who went on to bigger and better things. It was good and relaxing, in fact, to sit back and shoot the shit with someone you could trust, even if you didn't trust them. At least it was someone who had been there and done it. Not just cheap talk, but someone who walked the walk and talked the talk.

The sunlight faded away to the lights of night. Out on the street, headlights came on, the neon lights of curio shops, bars and restaurants beckoned to passersby. *Matagente*, the professional killer, looked like any of the other businessmen in the bar, downing a cool drink after a stressful day at the office. As he always did, he blended in with whatever the situation called for.

They put aside their drinks and ate steaks — big, juicy, rare, T-bone steaks. Julian sat back in his chair and burped. He fumbled through his pockets, pulling out his cigarettes, offering one to Allbright. "Smoke, my friend?"

"No thanks. Bad for the health."

"Let us get down to business," Julian said as he blew the smoke out of his nose. "You didn't come all the way down here to swap stories of your glory days. What is it that you want?"

"I think you know."

"Don't play games. It doesn't suit you. Spit it out. It has to do with the girl, doesn't it?"

"Not directly. It's what came after that. My friend. Mary Elizabeth killed him. Right?"

"So they say," Julian said as a wicked smile drifted across his face. "Do you want revenge? That's bad business, you know. You're never supposed to get personal in our line of work. You know that."

"So let's say I'm slipping." Allbright reached under his chair, pulling Mildred Hamilton's briefcase up on the table and popped it open. "Forty-five thousand now. Forty more when it's done."

"And to whom am I supposed to owe your favor, if I may ask?"

"Her and her fat ass lover. Do them both."

Matagente sat back in his chair, fumbling for another cigarette, taking his time to think. He took a deep breath, holding the smoke deep in his lungs, then exhaled slowly as he looked down at the stripped T-bone on his plate. He waited. He looked again at Allbright and shook his head. "Are you crazy, my friend? Why do you have to do this thing?"

"Because I'm getting tender in my old age." He shook his head as he continued, "Besides, yeah, for once in my life I would just like to get a little revenge. What difference does it make to you? I'll pay! You know that."

"Yes, my friend. I know you'll pay. It's just that you gringos are getting sentimental on me, that's all." *Matagente* reached over and closed the lid on the briefcase, pausing for a second with his hand on it, thinking. He knew it was now or never. Either do it or forget it, but the money wouldn't be there for him tomorrow. Slowly, he nodded his head as he pulled the briefcase to him and slid it under his chair.

"You have always been a man of your word, *Senor* Allbright. I'm sure the money is correct. Be back here thirty days from today. If it is done, I will be here. If I have run into problems, come back in another thirty days. By then, if I'm not done, I will return your money. No problem."

*

Reynaldo undressed in his bedroom while Mary sat on the bed and watched him. It was late and she wanted to go to bed, but he insisted on making love in the hot tub.

"C'mon," he insisted. "It'll be good for you," he laughed as he grabbed himself. "You need it."

Mary walked to the closet and nonchalantly undressed while he leaned against the door and watched. "You're good, you know," he said. He put his fingers to her breast as he continued to rub himself.

"Let's get in the water," he whispered when she stepped out of her panties. He took her hand and led her through the house, strutting and proud of his *machismo*. "Always a man," he bragged a thousand times when he was aroused. They walked through the dining room and onto the patio, naked in the comfort of his luxury, without shame or humility. He had already turned on the jets, so the water was hot and bubbly. He held her hand as they stepped in and sat on the bench.

"Ohh, so good," he said.

The bubbles massaged his back and feet. He put his arm around Mary's shoulders and pulled her close to him. She slipped in close, reaching down to take him with the gentle massage of practiced fingers.

He sat back, closing his eyes as she took him to the heights of the distant mountain peaks. As high as he had ever been before. His whole being became rigid — his heart pounded, his breathing was deep and gasping as the depths of his passion exploded into the water, where, just as quickly, the power of the chlorine killed every living organism in a matter of seconds.

Neither of them heard the bare feet as the skinny man came over the wall and padded silently toward them. They were lost in bliss, and the noise of the bubbles covered any sound. The man leaned down, placed the barrel of the tiny gun to the back of Guzman's head and fired. The bullet spun through the base of the skull and buried itself in his brain. Guzman's lifeless body pitched forward, then down under the water.

Mary Elizabeth was faster than the man anticipated. She screamed and jumped forward, twisting to see who was there. His second shot missed its mark. The bullet missed the back of her head and ripped into her jaw, angling up through her tongue, taking two teeth with it as it exited her lip. She lurched over the side of the tub, crying for help. Guzman's lifeless body caught against her legs and feet, causing her wet, naked body to fall onto the cool deck. She lay there quivering in pain and fear. Small drops of blood dripped from her mouth and stained the deck that Benny labored over so long and hard.

The skinny, barefoot man stepped around the tub, leaned over and whispered into her ear, "He told me it was a thin line between greed and friendship. And, for you? A man told me that you were a bitch, are a bitch, and always will be a bitch." Then he fired his trademark shot into the back of her head.

Made in the USA
Las Vegas, NV
28 June 2024

91634887R00154